Steel Time

STEEL BOOK FOUR
EMPIRES
SERIES

Steel Time © 2018
by J.L. Gribble
Published by Dog Star Books
Bowie, MD
First Edition
Cover Image: Bradley Sharp
Book Design: M. Garrow Bourke
Printed in the United States of America

ISBN: 978-1-947879-06-5
Library of Congress Control Number: 2018945590

www.DogStarBooks.org

For David, Julia, and Sarah

Also from the Steel Empires Series

Steel Time

J.L. Gribble

DOG STAR BOOKS

THEN

When she tripped over a jagged bone, Victory realized she'd expected to find more skeletons in what remained of the ruined city of Nacostina. Since the hydrogen bomb destroyed the lost British colonial capital almost a century prior, she'd never had reason to return. Until now.

A few yards to the side, Toria lifted her glowing quartz crystal higher. "All right over there?"

"I'm fine, just a misstep." With the toe of her boot, Victory nudged aside the bone. No other remains lay close to it, and the tooth marks gnawed into the bone made it likely an animal dragged it here.

The dim violet rays of her crystal provided enough light for Toria to see without impeding Victory's vampiric eyesight, though with Victory's enhanced senses, the magical talisman still shined like a beacon in the pre-dawn hour. It painted Toria's sun-tanned face with stark shadows, darkening her brown hair to black and reflecting silver from her gray eyes and the rapier at her hip.

Toria moved away and they settled into silence, broken by the scuff of boots over fragments of stone and asphalt choked with hardy weeds. Further off, Victory overheard snatches of quiet conversation between their other companions, Mikelos and Kane, as the two men prepared camp.

In theory, Victory and Toria scouted the area around the clearing in which they intended to camp for safety. In practice, Victory scouted, while Toria kept bending over to poke at things in the rubble.

Though the bombing had ground most of the city to dust, the occasional section of wall fought time and gravity. Gripping an outcrop of carving with her fingertips and scrabbling by her toes, Victory heaved herself onto a tenacious segment of stone construction. Once she'd doubled her standing height, she tossed her thick braid over her shoulder. With this much humidity so late at night, the upcoming summer day promised to scorch. Best they sleep through as much of it as possible, constrained to her nighttime working hours.

"This will be easier in the afternoon daylight, after you get some sleep," Victory said.

She pretended not to hear her daughter's aggrieved sigh. Or the muttered comment about who held this contract. They'd butted heads the entire trip, but she'd resolved to let Toria lead the way once in Nacostina. That hadn't worked out as well as she'd hoped.

"There's no point to searching in the daylight if we're not searching in the right place," Toria said, louder. She kicked another rock, sending it skittering away in the darkness. "Are we even close to where the museum was?"

From her perch, Victory surveyed the landscape. She didn't know. The long, flat expanse of overgrown weeds retained most of the original shape of the park at the heart of Nacostina's cultural and government center. Victory needed to find a better landmark tomorrow night, perhaps the towering monument built to honor the first governor-general of the united British colonies, to narrow down the location of the target of this contract. If she oriented herself there, she could use enough visual cues to dredge up hundred-year-old memories and figure out where Nacostina's old natural history museum might hide.

Her progeny Jarimis often haunted the museum in the city's heyday, whereas Victory had stopped by just long enough to drag him out of the archives. But she remembered enough to be willing to accompany Toria and Kane on this job.

Toria braced her hands on her hips, peering at Victory from the base of the stonework. Tension lined the skin between her eyes. "Anything?"

Movement caught Victory's attention, and she jerked to one side.

Nothing, other than shadows caught in shadows. Cracked cement and ruined stone reflected the meager starlight. Desolation surrounded them for miles, as weeds and insects reclaimed this once-thriving city.

"Mom?" Toria squinted into the darkness.

Victory dropped to the ground, absorbing the impact with bent knees. "I'm not sure we're close. Maybe tomorrow night, with more time."

They picked their way toward the cold camp as a meager breeze did little to shift the heavy moisture in the air. Victory got the better end of the meal situation this trip, since no sane traveler risked eating anything—flora or fauna—within miles of Nacostina, much less in the heart of the ruins. Toria, Kane, and Mikelos were stuck with surplus British military rations, heated via chemical reaction rather than over an open fire. Victory dined on bottled blood from her own private stock.

As Victory approached, Toria dimmed the light from her crystal. "I doubt anything is going to come eat us in our sleep. Unless you're seeing something I'm not?"

"You're the boss." Victory veered enough in her path to bump shoulders with Toria. "I'm the hired muscle." She didn't mention the shadows. She hadn't seen them in months, and they'd picked a hell of a time to play tricks on her now.

"That got old before we left Limani." Before Toria could launch into yet another rant about how she and Kane had subcontracted Victory based on her memories of Nacostina, not her more extensive combat knowledge, her boot landed with a sharp crack. Both women froze as it echoed into the night. Toria reignited her crystal. "Holy—"

Victory crouched and ran a hand over the nearest bone. It curved in an arc that stretched longer than her arm width, finger to finger. It wasn't alone—more bones surrounded it, along with shards of metal. Perhaps remnants of metal casings that held together displayed skeletons. Could they be this lucky? "Huh. I think we found the museum."

"You never said they had dragon skeletons." Toria knelt next to Victory and touched a cautious fingertip to another bone. "That's horrific."

"No, not dragons." Given the size of the bones, Victory saw how her daughter had jumped to the logical conclusion. "I remember an exhibit dedicated to the dinosaur skeletons found out west before the war started." The burgeoning British field of paleontology had fizzled when most of the lands where scientists discovered remains fell into Qin hands. On the off chance the dinosaurs shared any genetic heritage with the weredragons who ruled Qin society, the newcomers declared the areas sacred sites and halted all further exploration.

Now, of course, most people had better things to do than brave the Wasteland for piles of old bones.

"Perfect. Remember more. Where were the dinosaur skeletons in relation to the geological exhibits?" Toria's businesslike tone couldn't hide her excitement.

Before Victory could respond, Kane's voice echoed across the ruined landscape. "Food o'clock!"

"Damn it." Toria brushed off the knees of her jeans as she straightened.

"It's okay. What a stroke of luck." Victory hid her amusement as frustration wrinkled Toria's nose. "You three start searching once you're fresh this afternoon. I'll join when I'm able, if you haven't found it yet."

"We could take the long way back to camp." Toria's stomach gurgled, but something as low-priority as hunger would not deter her curiosity.

"Yeah, okay." Victory followed Toria, trailing the bones in the rubble.

These skeletal remains of prehistoric creatures would be worth a fortune if they could be returned to civilization. The party should also retrieve any of the more portable precious gems left in the geological exhibit. But Toria and Kane had accepted a contract by their mysterious sponsor for something specific: a particular piece of stone.

Taking blind contracts never appealed to Victory, but the kids were still building their reputation and hadn't hesitated at the job offer orchestrated through the head of Limani's Mercenary Guild. Since Victory needed to work off penalties acquired for breaking contract in Jiang Yi Yue a few years ago, she'd accepted the subcontract to guide them through the Nacostina ruins.

She waved her way through a cloud of midges as she followed Toria around another pile of masonry. If the kids wanted to spend the hottest part of summer treasure-hunting in what used to be swampland, well, Victory had accepted stranger contracts before.

The light of Toria's crystal reflected on a glint within the rubble, too bright to be another random metal casing. They both paused, and Toria knelt to shove away gravel. "Oh, cool—"

Toria's voice cut off as she blinked out of existence. The purple crystal fell to the rubble and darkened.

Victory froze mid-step as the area plunged into near-pitch darkness. She prayed her eyes were playing tricks on her. Perhaps the shadows—

At the campsite, a deep voice cried out in pain and shock. Dropped items clattered. Mikelos shouted, panicked.

Not a trick of the light. Toria was gone, and Kane was reacting through their magical bond.

Everything seized in Victory's chest. She scrabbled for the darkened crystal.

Pressure squeezed her torso, yanking her up and out and away. The night blackened as she hurtled through a void with enough speed to strip the skin from her bones.

Instead, she felt nothing at all as the shadows embraced her.

It's one of them.

Does the one see us?

Before Victory could latch onto the voice that echoed through the void, she crashed to a halt on unyielding stone. The impact reverberated through her tailbone and the back of her skull as color rushed into the world. Steady red emergency lighting glowed above her against a dark arched ceiling. The sudden silence rang in her ears.

BEFORE

Freezing cold alternated with searing heat against Toria's exposed skin. Any sense of up versus down vanished as her internal equilibrium was shot in this vast, colorless void. An immense weight pressed against her chest, anchoring her. Or was it pulling? Were her eyes even open? She heard nothing, smelled nothing, tasted nothing—

Wham.

She slammed into a solid surface, and her skull bounced. The pressure at her chest disappeared, replaced by sharp pain in her head and through her back and legs. She didn't remember falling, but whatever had happened would certainly leave her blanketed in bruises.

She kept her eyes closed, but a chorus of high-pitched voices and excited babble assaulted her ears from somewhere nearby.

Magic roared across and through her, soaking her being until her skin vibrated and her fingers tingled with excess power. More magical energy than she'd ever sensed in her life, even more than the stolen magic at the New Angouleme mage school, adding to the certain logic of a ridiculous occurrence. She remembered stumbling on a bit of rubble, losing her balance and falling forward. She heard Kane now: "Are you telling me you tripped and found the world's lost magic? Only you, Tor."

Their initial research into the museum's contents yielded spotty information at best. Too many records lost to time and war. They'd had no idea what they might find, but she never would have included getting knocked out and dumped into a maelstrom of magic on the list.

With a mental jerk, she turned off every inkling of her magesight before opening her eyes—seeing the amount of energy she sensed might blind her. Instead, sunlight poured through high windows. The shrieks and shouting subsided, much to the pleasure of her pounding head.

Sunlight? How much time had she lost? A moment of panic for her mother's safety seized her limbs, and an automatic move of distress sent her hand to grip her rapier hilt. Gasps echoed above her.

The world came into focus as a circle of curious young faces stared at her. The unfamiliar kids appeared about the age of Archer's youngest mage school apprentices, maybe nine or ten. Their dresses and button-up shirts looked like something out of a historical vid. Their faces swirled behind her rapid blinking.

Please, not another concussion. Her first, in a training accident over a year ago, took months to resolve even with liberal application of her partner's healing abilities.

Time sped up again, and the children whispered and poked at each other. Two older women, also wearing old-fashioned blouses and skirts, broke into the ring and hustled the children aside as they scolded them in gentle tones for staring and getting in the way. A man with nervous sweat glistening on his pale bald scalp pushed through the bystanders. He wore some sort of uniform, but the colors were wrong for Limani's police department. He knelt next to Toria, buttoned top restraining his middle-aged paunch. With this closer view, she spotted a badge on his chest—Central Security Contractors.

"Let's get you up, miss." With careful hands, he hooked Toria under the shoulders and eased her to a sitting position.

She swayed and caught herself against the cold marble tile with one hand. Though the two women had herded the children away, a larger crowd surrounded her. The adults, more circumspect, hid whispered comments behind their hands. Beyond them, glass display cases lined the walls, refracting sunlight to the high ceiling.

"Careful now, duckie." The guard's voice was kind rather than patronizing.

"I'm fine." But Toria didn't resist his help in leveraging her to her knees, then her feet. Her vision swam again and she clutched him for balance as he led her at a slow walk through the staring mass of people. "Okay, I'm not fine." Her brain reached over and over again for her internal link with Kane and came up empty each time, which made concentration difficult.

"Don't worry, I've got you." He kept her upright with a firm grip on her elbow and a protective arm around her shoulder against the crowd.

Even as she cataloged everyone she passed as a potential threat, a habit born of years, the clothing almost overwhelmed her. Full suits with dapper hats for the men, and more skirts and blouses for the women. The men wore subdued hues, but the women presented a riotous array of colors. She stood out either way in her khaki-toned hiking pants and navy tank top.

Ambient magic pounded her from every angle, but she battened down magesight for fear of worse pain.

They escaped the mass of people, and a second security guard ran up as her escort led her to an elegant stairwell. The skinny man, topped by a shock of red hair, stuttered to a halt a few marble steps below them. "Officer Comstock! Is it really a Code Gray?" He stared at Toria in amazement.

But it wasn't crass or sexual. Instead, it seemed to be genuine surprise at the rapier belted at her side, or perhaps her clothing. Toria stumbled again. Her hip crashed into hard metal at Officer Comstock's waist, and she jerked away from the revolver holstered there. What security guard had access to such specialized armaments?

"You think any other kind of emergency would drop a lass such as this in our midst?" Officer Comstock pointed down the hall. "Find someone to call Mr. Liam. I'll bring her to his office." When the other man didn't move, eyes still locked on Toria, Comstock snapped his fingers. "Jasper!"

He jerked to attention. "Right! Yes, sir." Jasper dashed down the steps, careening around a corner on black shoes polished to a high shine. Jasper also carried a revolver, and Toria couldn't fathom why.

Comstock prodded Toria forward into the stairwell with a gentle tug at her elbow, even bracing her with a small push every step. At the top of the sun-soaked stairs, lit by more high windows, he led her into a utilitarian side hall. No windows, and no more marble. A row of closed doors with nameplates and titles. Lee Stone, Publicist. Stephen Duvall, Assistant Archivist. Cole Burkehead, Head Geologist.

The memory of sunlight disoriented Toria. How much time had she lost?

Had she had these thoughts before? Her brain wandered in circles, too. *Not a good sign.*

Officer Comstock halted in front of a door labeled "Liamacorin, Deputy Curator." Elven name, with that many syllables and no surname. With a jangle of metal, Comstock unlocked the door with a cluster of keys hanging from his belt. After it swung open, he propelled Toria inside with another gentle nudge. "Go on, miss. Have a seat. I'll be right outside until Mr. Liam is fetched."

Two steps into the sunlit office, she stumbled against a wooden chair, empty and waiting for guests on the far side of a desk littered with paperwork.

Toria collapsed into the empty seat, leaning sideways to rest her head against the backrest. Comstock left the door ajar and stood watch in the hallway. But whether this was to keep her in the office or out of some measure of respect was unclear.

Her mind returned to the clothes. And the pistol. If she'd appeared in the middle of some sort of historical reenactment society, why continue the charade all the way here? The décor in this office looked straight out of a vid set, between the wooden desk and chairs and rickety metal filing cabinets. She didn't recognize the elven-style landscapes framed on two of the walls, but she found the bold jewel tones a comforting splash of color amidst the drab brown furniture, beige walls, and off-white curtains. Paper covered practically every flat surface, but there was no telephone or computer. Even the air smelled off, musty with hints of burned coffee and stale nicotine.

She recognized the writing on the files nearest to her side of the desk, at least. And Comstock and Jasper both spoke in Loquella, despite the odd accents. Where the hell was she? Not home in Limani. The British colonies? The Roman colonies? The sunlight meant time had passed, but how much? Days? Weeks?

If she did have a concussion, she might also have post-traumatic amnesia. So, how had she gotten here from walking through rubble in Nacostina with her mother?

Where was Victory? And where the hell was *Kane*?

She didn't need to risk blinding herself with magesight to use magic. The connection with her bonded warrior-mage partner was internal. She closed her eyes to block out the strange environment.

She stretched once more, searching for the part of her soul-mind-self that was also Kane. Where their power linked, no matter the distance. But she found imagined static instead of a solid radio connection.

No answering burst of earth magic buried within her element of storm. What should have been a link to a mighty forest protected by raging lightning was instead a mere seed buffeted by wind and thunder. No matter how she tried, she couldn't grasp the tiny kernel long enough to follow it to its source. Her connection with Kane was almost cut off. At least she could be sure he wasn't dead.

She already knew what that felt like.

But she had no idea why this block between them existed, or what might be its source. Had Kane been kidnapped and cursed, like in college? Even that memory of loss and fear felt nothing like this pure desperation.

At least he wasn't dead.

At least he wasn't dead.

He wasn't dead.

Her breath sounded loud in her ears. She pressed the heels of her palms over her eyes and hunched in the uncomfortable seat. She couldn't fall apart when she had so little information. She couldn't afford to show weakness. Officer Comstock appeared kind enough, but she knew nothing about the elf Jasper had been sent for. Tears leaked even as she managed to slow her hyperventilation to slower, shuddering gasps.

A younger voice than Toria had expected startled her out of her anxiety attack. "I'm sorry it took me so long to get here. It's astonishing how much traffic there can be on the weekend sometimes, really terrible—oh, no!"

She dropped her hands and accepted the handkerchief thrust at her face. The elven man appeared to be about her age, which meant at least two centuries older. He pressed the white cloth into her hand before wheeling his chair around the desk and dropping into it.

The man's light blond hair, pulled in a neat tail at the nape of his neck, accentuated the pale skin of a man who spent too much time indoors. He wore tailored slacks with a button-up shirt of summer-weight cotton, in a crisp blue that highlighted his eyes. The cut emphasized his broad shoulders and trim waist. Neat leather loafers. It all matched the clothing she'd seen so far, older than mere retro throwback.

Toria dabbed at her wet eyes and blew her nose. The man seemed like he didn't know what to do with himself while she pulled herself together. He resettled in the seat twice before unbuttoning his shirt cuffs and rolling up his sleeves. His unrehearsed awkwardness did not seem like part of an elaborate ruse.

Toria had plenty of experience with handsome elves who manipulated events to their own ends. But this one waited with patience while she collected herself. She balled the handkerchief in one hand.

He leaned forward, his elbows propped on his knees. "Do you feel up to talking now?"

"I think so, yes." She settled the storm-tossed kernel of earth within her mind.

"My name is Liamacorin, but you may call me Liam." Like Jasper and Officer Comstock, he spoke perfect Loquella with an odd accent.

"Toria. Toria Connor." She stumbled a bit over not returning the introduction in the elven manner, but perhaps humans and elves didn't have such a relationship here. Better to play it safe for now and avoid the questions her full name, Torialanthas, might evoke. "Forgive me for being blunt, but where am I?"

Liam rubbed his hands on his pant legs. "You're in the Museum of New Continental History, in the city of Nacostina—"

"Bullshit."

Liam jerked in surprise, startling Toria into a manic giggle. He seemed more relieved by her response than anything, perhaps because she hadn't broken into sobs again.

"Sorry, sorry." She waved the handkerchief dismissively. "But that's ridiculous."

"My guess is, you were brought to this location because you touched an item of magical energy that displaces people in time and space. The one we have here at the museum tends to fling people into the future." This part sounded more rehearsed, as Liam appeared braced for her to interrupt him again. "It's been under lock and key since the initial discovery of these properties, though not for the entirety of its existence. We've been studying it for years, but we don't even know how it works, much less how to control it. I'm going to guess by the expression on your face that you have no idea what I'm talking about, so obviously, you didn't accidentally trip over it while it's been under elven control."

Closer than you think, actually. "And you said I'm in Nacostina?"

"Yes."

Of all the damned luck. Toria slumped in her seat. "And this is an elven artifact?"

Liam's posture relaxed when speaking about a subject he had obvious passion for, as his hands traced an invisible sphere the size of two of his fists put together. "Well, no. There are no markings on the stone to indicate its origin or provenance. We've barely scratched the surface of what it might be capable of, because the risks are so great."

"Because you said it moves people through time and space."

"Yes. But we're going in unnecessary circles." Liam snagged a pen and pad of paper from his desk. "Do you mind if I ask some questions? I recognize that this is all a shock, but your answers will give me a better idea of how to proceed."

Toria shifted in her seat.

"You seemed surprised when I said that you were in Nacostina now. Where were you before the incident that brought you here?" He sat poised to record her answer.

Incident was a mild way to put it. "I was in Nacostina."

"That's fantastic! So you're already familiar with the city, to an extent." He wrote as he spoke. From Toria's angled perspective, his handwriting was a delightful scrawl.

"I guess you could say that." She stopped herself from making a quip about being familiar with a pile of rubble.

If all of this was real, and not some elaborate dream or fantasy, Liam couldn't know about Nacostina's destruction.

No one could.

The pressure in her chest returned.

Liam jotted down a few more items, then returned his full attention to her. "I don't recognize your style of dress, but your Loquella is easy enough to understand. Your sword is going to draw some attention, though, because people don't generally go about armed in this time. Especially human women."

"In this time. In the future."

"Yes. In every instance of the stone transporting a person, it has been from the past into the future. The time range is inconsistent though, so I'm a bit relieved that my first instance of this is a person who is not terribly far from the past. My predecessor once had to acclimate a man who traveled almost a thousand years." Liam twisted his pen in his hand as he spoke.

"How'd that work out for him?" Toria wasn't sure whether she asked about Liam's predecessor or the other accidental time traveler.

"It, erm, didn't." Liam did a terrible job at hiding a wince. "He had difficulty accepting many social aspects of life and ended up succumbing to influenza the next winter."

Toria forced down another set of disbelieving manic giggles. A hiccup came out instead. Liam rubbed the back of his neck and busied himself with more notes while she calmed herself.

This was too much. Only one explanation fit. She had tripped on a piece of rubble and landed on her head, knocking herself unconscious. This was all a weird, injury-induced dream. Victory had fetched Kane to help, and all the excess magic was her partner trying to heal her out of it.

Okay. She could play along. "What happens to me now? What do you need to send me home?"

"That's the bad news, I'm afraid." Liam paused, clicking the top of his pen a few times before noticing the nervous habit and setting the ballpoint on his notepad. "The trip is not reversible."

Nothing was irreversible, even elven superiority. "How do you know?"

"There are records, studies into the properties of the stone." Liam stood and, after dropping his pen and notepad on the desk, rustled through a stuffed filing cabinet. "I should have copies somewhere around here. Ah!" He withdrew a sheaf of papers, flipped through them, and shoved them back in the drawer. "That's not it. Hmm."

"It's fine. You can find them later." If she let Liam go off-topic, the two of them might never escape this office. Her stomach rumbled. A snack of dried fruit had been hours ago. Or several decades in the future.

Liam resumed his seat across from her. "Again, I haven't dealt with this before, so I apologize if I come off as frazzled. But let me assure you the museum has a policy in place for these circumstances. We'll set you up with lodgings and an allowance, along with training and instruction until you adapt here."

Not much she could argue with there. If this wasn't some fevered dream, it was nice to know Liam would not toss her out on the street at the close of this conversation. His adamant assertion that she must come from the past because no one had ever come from the future still grated. Her luck to be the anomaly.

Liam had his pen and notepad again. "If I may ask, what year are you from? It can't be too far in the past. Again, your Loquella is similar to ours, which is convenient, but more detail will allow me to figure out where to start with catching you up."

"Um." Toria's brain stalled. "I'm from Limani."

Brilliant. Not an answer to his question at all. Now Liam would think her an idiot on top of being an emotional mess. Or worse, her evasiveness would pique his professional curiosity. But no way in hell could she reveal being from the future. Paradox, thy name was Torialanthas.

Liam didn't press the matter, earning Toria's undying gratitude. "That's no issue. In fact, it will solve a lot of problems you might have with other people regarding any unfamiliarity with life here in Nacostina. Unless you wanted to consider returning home?"

"No!" Toria clutched the handkerchief, wringing it between both hands. "I mean, that'd be kind of strange, right? The city, ah, achieved independence a few years ago."

A safe enough point for her to claim. The Roman Empire had absorbed the last of the Greek city-states in Europa, leaving Limani, their sole colony, to fend for itself across the ocean. In the scramble to achieve self-sufficiency and resist the temptation to merge with the British colonies to the north or Roman to the south, record-keeping had fallen by the wayside. Liam had no way to verify her claim. But between college courses and family stories, she had a decent chance at passing as a refugee from the time period. It even explained the sword.

Speaking of. "You should know something else." She paused, as if she feared Liam's reaction. History had not always welcomed magic users, and she had to pretend as if she had no idea how this new world worked. "I'm a mage. Storm powers. Master-level. That's why I'm so interested in the object that brought me here. Not just idle curiosity."

Now the swept-hilt rapier at her hip drew Liam's complete attention. "But why, ah, if I may ask—"

"Family heirloom and awkward power focus." She drew a few inches of blade and sent a trickle of energy through the sword, which brightened with enough power to register to Liam's natural elven senses.

A regular mage, even one aligned with rare storm, had no reason to carry a sword, much less know how to wield one. No way could she reveal being half of a magically bonded pair, a connection allowing Toria and Kane to master the martial arts along with the arcane. Every empire in the world documented bonded pairs. Even Limani, teetering on the edge of disaster, would have kept track. Not acknowledging Kane pained her, but he was safe in the future. Or so she hoped.

"Oh! Well, then." Liam jotted a few more notes Toria couldn't make out. "Unusual, but not unheard of in this time."

She still lacked one important piece of information. Might as well rip off the bandage. "So, when have I ended up? How far?"

"Yes, that is a crucial detail, isn't it?" Liam retrieved a small flip calendar from his desk and presented it to Toria. "Without boring with you the calendar conversions, it's been approximately a hundred and ten years since Limani became independent. We are now at the start of what promises to be a hot summer."

Coordinating the British lunar and Roman solar calendars required extensive mental gymnastics at the best of times. She accepted the postcard-sized calendar in silence. The pressure on her chest bore down again, and the world closed in around her. Liam rambled in the background, his words a dim echo, something about acquiring modern clothing and settling her in with a friend. A promise he would personally make sure she became comfortable in this future and adapt well.

With shaking hands, she paged through the months of the calendar to the end of the current year. Liam didn't have any appointments listed on the page yet, but this calendar highlighted the date of the annual winter renewal festival celebrated throughout most of the known world.

Resolution draped over Toria's shoulders like a heavy coat as the truth of her situation sank in. If she was in the past, and this wasn't some sort of ridiculous hallucination, she couldn't stay in Nacostina.

But she couldn't go anywhere else either, because the world was about to end.

Liam had yet to say anything about it, but she was aware the Last War had begun a few months ago. Not that anyone called it that yet. Toria touched a date square with one finger. The day when the Qin Empire dropped a hydrogen bomb on the British colonial capital of Nacostina, launching the empires into nuclear war for control of the New Continent.

In just over six months.

Liam's hand clasped her shoulder, breaking her out of her daze. He stood above her, clutching a sheaf of folders in his other arm. "I said, are you ready to go? I'll escort you to where you'll be staying for now, give you a bit of a tour of the city on the way."

"Yeah, let's go." Toria willed away the numbness in her legs as she stood. She left the calendar on Liam's desk and followed him out of the office.

The past sucked.

After Liam stepped into another office for a moment to contact her new host, he led her out of the museum. She gave him half an ear as he described advancements in technology while she tracked their route out of the museum. She received a primer on electrical power, tried to appear impressed by the electric-powered lighting fixtures in the museum's hallways and lobby rather than gas or magic—which would have been familiar to "her" time—and bit her tongue before correcting Liam's elementary description of the internal combustion engine.

Her mind still whirled over Liam's revelations, and so much physical evidence around her seemed to back them up. Toria made the command decision to go with the flow until things felt steadier. Or at least until her headache passed.

She'd return to investigate the stone herself, regardless of Liam's assertions that getting home was impossible.

But she didn't have to fake astonishment when they stepped outside. The park across the street stretched to the left and right as far as the eye could see, and marble buildings glowed in the long afternoon sun. A warm breeze stirred her hair, and she pushed it away from her face while she surveyed the sheer number of town-cars. They rumbled down the wide avenue in front of the museum's grand staircase, at the top of which Toria and Liam stood between two of the many columns that fronted the building.

Cars, she remembered. The term "town-car" hadn't become prevalent until language needed a term to differentiate the smaller electrical vehicles from the larger transports, which still ran on rationed diesel. The shiny behemoths here spat noxious fumes. It didn't appear to bother the pedestrians who strolled the sidewalks.

A handful of passing pedestrians stared back. She knew now the whispers and nudges when she first appeared had to do with her strange outfit. It marked her as different among women who all seemed to wear knee-length skirts and neat blouses. Not to mention her rapier. Going without it in an unfamiliar city where she had no allies didn't appeal to her, since she'd had the misfortune of being snatched through time without any of her knives.

"This is wild." Toria settled on those words instead of more colorful language, her original instinct. She'd been raised on arguments that women should have class—her father—and women should say whatever the fuck they wanted—her mother. Time to learn how to be the sort of woman her father might speak to if she ran into him.

Holy shit. Her dad was alive right now, though bonded to a different vampire. Her mom was alive, too, and her grandfather. Mikelos would be across the ocean in Europa, but running into Victory or Asaron here was a genuine risk.

Liam checked his wristwatch and tapped the face once. "I'm sorry, I don't mean to rush you. But we are on a bit of a schedule. I don't want to keep Mr. Ainsworth waiting."

Toria followed Liam down the museum steps and kept close to his heels as he turned onto the sidewalk. The magnificent façade of the museum gave way to a garden filled with a riot of spring colors, and she spotted hints of statuary hidden among the greenery. "Your boss?"

Liam paused next to one of the steel giants parked along the street. "No, not at all. Your host. He said he'd have a spot of dinner waiting." He opened the passenger door of the deep blue sedan for her.

She searched for a seat belt while Liam crossed to the driver's side. There was none.

But she was supposed to have never seen a car in her life. As Liam settled himself and adjusted the rearview mirror, she slid her hands over the luxurious leather of the bench seat. If she wanted to get technical, she hadn't seen a vehicle like this before. It had little in common with the compact electric town-cars of her own time.

She didn't fake her startled exclamation at the gasoline engine's rumble when Liam turned the ignition. She gripped the seat in both hands as Liam pulled into traffic. Though both polite and deferential so far, this time he flashed her a mischievous grin. "Scared?"

"Never!" Toria foresaw a lot of explanation of the obvious in her future as Liam "educated" her about this new time, and the sooner she convinced him nothing fazed her, the better. She appreciated this glimpse of his silliness though, evidence the man was more than a stodgy academic. She wasn't sure she could be friends with someone so one-dimensional.

She spent the rest of the ride gazing in honest wonder as Liam delivered on the promised abbreviated tour of Nacostina, rambling about the history of the area. He swung by the Governor-General's Monument, white marble shimmering in the setting sun and the skyscraping phallic symbol even more impressive in person than through black-and-white photographs. As they drove along the tidal basin of the Patowmeck River, Liam pointed out the cherry trees, a gift from the Qin Empire about thirty years ago. "It's a shame you missed the Cherry Blossom Festival last month," he said. "But there's always next year."

Curious how Liam didn't mention the current conflict out west, where the British contested the Qin over control of the Magnus River.

The Qin, who would destroy Nacostina soon.

She dug her nails into the seat leather as she forced her breathing even. Either Liam didn't notice her stillness while he described various places they passed, or he was content to fill the silence and assume Toria needed time to get her bearings. They soon pulled in front of a large house in a quiet neighborhood. The sun had almost set behind the houses, and antique streetlamps flickered between the giant sycamores along the street.

To be fair, antiquity surrounded her. Toria needed to re-evaluate how she labeled things. The world descended into silence as Liam shut off the car's engine. She inhaled for a count of five, then exhaled for another count of five as Liam passed in front of the car to open her door.

Toria allowed Liam to take her hand to escort her out of the vehicle. His grip was warm and firm, and her rough calluses from years of sword work scraped against his smooth academic's palm. He released her to shut the door, and Toria resettled her sword belt around her hips. Windows in the three-story house spilled light across the manicured front lawn. "This is where I'll be staying?"

It didn't compare in size to Victory's manor house where Toria had grown up, or to the sprawling estate of the mage school in Limani where she kept a small set of rooms between mercenary contracts, but it was still a grander dwelling than she'd expected. Unless Liam forgot to mention the horde of relatives who lived with Mr. Ainsworth? Or worse, servants? All of whom for which she would have to keep up the façade of being from the past.

Liam pointed to a sign post in the landscaping and chuckled. "Mr. Ainsworth retired from the museum to open a bed and breakfast about two years ago and has been refurbishing this place ever since. Maybe having his first guest will help him speed along the construction process."

She tried to return his smile as they mounted the steps of the wraparound porch, even if she didn't get the humor. White shutters gleamed against the stonework exterior even at dusk. The wooden porch was painted the same bright white, and she envisioned herself relaxing in one of the rocking chairs with a cool drink on a hot summer's day.

An older gentleman flung open the front door as Liam lifted his hand to knock. "Come in, come in! Supper is on the table." Despite his balding head fringed with short graying hair, and a few age spots faded into his tanned hands, there was nothing frail about the human who herded them inside. He towered a few inches over Liam, and the width of his chest could be described as muscular rather than portly. After exchanging a handshake with Liam, he turned his sharp gaze to Toria. "You must be Ms. Connor, my first tenant! Please call me Hugh. I hope you can excuse the mess." He shook Toria's hand with a firm grip, acknowledging the sword at her waist without batting an eyelash. His paint-stained canvas pants and rumpled shirt also led Toria to relax, despite the grandeur of the foyer. But though the hanging chandelier gleamed, the wooden floors and staircases needed a desperate polish and half the atrocious floral wallpaper remained unstripped.

His good humor was infectious. She returned a genuine smile. "Thank you. And call me Toria, please."

Liam shut the front door behind them. "Hopefully she's your first tenant of many. How long since your retirement party?"

"Now, now," Hugh said. "You can't rush a man's labor of love."

They followed Hugh down a long hall toward the rear of the house, and Toria glimpsed more half-finished rooms and sheet-covered furniture. She saw a lot of renovation work in her future to repay this kindness, at least until… until… too many thoughts crashed about in her head, too many possibilities to contemplate now. Her stomach gnawed at her spine.

Their final destination was a welcoming kitchen, filled with warm woods and gleaming, brand-new appliances. Toria assumed the range and refrigerator were state-of-the-art, even as the absence of a microwave struck her. Hugh had placed three silverware settings at a trestle table, and he bustled around the kitchen filling water glasses and retrieving a basket of steaming rolls from the oven. Toria unbuckled her sword belt and leaned the weapon against the wall, and she and Liam settled on opposite benches.

It was simple bachelor's fare—the long pasta in a red sauce hinted at Roman influence despite Hugh's very British name. But once the food sat before Toria, the outside world all but disappeared. Liam and Hugh seemed amiable to gossip about current and former museum coworkers while she inhaled the pasta and worked her way through half the basket of rolls. Once she couldn't eat another bite and pushed her plate away, Liam offered to help with cleanup.

"Thank you for the kind offer, but we'll manage." Hugh cleared his dishes from the table and piled them on the counter next to the sink. "You'll be back tomorrow?"

"Yes. Toria had good timing in arriving during the weekend." Liam leaned against the counter as Toria finished her glass of water and Hugh started on the dishes.

"I do what I can?" It wasn't as if Toria had intended to trip over a magical artifact and end up in a world poised for catastrophe. She carried her empty glass to the sink and retrieved the dishtowel Hugh pointed out to dry the clean dishes.

"Well, I'll be here around eleven in the morning. I'll treat you both to lunch and we can put together a curriculum of things you need to know. Perhaps show you around the city a bit more?" Liam pushed off the counter.

"I can loan a shirt for you to sleep in tonight, but some clothes shopping would also not go amiss." Hugh cocked his head at Toria, and her face heated when both men appraised her garb.

"Yes, right. I suppose we'll manage something." All of a sudden, Liam seemed in a rush to leave, checking his watch and glancing at the darkness outside the kitchen window. Hugh wiped a hand dry to exchange a handshake. Liam assured them he could show himself out and fled from the kitchen.

"What the hell was that about?" Toria wiped dry the final glass and set it on the counter. Too late, she hoped her language didn't offend Hugh.

Hugh tossed his head with a laugh. "My fault, there. I reminded the kid that you're a person instead of an academic curiosity."

Toria handed over dishes, paying attention to where Hugh placed each item in cupboards. "He's an elf. Not much of a kid." Estimation became difficult after a certain point, but Liam might be Hugh's elder by at least a hundred years.

"But not my boss anymore, so I'll call him what I want."

During dinner, Toria learned Hugh had worked at the museum in an artistic capacity, designing and building exhibits based on the curators' needs. It explained why he thought house renovation counted as a relaxing retirement, she supposed.

Hugh closed a final cupboard. "Let me show you around the place. Don't worry, the third floor is finished, like this kitchen. I'm only taking my sweet time with the guest areas."

Toria leaned against the counter and tried to act casual. "I thought I'd explore the neighborhood a bit first, before it gets too late. Check out the shops we passed around the corner."

Hugh mirrored her position, hip cocked against counter and arms crossed. "I'm not sure that's a good idea." His lips pressed into a fine line.

She bristled. "Why not? I can take care of myself." Did she give the impression of fragility? She'd crashed into this time period wearing a sword and declared herself a master-level mage, for crying out loud. Except she'd told Liam the rapier was nothing more than a magical focus. Keeping this straight was a nightmare.

Hugh lifted his hands. "That's not what I meant at all. Call me old-fashioned, but you might get more attention than you bargained for in that get-up. And I think you're looking to scope the place out, not become the talk of the town."

Astute, and yet another reminder of the drastic societal changes after the Last War. Hugh might be older, but he was no fool. Toria sagged against the counter, the adrenaline crash sapping her energy. "I can deal with the fancy tops, but please tell me that some women in this time period wear pants."

"I promise pants in your future." Hugh placed one hand over his heart in vow. His eyes shot to Toria's rapier for a split second before settling on her. "Now, I'm not used to seeing ladies with their arms uncovered unless they're in a ball gown, but something tells me by the state of your muscles you know how to use that pointy toy over there."

"You could say that." Toria crossed to the table and hefted the sword. It wasn't a crutch, but having contact with it soothed something in her. "It's not exactly a toy."

"I might not be a fancy curator like Liam, but I've enough experience to see it's the real thing." Toria's opinion of Hugh increased yet another few notches when he made no move toward the sword, but seemed content to admire from afar. "You mentioned during dinner that you're also a mage?"

"Correct." Further elaboration didn't seem necessary, but she braced for a barrage of questions. She wanted to like and trust this man, but magic could throw a wrench into anything.

"Don't suppose you know any magic spells for removing wallpaper older than my mother?"

Her optimism lasted until Hugh left Toria in her new bedroom, wishing her a good night and agreeing whoever woke first made the coffee.

She prowled the room beneath the eaves in the rear of the house. A small bed tucked against the wall where the ceiling sloped the farthest. The bedside lamp cast shadows against the irregular angles of the room. Empty wardrobe. No surprises.

Toria loosened the laces of her boots and tugged them off. Her hiking socks followed, and her toes sank into the plush area rug over the refinished hardwood floor.

She propped her rapier against the nightstand, though she doubted any sort of attack would come in the night. Still, this was an alien place filled with dangers she couldn't predict. She stripped off her modern clothing and still felt naked even after she pulled on the soft nightshirt Hugh loaned her.

The room wasn't stuffy, but the air contained traces of the paint and floor polish Hugh used during his renovations. Toria pushed open the window for the late-spring breeze, bringing with it the aromas of gardens and fresh-cut grass. She switched off the lamp and curled under the soft quilt and lavender-scented sheets.

After her minor meltdown in Liam's office, Toria had drifted with the flow. Taking in information. Figuring out what was safe to say and which appropriate questions to ask. React, instead of act.

Now, in silence broken by cicadas outside, she had time to think. Thinking meant strategy. And strategy meant figuring out the facts and the questions.

Fact: She had travelled back in time.

To believe otherwise right now would be to disconnect from apparent reality, and that wasn't a road Toria was prepared to travel.

Fact: In six months, the Qin Empire destroyed Nacostina in a surprise aerial attack. This attack on the colonial capital was in retaliation for the British bombing of Wan City on the western coast of the New Continent. The Qin hoped this would destroy the British ability to mount an immediate offense.

Fact: An artifact, which may or may not be the artifact she was hired to find, sent her to the past.

Fact: She had to pretend to be from the past in order to prevent damage to the timeline.

Or did she?

Didn't her mere presence affect the timeline? How much had she already changed? What if she had interrupted plans Liam or Hugh had for the evening, influencing other events down the line?

Sharp pain lanced between her temples, and Toria jerked upright. She pressed her face between her knees and tried not to hyperventilate. She made her living as a warrior, but she was a scientist at heart. This sort of theoretical physics was way above her paygrade, not to mention outside her realms of chemistry and metallurgy, but the same logic might work here.

Theory the first: Every moment, every word, every action she made from this point forward had a ripple effect that altered her future.

Theory the second: Travelling back in time had created a parallel universe, branching off from the world she knew. When she made it home, everything would be as she left it.

She didn't know which was more depressing. She could save the city and avert a world war at the expense of ever seeing her family again. Or perhaps Nacostina's destruction was inevitable.

More permutations existed, such as traveling forward and creating more parallel times, or even the basic fact that she might never make it home. Did a malleable future exist at all, even if she'd already been there?

Sweat coated her skin, so she threw off her blanket. The room didn't give her much area to pace, but at least the rug muffled her footsteps. The breeze cooled her sweat-dampened limbs.

But no way existed to establish which theory was the correct one. To be on the safe side, she had to make as few ripples as possible.

First: She could leave Nacostina. Take advantage of Hugh and Liam's generosity until she was kitted out in contemporary clothing and slip away in the night. She had her sword and her magic. All she needed, in the end.

Don't think about Kane. Don't think about Kane. Don't think about Kane.

The biggest trick would be staying away from familiar faces. Staying in the path of the oncoming war was dangerous, but so was escaping to Europa.

Second: She could stay in Nacostina. Take advantage of the hospitality until she made her own way. She knew Victory had visited the city at least once in the year prior to its destruction, but no reason existed for them to cross paths if she kept to herself.

She knew the exact date of the city's demise. Where she came from, everyone in the modern civilized world knew the date. Toria could collect a nest egg and disappear a few days prior. Head south for the neutral Roman colonies and hide out along the coast until the war ended.

This option was safest and caused the least amount of impact in the long run. All she had to do was acknowledge she would spend the rest of her life in a backwater town. Once the British and Qin decimated the interior of the continent, she could find a job protecting a small farming settlement from mutated monsters, which crawled out of the Wasteland even decades in the future.

After another turn on her heel, Toria drew to a halt. Yeah. That would be the plan, at least until she felt more comfortable with her surroundings. She settled on the edge of the bed. Her surging adrenaline meant sleep was no longer an immediate option, but at least she had a tentative plan.

The plan sucked, and she despised it, but she saw no other immediate options as the air in the room stifled her, and her breath came in short, hard gasps. Not unless she woke in a pile of rubble with Kane and her mother standing above her. Or better yet, home in Limani, to find this entire thing a vivid, distressing nightmare.

Now, her other problem.

She cleared her lungs and centered herself.

The good news: she wasn't dead. She already knew from experience—a memory she shuddered away from—that if Kane died, she would soon follow. Since she wasn't dead, it meant the connection between them existed across time.

With deft mental fingers, she sought the internal seed she recognized as the earth element of her partner. Cupping hands of power around the seed, she poured energy in and around it. Even if she couldn't reach Kane, her life depended on protecting that tiny connection.

So much ambient energy flowed around and through her that she never touched her internal reserves. If this was the state of magic in the world that was, no wonder so few mages remained in her time. Though she and Kane had disrupted the world spell limiting future technology, the amount of power it sucked away in less than a century staggered her. Generations would pass before mages saw power at these levels again, if her kind even survived that long.

The last time they were magically separated, when he'd been kidnapped in college during Roma's futile takeover attempt of Limani, Syri used her power to connect them and access Toria's magical ability.

She didn't have Syri this time.

How much more could the world steal from her?

This time, she collapsed onto the bed and allowed the tears to come, burying her face in her pillow to mute the sobs. The pain of clogged sinuses warred with the ache still lingering at the back of her skull. She clutched her left wrist with her opposite hand, digging nails into delicate skin as she tried to draw metaphorical strength from the tattoo there.

When she, Kane, and Archer reunited in Limani after Syri's death, they had each gotten inked with the names of the other three. To honor Syri's memory and as a reminder they were stronger together. That they faced the world together.

Now, she traced the elven runes naming Kane Nalamas, Syrisinia, and Archer Sophin. It was a promise broken.

Now, she was alone.

BETWEEN

Victory reined in uncoordinated limbs and staggered to her feet, drawing her sword and ignoring the ache in her tailbone. She dropped into a defensive position and turned full circle, bracing for attack.

None came. She stood alone in a long gallery. Moonlight poured in from high windows, and red emergency lighting at the far end of the hall reflected on marble floors. Display cases lined the walls, and her enhanced eyesight picked minerals and gemstones out of the darkness. Even as the back of her mind cataloged karat weights and worth, the rest of her brain noted something much more urgent.

She was alone in this museum gallery. No heartbeats. No Toria.

The muted sounds of a city at night penetrated the gallery. Including, of all things, more liquid-fuel engines than she'd heard in one place since her visit to Jiang Yi Yue, a city where the vehicles ran on ethanol.

A museum gallery. Gasoline-powered engines.

Even inside, she scented the tang of gasoline below the harsh aroma of cleaning supplies and traces of body odor from those who had passed through this hall today.

A museum gallery, with a type of emergency lighting she hadn't seen in years. *Gasoline* engines.

It was like she'd gone back in time.

Ridiculous.

Buried among the smells of other people, she plucked out one in particular. After so many years, she knew her daughter's unique scent—her skin, her hair, her sword. Even if Toria wasn't here now, she had been in the recent past.

With no immediate attack imminent, Victory sheathed her sword.

The long hall had exits at either end. Flipping a mental coin, Victory picked a direction. It was child's play to pick the basic lock on the massive metal door and haul it open.

Once through, she found herself on the second-floor balcony of a tall rotunda. Moonlight filtered into the large windows closer to the ceiling, and the marble architecture shimmered in the pale light. The entrance to another exhibit gallery sat opposite the wide expanse of space, this one advertising the flora of the New Continent. Victory stepped to the edge of the balcony and peered down, onto the dusty top of a giant stuffed mammoth.

"Hank." Her voice, no more than a whisper, seemed to echo in the emptiness. She recognized the animal, or at least the affectionate term by which visitors had known it. She knew this museum, which was why Toria had asked her along on this job.

She could no longer pretend this was anything else. She had returned to Nacostina before the Last War, before the destruction of the city. Her fingers gripped the marble railing at the balcony's edge. Of all the things, her first worry was how pissed off Asaron would be when she disappeared off the face of the planet. Whenever she left Limani, he assumed the role of Master of the City. He did so with lots of begrudging complaints, but deep down, Victory knew he enjoyed the change of pace from traditional mercenary life.

But the kids lived dangerous lives, having followed in the footsteps of their adopted mother and grandfather. Victory always took the chance to spend time with them, even if it meant traipsing around a ruined city hunting for a rock.

Victory was hundreds of years old. She had seen the rise and fall of civilizations. She had already experienced one complete paradigm shift when the elves blocked the progress of technology. It wasn't so far-fetched that she might experience another.

Time travel. Who'd have thought?

So, two goals. Find Toria. Find the way home.

But first, she had to break out of a museum. Victory examined her options, what she could see and what she could remember. Lots of windows in the gallery she had come from, but they consisted of many panes. The heavy leading would be a chore to break through. Massive front doors out of the bottom of the rotunda where Hank surveyed his domain would also be tricky to disguise an escape.

There had to be other ways out of the building. Staff entrances. Loading docks. Things she'd never had reason to pay attention to, and therefore had no reason to remember now.

At least security cameras were not a concern in this era.

The *thud-thud* of a heartbeat shattered the silence, accompanied by boots sauntering across marble flooring and relaxed breathing.

Security guards, however, were a concern.

BEFORE

For a girl spoiled by lattes, coffee circa one hundred years ago was a shock to the system. But caffeine was caffeine, so Toria entertained Hugh with a wide variety of facial expressions as she choked down the bitter brew, harsh despite copious amounts of cream and sugar. After, she helped him shove the parlor furniture to the center of the room in preparation for removing the rest of the atrocious wallpaper as they waited for Liam.

When a car honked outside, Toria freed her hair from its borrowed handkerchief.

"I'm not sure that's a good idea," Hugh said as she reached for her rapier, propped in the corner of the foyer.

Toria knew he was right. If she was determined to remain as low-key as possible, she didn't need to make her social entrance to Nacostina as the armed woman in weird clothes. She dragged reluctant fingers across the hilt as she stepped away.

Hugh pulled open the front door. "Besides, I doubt you're helpless without it."

Toria followed him down the front walk toward Liam's idling vehicle. "I accept the compliment."

After her swift comfort with Hugh, a bout of shyness bit Toria at meeting Liam again. She ducked into the backseat before Hugh insisted otherwise and spent the drive in silence, now seeing the city in full daylight. Families out and about, young couples strolling the boulevards.

Because she knew the conflict with the Qin Empire was inevitable, Toria couldn't help but see the specter of death hang over everyone they passed. She drew away from the window and slumped against the leather seat with her eyes closed. Trying to ignore it was like the chorus of a song on repeat, or trying not to think of the word "yellow." Her brain kept circling. If everyone was already dead, did that absolve her of the responsibility of warning them? What cost would the protection of the timeline incur on her very being?

"Toria?"

She jumped at Liam's voice. When she opened her eyes, the car was still and he and Hugh twisted in their seats to stare at her. Liam must have called her name more than once. "Sorry. Long night. Didn't sleep well."

"I can't even begin to imagine."

His concern was harder to accept than Hugh's. Toria pushed open her door. "Shall we? I'm starved."

They followed her out into a quiet neighborhood. A few parked cars lined one side of the street, but an elven woman riding a horse trotted down the road. For a brief moment, Toria imagined herself home in Limani.

She blinked again, and Nacostina crashed back harder than ever.

Liam stretched out an arm, as if encompassing the entire boulevard. "I thought it might be easier to handle all of this in Nacostina's elven district. No one here will look twice at what you're wearing, and we have an appointment with my clothier to fill out your wardrobe."

Without waiting for agreement, he led them to a café with elven script on the plate-glass window. He greeted the waitstaff by name, and soon the trio nestled in a corner. Without any of them ordering, a waitress carried plate after plate from the kitchen, presenting them with an elven high tea.

Even with the gorgeous weather outside, the spice tea warmed her from the inside out. As Toria reached for the teapot for a second cup, Liam's hand darted across the table and caught her wrist in gentle fingers.

"What's this?" He pulled Toria's palm up, tracing the delicate runes on the inside of her wrist. "I didn't notice yesterday."

Hugh lifted the teapot and refilled Toria's delicate cup. "A lot was going on yesterday."

Liam's fingertips warmed her skin with five points of heat. "They're names, but I don't recognize them."

Because they hadn't been born yet. Toria suppressed both her initial retort and the shiver caused by Liam's light touch. "They're friends. I guess they didn't make the history books."

He didn't resist when Toria withdrew her arm. She cradled her teacup in both hands, distancing herself from the table and the latest waves of sympathy from Hugh. The pastry settled heavy in her stomach.

"I'm sorry, that was indelicate of me." Liam nudged a plate of candied fruit closer to Toria. "You must miss them terribly."

"One of them passed away a few years ago." Toria accepted his apology and selected one of the treats. "But yes. The other two are…were close to me." Understatement of the century. Her brothers in all but blood.

Oblivious to the sudden awkwardness at the table, their waitress returned to ask how everything was. Liam requested the check, which prompted a small argument with Hugh. Toria shrank further in her chair, reminded once again of her reliance on the charity of these strangers. Whatever Liam said about the museum's budget for such circumstances, Toria would feel better when she could care for herself.

Once the bill was settled, the last of the tea sipped, and the table cleared, Liam led them out of the café. True to his word, not more than a handful of people exclaimed at Toria's appearance—each of them human. The elves they passed favored the group with pleasant expressions.

"Don't let them fool you. They're all dying of curiosity." Liam held open a door tucked between two storefronts labeled with elven runes Toria couldn't read. She and Hugh climbed steep wooden steps as he continued speaking over his shoulder. "The head curator at the museum is also elven, and I telephoned him about you last night. His wife is a bit of a gossip, and it's not a huge community."

"Nothing's changed, then." In Toria's experience, gossip was an essential elven food group.

Liam's entire face lit at her quip, but before he responded, the door at the top of the stairwell burst open and a face peered at them. "Come in, come in. Don't dawdle."

In a whirlwind of activity that left almost no time for Toria to breathe, she received a hearty greeting and handshake from a tiny elven lady with skin as earth-dark as Kane's and hair as silver as Toria's rapier. The elderly woman—"Kearestia, but call me Granny Tia, dear"—was so old she even had smile lines that deepened the corner of her eyes. And Toria had the immediate impression Granny Tia did a lot of smiling.

The shop could be mistaken for a cozy sitting room if not for the wall plastered with fabric samples. After she shuffled Liam and Hugh off to a table in the corner, Granny Tia settled Toria next to her in a loveseat and spread a selection of catalogs on the low table before them. "First things first. Liam has told me of your interesting circumstances, and I thought it would be more helpful to give you an overview of current clothing styles before overwhelming you with garments."

Toria could have kissed Granny Tia. She had braced for such an experience. "That sounds perfect, thank you."

The conversation that followed might still have overwhelmed her if not for how hard Granny Tia worked to put Toria at ease, joking with her about atrocious color combinations and agreeing the fashion industry left much to be desired regarding unrealistic representations of the female body. But the clothier balked when Toria suggested she might be more comfortable in some of the available men's patterns.

"Unacceptable." Granny Tia sniffed in disdain. "Perhaps a few pairs of tailored slacks, but I'm not sure where this fascination you have with denim comes from. Suitable only for farmhands and ruffians." She peered at Toria and plucked at her hiking pants. "Unless you were a farmhand. I'm unfamiliar with this material, but it seems sturdy enough for manual labor."

Toria laughed, aware when Liam stopped all pretense of paging through a pattern book to listen. Hugh had tilted his head against the wall to enjoy a post-lunch snooze. "Not a farmhand, no." She wasn't about to explain sweat-wicking fabric. Her mind raced in another direction. What had she told Liam so far? She was from Limani. She was a mage. "I was a tutor, I suppose you could say. Teaching children with magical ability similar to my own."

Close enough. When Kane and Toria spent time at home at Limani's mage school between contracts, Toria did tutor two particular students, with Archer happy to relinquish the subtler aspects of storm magic to her expertise.

Granny Tia patted her hand again. "My mother was a teacher, too. Now what do you think of the neckline on this blouse?"

After they finished perusing the catalogs, Granny Tia led Toria into a dressing room to measure her in privacy. She clucked over Toria's broad shoulders and curves but assured her the slim, boyish silhouette was on its way out of fashion.

She didn't say anything about the tattoo on her wrist. Her sports bra concealed most of the second tattoo between her shoulder blades, her rapier crossed with Kane's scimitar. Toria wasn't sure how she would have explained it.

When she emerged from the back room, Liam and Hugh both rose from their seats. Granny Tia had provided her with simple black cotton slacks, which fell straight from her hips to brush the tops of ballet-style elven slippers. The plum button-up shirt strained across her breasts, now supported by a full-coverage brassiere. Toria wanted to force the invention of the underwire, but the blouse's light silk would be comfortable on her skin as the weather warmed.

Liam cleared his throat. "You look nice, Toria. Much more appropriate to this era."

Granny Tia bustled around the room, pulling fabric swatches from the wall and selecting pattern books from a shelf. "I know it's cliché to put a storm mage in purple, but that blouse does bring out her eyes. I couldn't resist." She paused in her whirlwind of activity to smooth the fabric on Toria's shoulder. "These will do for now. I'll have a few more things altered by this evening and have them sent to Mr. Ainsworth's. Have one of your young gentlemen bring you back in a few days so I can check the fit on the rest."

Heat rose in Toria's cheeks. Neither of the men were young, though everyone was perhaps young compared to Granny Tia.

Liam's ears reddened. "I'll arrange something, Granny Tia. Thank you again for fitting us into your schedule."

Granny Tia reached up to pat him on the cheek. "It is my pleasure. You go on now, and finish getting our girl settled in to her new life."

Toria gave her thanks as well. Emotion choked her throat when Granny Tia ignored her offered hand and swept her into a hug. Maintaining a stern mercenary image was hard when you couldn't even tell anyone you were a mercenary. She regained her composure by the time they left the clothier shop. Hugh once again tucked her hand into the crook of his arm. He slowed his pace until they dropped a few steps behind Liam on the way to the car, leaning over to whisper in her ear. "I'm proud of you, kid. I'm not sure I could hold it together this well."

"Thanks, Hugh." She hugged his arm. "You missed my meltdown last night."

"I'd be more worried if you hadn't confessed to a meltdown." They drew even with Liam before Hugh said more, and she didn't resist when he offered her the front passenger seat for the trip home.

The drive began in silence, but Toria didn't miss the glances Liam made, as if he wanted to say something but didn't know how. As if he'd had a better idea of how to handle her when she was an intriguing artifact to be studied, but now that she blended into his normal surroundings, he was more inclined to treat her like a boring human woman.

Well, that wouldn't do. Toria might be in over her head, but she was never, ever boring. "Thank you for the delicious lunch today. And for orchestrating the appointment with Granny Tia. I'm not sure how I would have handled this on my own."

"Lunch was my treat. You're very welcome." Liam maneuvered the large vehicle around a slower car. "So, you're a governess?"

Ah, the next round of interrogation. "Something like that."

"Is that something you were interested in continuing?"

Toria twisted herself to face him. Behind them, Hugh stared out the window as if the passing scenery was the most interesting thing in the world. "It's an option I'd considered. I'm trained in a variety of things, so there has to be something I'm qualified to do here."

"I hope you're aware that it's not necessary." This time, Liam gripped the steering wheel with both hands, and tension strained his shoulders under his tailored sport coat.

"What the hell else am I supposed to do with my time?"

Liam flinched at her language, but didn't respond until after he'd shifted gears and pulled into Hugh's quieter neighborhood. "First of all, it might be a good idea to give you some lessons on the particulars of the future. You have some history to catch up on, and it might help you blend in better."

"I see." Toria tilted her head forward, as if eyeing him over the rims of the sunglasses she'd left behind in the future. "Teach me how to be a proper lady, is that it?" When the length of Liam's silence made it obvious he had no immediate response, she gave an unladylike snort just to see him flinch again. "Okay, fine. Civilization lessons it is. When do we start?"

Liam slid the car to a smooth halt before Hugh's house. "Will it suit you if we meet for lunch again tomorrow?" His fingers tapped the gear stick, and he avoided her gaze.

"I'm sure I'll manage to fit it into my busy schedule." Without waiting for a response, Toria exited the car and stormed toward Hugh's front door. The door was locked, of course, so she threw herself into a rocking chair while Hugh exchanged his farewells.

Instead of unlocking the door, Hugh set the package of Toria's clothing in front of it and settled into the other rocker. He lifted one arm in a wave, and Liam pulled away from the curb. When the car disappeared around the block, Hugh turned to Toria. "Gonna tell me what that was about?"

She tucked one foot under herself and pushed the rocker with the toes of her other. "I can't imagine that Liam expects me to fritter away the rest of my life as a woman of leisure, even after he trains me to be a proper woman by Nacostina's standards."

Hugh matched her pace with his own rocking chair, lacing his fingers together across his stomach. "You have to remember that nothing like this ever happened during my time at the museum, and I started a good decade before Liam moved here from Europa, along with the head curator. But I know the annual budget includes funds for such incidents. I bet the compounded interest is...extensive, at this point. So, yes, you could be a woman of leisure for quite a while."

The streetlights flickered on one by one, and down the street, an unseen mother called her children for dinner. "That doesn't sit well with me."

"And that right there is another reason I like you."

Hugh seemed content to enjoy the warm evening air while Toria brooded. How much to tell him? Even though he agreed with her side of this odd moral dilemma, some context would not go amiss. But how much could she explain about her past in the context of the history she was creating for herself? What could she say without compromising the secret she must protect?

She could begin small, then gauge the rest from Hugh's reactions. "I've never been a woman of leisure, though you could say I come from an upper-class background." A quick glance to Hugh, who dipped his chin once in encouragement. "I have a college degree. More than one, if you consider I graduated in multiple specialties. I'm also a master-level mage, a status I obtained before college. And I have master-level status in the Mercenary Guild." She held her breath. If he asked for details, her cover might fall apart. Her life story was colorful enough even without throwing in the warrior-mage thing. Or the adopted-by-a-vampire thing.

Hugh's expression was more thoughtful than confused. "That does explain the muscles."

His response startled a laugh out of Toria. "Like I said, the sword's not just for show."

"Can I ask why you won't share all of this with Liam?"

"I don't know." Some of the tension bled out of her skin at Hugh's calm responses. "I guess I don't think he could handle it? He has such strong expectations and ideas about what he thinks is right."

"Sounds like an elf to me." Hugh shrugged one shoulder.

Toria curled her lips in a smirk. "Sounds like a man to me."

He roared in laughter, leaning forward and slapping his knees. "You got me there, kid!" After pushing himself out of the rocker, he dug in his pocket for his keyring. "Ready to go in? I can throw together something for dinner."

"Actually…" Toria brought her rocker to a stop and stood, stretching her arms toward the porch ceiling and twisting her spine until it popped. "Can I borrow some cash?"

Hugh had already stepped inside, but he poked his head out the door. "Of course. You don't have to tell me, but can I ask why?" He'd already pulled his wallet out of a back pocket.

Toria reached past him, inside the door, and snagged her sword. Slinging the belt over her shoulder, she considered how to answer. Lying wasn't worth it in the long run. She had no idea how long finding a way home would take, and she needed a more reliable source of income in the meantime. "Because I can't be a woman of leisure, and I have to figure out how to make my way in this world. I'm going to go try my luck with the Mercenary Guild first."

Once again, she steeled herself for a negative response, and once again, Hugh surprised her in the best way possible. He handed over a wad of bills and pointed down the street. "I'll put your things in your room. Best place to find a cab is about two blocks that way. Good luck."

Toria stretched on tiptoes to press a kiss to Hugh's cheek. "Thanks."

In the timeless manner of cabbies everywhere, the driver didn't question Toria's sword or her requested address. The city slid by as late afternoon darkened to dusk, and when the taxi halted before a squat brick building, Toria picked out the door plaque highlighted by an overhead lamp: Nacostina Mercenary Guildhall.

She paid the driver, with what she hoped was a decent tip, and stepped out of the car with a deep breath.

A middle-aged human couple gave a wide berth as they passed her on the sidewalk. Between the sword and elven slippers, Toria was a walking anachronism. She dashed up the Guildhall's front steps and tugged on the brass door handle polished to a golden sheen by years of calloused merc hands.

The familiar scents of mingled weapon polish, sweat, and alcohol assaulted her. She pushed the door closed and crossed the foyer to the large desk, where the evening's administrator on duty waited. The man showed all the typical signs of a retired merc. Receding hairline. Two missing fingers on his left hand. Leathery skin from the wear of outdoor-living.

He leaned with his wooden chair balanced on two legs, boots propped on the desk. He let his magazine drop and righted the chair with a slam on the linoleum flooring. "Can I help you?"

Toria's fingers itched to pull her Guild ID from her wallet, but why carry her wallet when nothing in it could pass as real? "Good evening. I'd like to inquire about joining the Guild."

The man made no effort to hide the way he scanned her body, making her fingers itch in a different fashion. "Yeah. Right." He sat back in his chair again, magazine in hand.

Toria leaned across the desk and plucked the magazine away. "Good evening. I'm here to join the Mercenary Guild. You must not have heard me the first time." She set the magazine on the desk with her hand flat, so he couldn't dismiss her outright a second time.

"You're kidding, right?" At least this time, Toria recognized a professional appraisal under his leer. "You can't walk in with a fancy sword you stole from Daddy and sign on the dotted line. There are qualifications. Hoops to jump through."

"The sword is mine." Toria hitched the belt higher on her shoulder. Wearing it on her hip looked better, but these damned pants didn't have belt loops. "And I guarantee I can pass every apprenticeship test within a week." Three forms of armed combat, two forms of unarmed combat, firearm accuracy, survival skills, horseback riding—which didn't even take her magic into account.

That gave her an idea.

Though the extra flourishes of showmanship weren't her usual style, Toria snapped her fingers once. The man jumped as a spark of electricity danced across her fingers and disappeared in a tiny starburst of ball lightning. The smell of ozone charged the room. "Also, there's that."

His mouth had gaped open at her display, but he shut it with a snap. "What the hell do you think you are? Some kind of warrior-mage?"

Abort! Abort! Toria made a show of dismissing his question with an amused snort of laughter. "Don't be silly. I lucked out, and all my abilities are combat applicable."

"Yeah, lucky." The merc tugged his magazine out from under her hand. He flipped it open with a snap and smirked at her. "But I bet you still can't grow a dick with them."

Oh, for crying out loud. "I can't join the Guild because I'm a woman? Ridiculous. I know at least one woman who's an active member right now."

"And who might that be?"

"Victory."

It was the merc's turn to laugh, but at least he lowered his magazine again. "Because she's a vampire, kid. I doubt they were going to turn her away when the Guild charter finalized worldwide, oh, a few centuries ago. If you were serious about this, you'd already know human women aren't allowed membership."

As a matter of fact, Toria was familiar with some historical versions of the Guild charter. But she hadn't figured the "no human women" clause also applied to those with magical ability, since women of the supernatural variants were admitted. Not just vampires, but elves and werecreatures, too. This outdated version lived up to the societal expectations of its time. So much for Liam's claim that this shiny new future was so civilized compared to where Toria claimed to be from.

She drew herself straight. Arguing with the guy was no use, at least not right now. Later, if the situation called for it, she would return at a more reasonable hour and make an appointment with the Guildmaster like a professional. "Thank you for your time. Have a good evening."

"Whatever, lady."

Toria left the Guildhall and leaned against the brick wall, still warm from the setting sun. She closed her eyes to block out the world. Evening traffic rumbled, and music blasted from the open doors of the bar down the block. She didn't want to return to Hugh's yet. Not with this failure still ringing in her ears.

The Mercenary Guildhall wasn't in the best part of Nacostina, which suited what she knew of the Guild's status during this point in history. With more advanced military technologies like planes and rockets, mercenaries reduced their niche to private security. Not a stable way to make a living for more than a handful of skilled people.

She resettled the belt on her shoulder and ambled in the direction of the loud bar, which seemed to draw her in. She wasn't sure what appealed to her, once she got closer and found what she expected: a seedy merc bar with a dim interior.

Toria fingered Hugh's cash in her pocket. Should be enough for at least one drink. Anything bottled had to be okay, despite the shoddiness of the furniture. The sticky floor sucked at her thin soles as she crossed the threshold.

The place wasn't packed, but the evening was young. Toria slipped between tables of men interchangeable with the merc at the Guildhall. She settled herself on an empty stool at the back, propping her sword against the bar between her knees and rolling her shoulders loose. The sword belt had dug into the strap of the awful brassiere, and the lack of weight was a relief.

Something pinged the edge of her consciousness, the sensation of eyes on the back of her head. But when she peeked over her shoulder, the curious glances diminished as the bar patrons realized she wasn't going to be an interesting distraction.

The bartender made her way down the opposite side of the used and abused wood to stand in front of Toria. The petite woman's skin was a deep sepia, and her dark eyes disappeared around the black of her pupils. She jabbed her thumbs into the top of the apron tried around her hips, and her left eyebrow tried to join the mass of wild black curls tied back with a scarf. "I think you're in the wrong bar, lady."

But her eyes flashed with protectiveness, so on impulse, Toria decided to try for humor. "There's alcohol here, so I'm pretty sure I'm exactly where I intend to be." She pointed at the display of empty beer bottles positioned above the liquor shelf. "I'll try that red ale, please."

The bartender didn't seem impressed. She crossed her arms instead of fetching the drink. "No offense, but I'm asking for cash up-front. I've had my share of thrill-seekers here to lead on the men. It always ends with tabs the men refuse to pay when the ladies disappear rather than go home with them."

"Good to know some things never change." Keeping her wad of money unseen beneath the bar ledge, Toria peeled a bill out of the stack and handed it over. A spark of electricity jumped between the two women when Toria's fingertips brushed the bartender's palm.

"Ow!" The woman snatched her hand away, dropping the crumbled bill to the bar and shaking her fingers. "What the hell?"

Toria had no idea. Nothing like that had ever happened. But that wouldn't fly if she didn't want to be kicked out for shocking the bartender. "Sorry, sorry." She shoved the money back in her pocket and held up both hands in apology. "Residual energy from a trick I did earlier. Won't happen again."

The woman pursed her lips, but said nothing as she turned away. She pulled a bottle of beer out of a cooler and popped the cap, then slid it to Toria, careful not to get anywhere near her. After a quick visual check to ensure none of the nearby patrons needed her attention, she leaned her hip on the bar across from Toria. "You're a mage, then?"

With a half-shrug, Toria took a pull of the beer. This was a merc bar, so the same cover she'd presented at the Guildhall might be the best idea. "Just a bit of the blood, a few minor skills."

"I know what you mean." The bartender pulled a rag out of her apron and rubbed circles on the bar top. "My mum wasn't an earth mage, but I swear she could make anything bloom."

Out of habit, Toria flicked the mental switch for her magesight. Ambient energy blared into view, and she gritted her teeth against a flinch. Toria fought through the brilliance until everything evened out, the way eyes needed time to adjust after removing sunglasses on a bright day. She picked out the bartender's aura at once. Most of it showed typical human shades of silver and gray, but sparkling motes of green surrounded her like a shimmer of emerald dust. Toria's adrenaline surged. "I don't know—you might have a bit of earth magic in your blood, too." She dismissed her magesight in time to see the woman frown.

"Did you just check my aura?" Her hand stilled on the rag.

"Yes. I'm sorry?"

"Seems a bit impertinent to let someone look inside my skin when I don't even know her name." The bartender offered her hand across the bar, but paused midway. "Are you going to zap me again?"

"I promise not to." Toria shook her hand, happy to note the woman's firm grip in a meeting of equals. "Toria Connor. Thanks for the drink."

"Lyra Brownlee. It's my pleasure." A drink order summoned her attention, and she held up one finger in promise to return before darting away.

Toria sat in silence and enjoyed her drink. The initial sensation of being watched had vanished, so she seemed to have lost her "mysterious stranger" intrigue. Lyra was right, though. This was a merc bar with typical mercs. She grew up with modern mercs in Limani, who viewed her as half stalwart equal and half little-sister-combination-mascot. These were pre-Last War mercenaries, a different breed. They would show her no more respect than the man at the Guildhall. There was a good chance they would show even less, regardless of her skill with sword or magic.

She twisted the beer bottle between restless fingers. If she couldn't be a mercenary in this "enlightened" era of women's rights, what alternative money-making opportunities did she have?

This was dumb. She was twenty-four years old. She had the equivalent of multiple degrees. There had to be something else she could do.

Magic? Leave the sword at Hugh's and present herself to the local mage school? Make up a history from the Roman colonies to the south, which had less of a formal magical education system. Ask whether they had any openings for a "house mom," in-residence mentors who supervised boarding students and assisted apprentices one-on-one with everything from magic to mundane homework to how to do laundry. Storm mages were rarer than the other four elements, so she had an advantage there.

Or, her actual college degrees. Political science. Combat had already broken out, and there was about to be a war on, whether the city knew it or not. A job with the local government was a possibility, but that presented a new set of problems. She had no idea how foolproof the identity Liam built her was, and governments tended to like things like background checks. There would also be the temptation to nudge things a bit, based on what she knew of the past. A road she couldn't risk following.

Her chemistry degree posed the same issues. She knew too much about the future of technology to fake her way as a lab assistant now.

Toria pushed the empty beer bottle away and slumped over with a groan, burying her face in her arms. This sucked. The past sucked. The Guildhall merc sucked.

She missed Kane.

A throat cleared above her. Toria lifted her head to find Lyra on the other side of the bar.

"Need a refill?" Lyra chucked her empty bottle into a bin, where it clinked against other empties.

"No. I need a job." Toria made a show of surveying the other patrons. "I don't suppose you know if any of them are hiring?"

"Honey, you wouldn't want to work for any of them." Lyra pointed at different groups in turn. "You don't strike me as a whore or a drug runner, so that crew will want nothing to do with you. Forget subcontracting as a merc with any of the lot by the door—there are too few jobs to go around as it is. If you've any luck with cards, you might have a shot in the back room. But they're not open to female players, no matter how good your money is."

As Toria evaluated each set of men by turn, she agreed with Lyra's assessment. This wasn't her crowd, and she wasn't about to lower her standards unless her actual survival was on the line. This was just her pride. "Maybe I do need another drink."

Lyra laughed, a bright peal of sound that seemed out of place in the dark bar. "There I can help." She retrieved two bottles of the red ale and opened both, handing one to Toria and clinking it against hers. They drank together, and Toria giggled at the face Lyra made.

"Not a beer fan?" It wasn't bad, considering Toria favored cider. At least it wasn't as heavy as Kane's stouts, which always made Toria feel like she'd eaten a loaf of bread.

"Not much of an alcohol fan." Lyra held up her hands. "I know, I know. Funny thing for a bartender to say. But Kojo wants me to keep trying."

"Kojo?"

"Boyfriend. Owns the bar. Thinks having me drink the wares will help sales."

"Does it?"

"No idea." Lyra sipped her beer with more caution this time and suppressed most of her shudder.

They drank in a silence Toria found comfortable, as if already longtime friends who didn't need to fill the air with pointless chatter. She finished her drink faster than Lyra, so she put the woman out of her misery by trading bottles and draining the second as well.

Two and a half beers on an empty stomach made itself known as Toria swayed when she stepped off her barstool. She pulled another few bills from her pocket and handed them to Lyra, waving away the change Lyra tried to return.

Lyra grabbed Toria's wrist with stern fingers and pressed one of the bills back. "No, this is too much. And you said you needed a job, so I'm not accepting an unearned tip."

Toria wrinkled her nose. Alcohol always brought out her inner angst. "It's not so much that I need a job…. It's a long story. I'm having an interesting relationship with money right now." She snapped her mouth closed before she confessed too much in her inebriated state. She grabbed her sword and stared at the latched belt. Right. No belt loops. She draped it over her shoulder again.

Lyra fiddled with the gold chain at her neck. "I know you said the Guildhall turned you away. Do you have a place to stay tonight?" Toria rattled off Hugh's address. "Okay. I'm calling you a cab."

"The walk will do me good." Long, though. Her ridiculous shoes might not make it. The belt slipped off her shoulder, and Toria snagged her sword before it hit the ground.

"Stay there. Don't be daft." Without waiting for assent, Lyra stepped to a telephone in the corner. She picked up the handset and narrowed her eyes at Toria.

It was kind of funny. Her expression reminded Toria of when it was time to stop arguing with Kane and do as her partner said.

Toria sat on the barstool to wait for a cab.

Light shone from the kitchen when Toria crept through the bed and breakfast. Hugh sat at the kitchen table with a mug of tea, but he'd closed his book and set it aside by the time Toria entered the room.

She had a momentary flash of irrational panic, to nights in high school coming home late to find Victory and Mikelos waiting up. They had never enforced a curfew, but there was always the fear she'd pushed an inch too far this time.

At least she'd sobered a bit in the cab. Hugh saw her in the doorway and gestured to the kettle. "Water should still be hot. Would you like some tea?"

"Sounds perfect." Toria pressed a hand to Hugh's shoulder before he rose. "No, I'll get it." She rested her sword across the other end of the table.

Hugh resumed reading while Toria puttered around the kitchen, slathering butter and jam on plain bread while waiting for her tea to steep. He placed the novel on the table again when Toria settled across from him, but waited to speak until she finished half her snack. "Any luck?"

She washed down the thick bread with a sip of tea. "No. Guildhall wanted nothing to do with me. I brainstormed a few other ideas at a bar nearby." Again, she waited for any reproach from Hugh, but his commiserating frown showed no judgement. She pulled the remainder of the cash from her pocket and slid it across the table. "Thank you."

Hugh ignored the crumpled bills and placed his hand on top of hers. "Anytime."

Toria fiddled with her bread crust, then returned to her substitute dinner. They sat in companionable silence until she pushed the plate away and clutched the cooling mug between both hands. "Liam's picking me up again tomorrow?"

"Yes, around lunchtime. He called earlier, but I told him you were walking around the neighborhood," Hugh said, and Toria stifled a snicker in her tea. "And the first delivery of clothing arrived. I stuck the whole lot in your room."

"Thank you." Toria paused, considering. "I seem to say that to you a lot, but I want you to know I mean it every time."

"It's my genuine pleasure, kid. And I mean it every time, too." Hugh clinked his mug with Toria's.

The first "history lesson" with Liam was an exercise in patience for both of them. Liam hosted Toria at a table in the museum's café, which he covered with notes and copies of newspaper clippings. Toria's reluctance to identify a specific date from which she came frustrated Liam. His high-handedness regarding how much better he expected Toria to find this new world irritated her.

Internal combustion engine. Smallpox vaccine. Long-range telecommunications systems. Faking enthusiasm for these "new" developments was difficult when she knew technological progress soon ground to a halt.

On the other hand, she didn't have to feign excitement when Liam told her about the museum's interest in funding expeditions to the center of the New Continent for paleontological research, "once we get a spot of trouble sorted out with the Qin regarding land use." If Liam found it weird that dinosaurs prompted more discussion than airplanes, he hid behind a veneer of politeness and typical elven superiority.

They exchanged terse goodbyes. Liam thrust a giant pile of reading at Toria and escaped upstairs to his office.

Of course, it wasn't as if the man was a total asshole. If they'd met under any other circumstances, she'd turn on the charm. Even under his frustration, he was kind enough to not give up on her.

And on a physical level, she didn't mind watching him walk away.

She clutched the books and folders to her chest as she entered the geology exhibit where she'd arrived to such fanfare. Now, with her period-appropriate clothing, she blended into the crowd admiring the displays.

Most visitors lingered by the more spectacular stations near the exhibit's entrance, featuring gemstones native to the New Continent in both their raw and cut forms. But Toria beelined for the less-attractive minerals on display farther down the hall.

She opened her magesight to the slightest trickle of energy. All of the glass cases shimmered with passive security wards, and a handful of the gemstones toward the exhibit entrance burned with magic, but magical power also exuded from a single boring specimen in the back half of the room.

She passed cases of gems and minerals, and here it was with the meteorites. An unimposing gray chunk about the size of Kane's large fist. The igneous stone's interior shimmered in the light where a corner had been sheared away.

The placard below noted it was a gift from another museum in Britannia, featured here with examples of other meteorites found on the New Continent, but made no mention of its more obscure properties. It didn't even specify the original location of this particular meteorite, whether in Britannia or elsewhere.

It was as if its display were an afterthought, meant to heighten interest in the other specimens in comparison.

Toria would give anything for Kane or Archer at this moment. She could learn little from the rock's magic signature alone, without the time and space for a full ritual. Her partner's earth affinity would tell him so much more with a glance, and Archer's sheer knowledge of magic itself might fill in the blanks.

Instead, she could stare at the rock, and do nothing. This wouldn't help her get home.

She exited the museum and summoned a cab. Once inside, Toria slumped against the seat and groaned, ignoring the curious glances the driver shot in the rearview mirror. With no immediate alternatives, she relied on Liam's charity to survive, which was a significant wrinkle in any relationship.

Relationship? He was hot, but attractiveness did not form the basis of a real relationship.

The last time she'd gotten laid was six months ago (or decades in the future—at some point she had to figure out how to measure her current nonlinear time stream). A one-night stand with a cute grad student in Oxenafor before she met Kane in Londinium for a courier job.

The last thing she needed right now was an inopportune crush on the man who knew nothing about her. On the man she must keep on her good side if she wanted continued access to the artifact, along with further opportunity to study it.

To be fair, it was her usual pattern when it came to emotions. She envied Kane, who fell in love straight out of college and enjoyed an unwavering relationship with Archer. Another reason to miss her guys, her voices of sanity whenever she experienced these hormone-induced lapses in judgement.

Stress for another day. She had research.

Toria made herself at home in the kitchen when she returned, scattering the readings around her. Her brain slipped into research mode right away, a headspace she'd developed in college. She scoured the documents and sorted them into relevant piles ordered by how closely she would need to re-read the material later.

Most of it was refresher, compliments of her liberal-arts education. This was not the first time she had cause to thank her mother's insistence she and Kane go to college before their journeymen time, even if it did delay their mercenary careers.

By the time she had a full page of notes, research she needed to solidify a persona from the past, the kitchen had grown dim in the evening light. She'd seen no sign of Hugh since she got home, but when she wandered upstairs to her room, she found a note with cash on her nightstand. Hugh was away on errands and would spend the evening out at his weekly card game. The money was for Toria to order dinner at a nearby shop, according to the rough map sketched beneath his text.

She changed from her prim knee-length skirt into more comfortable trousers—for various degrees of comfort, considering the horrific undergarments available to women in this era. She even walked to the tiny commercial district in Hugh's neighborhood and enjoyed a sandwich and iced tea at the local café. But instead of returning to the bed and breakfast afterward, she hailed a cab and gave the driver the address to the Mercenary Guildhall.

Not that she planned to try again at the Guildhall. The defeat from the night before still stung. Instead, she paid the driver and wandered toward the bar.

More people crowded the dim room tonight, but Toria didn't warrant more than a passing glance without her sword.

She parked herself at an empty spot at the bar, and Lyra appeared in front of her as if by magic not two seconds later.

"You're back."

"I'm back." Toria steeled herself, but Lyra maintained a neutral expression. "I'm not in a beer mood tonight. What can you recommend?"

"I don't know whether you've noticed, but this isn't the fanciest of establishments." Was it Toria's imagination, or did Lyra's mouth quirk in a smile?

"Surprise me, then." Toria propped her elbows on the bar and leaned forward.

"I trust you."

Lyra seemed startled by her response, so she stalked down the bar. At least she didn't demand Toria pay up-front this time.

Toria twisted in her seat enough to people-watch while she waited. The same sort of crowd from the previous night filled the bar. Drinkers, card players, and clusters of men engaged in furtive conversations and ready to lash out at the merest hint of conflict.

Typical mercs. Perhaps why she felt right at home.

After Lyra poured beers for a waitress to deliver to the floor, she mixed various liquor bottles into a tall glass. As Lyra carried it toward Toria, her face lit up as she spotted someone darken the bar's entrance. She deposited the drink in front of Toria and, without waiting for thanks, ducked out from around the bar and greeted the tall man who entered.

With nothing better to do, Toria watched them as she sniffed her drink and sipped with caution. No olives, and the wrong style of glass, but a martini was a martini. She preferred them sweeter, but once again, she was in the wrong bar if she wanted high-quality liquor.

The kiss the man exchanged with Lyra was perfunctory, and he soon brushed past her toward the back where the card players gathered.

Lyra stared after him for a moment, her expression distant, before she resumed her position behind the bar. Her demeanor showed no hint of displeasure. "Sorry about that. What do you think of the drink?"

"Delicious, thank you." Toria sipped again as proof of her appreciation. "Exactly what I needed."

"Rough day?" Lyra kept an eye on the room, but appeared content to chat with Toria. Considering the majority of her customers were male, perhaps Toria was a nice change of pace. "How's the job hunt going?"

As much as her dependence on Liam and the museum galled her, she had a lot of work to do before she was comfortable enough with her cover story to consider more gainful employment. "On hold, for the moment."

"Should I have asked for the cash before I mixed the drink?" Lyra asked, but her tone was teasing, not suspicious.

"I promise I'm good for it." Toria toyed with the stirrer in her cocktail. "The money's not the problem. Just my pride."

The man Lyra kissed settled himself on the barstool next to Toria in time to catch her last words. "Cute thing like you shouldn't have any problem finding work."

Before Toria could defend this dispersion against her honor, Lyra beat her to it. "Kojo! She's not a whore." Rebuke and embarrassment warred in her voice.

Kojo plucked his hat from his head and dropped it on the bar, revealing a shaved scalp. The deep umber of his skin glowed with golden undertones in the bar's lighting. "What's she need money for?" His sharp suit seemed out of place in the dingy environ.

Toria missed her partner, but not enough to give the man's rudeness a pass despite his superficial resemblance to Kane. The shaved head, and something in the shape of his jaw, perhaps. "She needs money because needing money is the human condition."

Though he didn't apologize for his prior insult, the man had some manners. He held out a hand and Toria accepted it after a slight pause. His handshake was the limp, delicate grip some men reserved for women. "Best of luck with that. Welcome to my establishment. Kojo Vitalis." The Roman last name explained his lighter skin tone, if his mother had been British.

"Toria Connor." She knew her smile didn't reach her eyes.

"Pardon me while I borrow my girl." He jerked his head toward the back, grabbing his hat as he stood. He set off without waiting for Lyra to acknowledge his indirect request.

She lingered as Kojo sauntered away. "Sorry. That was uncalled for."

"No worries." Toria was a female merc. She sold her life for a living, after all, not just her body.

Lyra hurried after Kojo. Toria enjoyed the rest of her drink in silence, but as time dragged by, the bartender never returned. The two waitresses exchanged furious whispers, both of them casting nervous glances toward the back room, before one of them positioned herself behind the bar to mix drinks and pour beers.

Martini finished, Toria left money with her empty glass and wandered into the night. This time, she noted the bar's address before she strolled downtown, where taxis were more abundant.

The next time she returned, maybe Kojo wouldn't be around. Despite her poor taste in men, Toria like Lyra. Right now, she needed all the friends she could get.

She spent the next few days in a whirlwind of activity. Hugh took full advantage of both Toria's magical ability and younger back. They made progress restoring and updating the house's formal front parlor and dining room, spending mornings ripping out wallpaper, sanding, and painting, and they discovered different tastes as they bickered their way through furniture stores. The neighborhood library was in walking distance, so Toria ensconced herself there in the afternoons. She told Hugh she was doing assigned readings for Liam, and at least half her words were true.

When she met Liam the next weekend for another lunchtime "study" meeting, Toria was prepared. She had solidified her personal history in Limani, verifying dates of events and researching enough details to pass if pressed.

If Hugh and Liam ever spoke without her knowledge, Hugh seemed to keep what truths he knew about Toria to himself. Liam never indicated he thought Toria was anything other than a garden-variety mage, and she stuck to her fabricated story. She made sure to sprinkle in occasional personal details, mixing her memories of the house in which Victory and Mikelos raised her (a former tobacco plantation manor already a century old before Victory acquired it in retirement) with stories about the current crop of kids at Limani's mage school.

Even as Toria became more comfortable lying to Liam, she felt worse for it. On the morning of her fourth meeting with Liam, almost one month since arriving in the past, she considered pleading sick and staying in bed.

The virus might be fake, but the time she spent vomiting in the toilet from anxiety-induced nausea wasn't.

Hugh made no comment about her extended time spent in the bathroom after she stumbled into the kitchen and choked down a slice of dry toast. But he searched her face when she declined coffee.

Toria retrieved a glass of cold water from the faucet. "Caffeine would be a bad idea right now. Um, woman's troubles." A blatant lie, considering her modern form of birth control meant such monthly issues were no longer a concern. But Hugh was a single man who'd never married, in a world with strict gender roles.

He reacted as anticipated, lifting a hand before she could explain further. "Say no more. Do you... do you need anything?"

Toria read his discomfort in the way he toyed with his empty coffee mug. She took pity on the man who'd grown into a dear friend. "Nope. Everything's handled. Just wasn't feeling well this morning."

"Good, good." Hugh refilled his mug with her share of the coffee. "Liam called while you were in the shower. He asked if I could drive you to the museum today. He has an afternoon meeting with his boss."

"Don't worry about it." Toria leaned on the counter, fighting the urge to sit and curl around her painful stomach. "A walk would do me good. I'll head downtown until I find a cab for the rest of the way." She kissed the top of Hugh's head on her way out of the kitchen. "See you for dinner!"

Even if she'd lied to Hugh about the cause of her intestinal distress, the fresh summer air did refresh her. Her appetite returned by the time she'd left Hugh's residential neighborhood, so she stopped at a café for a pastry and coffee and watched the world go by from a seat outside. With her wardrobe one hundred percent contemporary, she blended in seamlessly. Even her hair had grown, and though she refused to waste the time necessary to curl it, society also accepted a loose knot at the base of her skull.

She missed the weight of her sword at her hip, but her magic meant she was never defenseless.

A cab deposited her in front of the museum a few minutes ahead of her session with Liam. She waved to Jasper at the front desk, who wished her a harried good afternoon before returning to a clutch of mothers who peppered him with questions in between corralling hyperactive children.

Toria climbed the three flights of stairs to the private office corridors. If Liam was buried in paperwork, it would be more efficient to search him out than to cool her heels in the café until he remembered their meeting. She kept to a sedate pace and dragged her fingers along the wall as she traveled the halls. Though the visitor galleries bustled with activity, most of the museum's research section closed for the weekend. She waved to a lone botanist and held a door for a janitor.

She heard Liam before she rounded the final corner, his smooth tenor contrasting with another man's deeper bass. Loud enough that they must have stood in the hallway outside Liam's office. Since no one was around, Toria spared a moment to smooth her hair and tug her blouse straight. The anxiety butterflies had returned, but she was a big believer in "fake it 'til you make it."

It was just Liam. A bit pretentious, a lot handsome, and kind of a history nerd, befitting his position at the museum.

Toria was a badass warrior-mage. She could deal with this. She stepped around the corner, raising her hand to wave—

And instead gripped the nearest doorway, digging her nails into the wood of the doorjamb. She locked her knees to avoid collapsing or turning to run. The butterflies turned poisonous, and she bit her tongue as bile rose in her throat.

The two men stood in profile, and one drew her gaze like a roadside car accident. The elven man, in a tailored suit much more expensive than the one Liam wore, nodded at Liam's words unheard through the roar of blood in Toria's ears. He kept his hands folded atop a walking stick, but when he opened his mouth to speak, he lifted one to tuck a lock of blond hair behind a pointed ear.

The walking stick was an affectation. And the last time Toria encountered him, his hair had been cut much shorter and deepened to a silvery gray.

The last time, his head snapped back as a bullet hole appeared in his forehead and bits of skull and brain matter splattered the floor of the Parisii Catacombs.

"Ah, Toria!" Liam smiled at her. At any other moment, it would have brightened the hallway and her day. "Your timing is perfect. I'd like to introduce you to Rubinaril, the head curator."

Liam and Rubin approached before she convinced her legs to be more than lead weights. Rubin extended a hand, and Toria raised her own palm.

She swallowed the sour taste in her mouth. Instead of blasting him with pure electric energy, Toria turned the angle of her palm at the last moment and shook the man's hand.

The man responsible for setting the world spell that limited technological advancement after the Last War.

The man responsible for destroying magic in the world.

The man responsible for the death of her best friend.

"It's a pleasure to meet you, sir." The words stuck in her throat, but at least she didn't gag on them.

"Please, call me Rubin." This was a different man from the one who'd dismissed them from a Parisii museum five years ago and decades from now. "I'm delighted to make your acquaintance, Ms. Connor. I hope things are working out with Mr. Ainsworth?"

At least she could answer truthfully. "He's been kind. Anyone in these circumstances would be lucky to have such a host to help them make their way."

Rubin patted Liam on the arm. "And I trust young Liam has done his part as well." He tucked his walking stick under this arm and checked the flashy watch on his wrist. "Ah, I must be off to my next meeting. I'll expect your review of O'Toole's exhibit proposal on my desk soon, Liam."

"Very good, sir." Liam half-bowed to Rubin, who acknowledged it and strode away.

Toria could kill Rubin right now. He'd turned his back on her. He might be shielded, but he'd have no reason to expect an attack. One full-strength blast would obliterate him. She could save Syri.

But at what cost? The same damned question, over and over again. Toria grounded herself in the sharp bite of fingernails digging into her palms. Once Rubin disappeared around the corner, she collapsed against the wall.

Liam grabbed her arm before she slid to the floor. "No, no. Come sit in my office." He tucked her to his side and supported her to his door. "You were already pale when I first saw you. Are you feeling okay? I hope you didn't feel like you had to put on a show for my boss." Once Toria settled into a guest chair, he shut his office door and fetched her a drink from a flask in a desk drawer. "Here. Even I need a drink after dealing with him sometimes."

Toria tossed back the shot in one gulp. As the brandy's burn worked down her throat, she set the glass on the edge of Liam's desk and buried her face in her hands, hunching until her elbows rested on her knees. The brandy hit the remnants of her breakfast, and the pastry and coffee curdled in her stomach. She took shallow breaths and tried not to vomit.

Liam sat next to her in silence.

She thought she'd been okay. It'd been a month. She laid low, keeping her head down, playing along with Liam and Hugh's expectations of her. She hadn't blown her cover by not knowing something about the past, and she'd resisted the urge to act on her knowledge of the future. It all sucked, but it was her life for now, and she'd accepted it.

Until she saw Rubin, and remembered everything she'd lost.

Everything she could change.

Hot tears leaked from her eyes, and she inhaled a ragged breath.

Liam placed a hand on her back. The heat of his palm bled through the thin silk of her blouse and spread to her core. The dam burst, and Liam scooted his chair closer and pulled Toria to his chest as her body shook with sobs. He wrapped both arms around her, and she buried her face into his shoulder and let go of all the tears she'd kept trapped in a steel cage after her first night in Nacostina.

Liam whispered into the top of her head, pressing his forehead to her hair. "I have no idea what's going on, but I'm here. I'm here."

Toria tried to speak, but the words stumbled against each other and broke. "I can't.... This is so wrong.... I can't handle this."

Liam rubbed circles on her back, even as he held her close with his other arm. "I know this isn't how you imagined your life going. But you're here now. You have people who care for you."

Her burgeoning friendship with Hugh was real. So was the one with Lyra.

Maybe she even had Liam.

But that wasn't the problem. The problem was that monster. How was a person expected to face such a villain twice in her life? Even if he wasn't a villain yet. Toria had no idea what might happen to Rubin during the Last War to prompt such a drastic measure as the world spell.

"You don't understand." Toria pulled away from Liam and wiped her nose with the back of her hand. He let go at once, and she was glad she'd left tearstains on his shoulder instead of snot.

"Then help me." Liam pushed a tangle of hair out of Toria's face.

She cringed away from his familiar touch. Not fair. He couldn't sit there looking handsome and sympathetic. She couldn't afford to get close to this man. "It's complicated."

Liam gripped his knees, as if avoiding the temptation to reach for Toria again. "I know there are some things I can't even imagine. But I'm here for you."

Toria jerked away and scoffed. "It's your fucking job to be here for me."

"No." The snap in Liam's voice was fierce and immediate, and for once he didn't wince at her profanity. "Because I care about you. My job was to teach you enough to fit in and make sure you wouldn't cause any trouble. But it turns out that you're smart and interesting, and I've learned as much from you these last few weeks as I hope you've learned from me." He grasped Toria's hands in both of his, and this time she let him. "You can trust me."

It would be so easy.

He was gorgeous and smart and kind and if this was real life, Kane and Archer would have already staged an intervention or locked them in a room together. But this wasn't real life. This was the crazy reality she'd found herself in. The nightmare she would never wake from.

She could embrace the nightmare. Take everything Liam offered her. Let him take care of her the way he seemed to be offering. Financially, and maybe even emotionally. She could forget the past, and embrace this strange present. Her old life was gone, but this might be her chance at a fulfilled life.

A short life, considering the countdown clock in her head.

"Toria? Are you okay?"

"I'm sorry. I… I do trust you. But you're right. It's hard to explain. It's too big, and too difficult." And full of lies upon lies. Her stomach clenched again, but she bit the inside of her cheek.

Liam stroked her hands with his thumbs. "I hope you'll let me be here for you when you're ready."

Though her stomach still heaved, something in her chest glowed warm and content. As if Kane couldn't be here to shove her into Liam's arms, but the tiny kernel of earth magic within her had to make his opinion known.

Or she was losing her mind.

One deep breath, then another, and another. Combat breathing to slow her racing heart and calm the anxiety bubbling under the surface of her skin. "I promise you're on the short list."

"I'm glad." He squeezed her hands again and released them. "Today's notes can wait. Let's get lunch. Not the café here. Someplace real."

Toria rubbed her palms on the linen of her skirt, wiping away the distracting echoes of Liam's touch. "I thought you had meetings?"

"No. Today I have a pretty girl who deserves a glass of wine in the sunshine." He rose to his feet and offered Toria a hand. "Will you join me?"

It would be so easy. All she had to do was take his hand. She could be a pretty girl with a handsome man and enjoy this life.

She pushed herself out of the chair and inhaled to her diaphragm, clearing her lungs and steadying the roiling in her gut. Or she could be a pretty girl with a handsome man and enjoy a glass of wine in the sunshine and figure it all out tomorrow. "Sounds perfect." She slipped her hand into Liam's.

He entwined his fingers with hers. After they left his office, he rambled about the current gossip among the historians in the anthropology department. The story didn't seem to require any input on her part, which she was thankful for as she dragged the final pieces of her composure together on the walk out of the museum.

The itch between her shoulder blades didn't ease until they stepped into the bright afternoon sun, and she knew the source of her lingering discomfort.

She had no way to avoid Rubin forever. Not when he held her financial security in his hands. She couldn't afford to melt down and raise any suspicion the next time she saw him.

She could figure that out tomorrow, too.

BETWEEN

A human wearing a security uniform, his cap perched at a jaunty angle over red hair, sauntered through the museum rotunda. He twirled an unlit flashlight in one hand, whistling off-key. Victory stilled her body to perfect silence, but the man never so much as glanced in her direction. After walking the long way around Hank, he patted the faux-marbled finish of the mammoth's base and disappeared under the balcony where Victory stood.

The relaxed staccato of his heartbeat faded, along with his footsteps, as the guard made his rounds.

Victory was a mercenary, not a thief. She didn't have the faintest idea how to break into a museum, much less out of one. But over the centuries, she had been a bodyguard, a courier, a spy, and a special combat operative. She could figure it out.

She made her way along the balcony until she found a staircase and picked her way down the marble steps. On the main floor, she peered around the corner to survey the rotunda from her new angle. Giant mammoth on his stand. Information desk. Multiple sets of doors leading out to the street, bolted shut at this late hour. Victory slipped in the opposite direction of the guard.

A giant stuffed mammoth of which she had dim memories was one thing. An entire hall dedicated to mounted animals common to the New Continent, all cloaked in the odd shadows cast by the emergency lighting, became downright creepy. As Victory passed under a mountain lion lounging on a tree limb arched over the walkway, the heartbeat and footsteps returned.

She ducked behind a glass case featuring a variety of rodents and crouched low. Not the same heartbeat as before. This one beat a hair faster, and the echoed quality of the breathing was heavier, more labored. An older man came into view, one who carried more body fat around his middle.

This guard performed a few perfunctory checks from side to side as he passed through the exhibit, but missed Victory altogether. She waited another thirty seconds after he left the long hall before reemerging.

The skunk kept staring at her. She wrinkled her nose at it. She much preferred her version of life after death.

The guard had patrolled toward another gallery, but she'd watched him pass a separate entrance. She slipped under the rope from which an "Employees Only" sign dangled and twitched aside the heavy black curtain.

Nothing. Staff hallway, as advertised. Abused wooden floor and scuffed walls, dinged and marked by the passage of storage crates like the ones piled near closed double doors. She crept toward it, keeping her senses peeled for evidence of the security guards.

A sign next to the closed doors marked the east loading dock. She opened one door with a gentle nudge and scanned the room before entering. The long space, lit by a single emergency light high in a far corner, was empty of both people and vehicles. The wall inside the door held a box with a row of small levers, all connected to the electrical system that ran up to the ceiling and spread through the room. She squinted in the darkness, but the labels to the individual levers had worn away with time and use.

She'd seen systems like this before. Each of these levers controlled the locking mechanisms on the individual garage doors. If she released one, she'd be able to lift the door and roll under, escaping the building.

Picking a switch at random, Victory flicked it up. She froze, as sound roared through the room.

She'd made a terrible mistake. It wasn't the switch for the lock. She'd activated the hydraulic system for the doors themselves. One heavy metal door inched open at a snail's pace, broadcasting her unauthorized activity. She hit the lever again, but the door didn't stop.

There. A heartbeat over the rumbling. A door on the opposite side of the loading dock slammed open as the red-haired guard burst into the room. With his flashlight lit, he waved it around the room until he found Victory. She drew her sword, hoping to intimidate the guard and avoid a fight.

"Stop!" His voice cracked.

The garage door rumbled to a halt in its open position. The room filled with the frantic pounding of the guard's heartbeat, wild from adrenaline. He stood closer to the exit, but he was no match for Victory's speed. She launched herself off the ledge of the walkway and sped toward the gaping mouth of freedom.

But as she passed, the guard hurled himself off the walkway as well. He hooked his flashlight out and it caught on her sword. Victory unbalanced, tripping on an uneven patch of concrete, and crashed to the ground.

He staggered forward enough to hurl himself atop her. The flashlight flew from his grasp, arcing its beam of light through the room.

The guard elbowed Victory in the side, but he was too uncoordinated or too inexperienced for more. She shoved his body away, pushing against the ground and rocketing to her feet. The guard flew off her with a cry, which cut out when he hit the side of the loading dock platform. He slid down the wall.

Before she saw him land, Victory scrambled to her feet and sprinted outside. Moonlight lit the gardens she sped through with traces of soft color in contrast with deep shadows. She ignored the meandering paths through banked flowerbeds prepared for winter and large, abstract sculptures. Guilt stabbed through her. She had no idea whether the guard lived or not. She hadn't waited to confirm a heartbeat.

If she broke an innocent man's spine within moments of arriving in the past, she had no idea what the ramifications might be.

She had to find her daughter.

She left footsteps through the frost-laden grass, but her passage would become untraceable once she made it to the city streets. She hauled herself over a decorative wrought-iron gate.

And found herself in the capital of the British colonies on the New Continent.

The buildings in the heart of the city didn't touch the sky like the skyscrapers in New Angouleme. Instead, they sprawled through former swampland. Where New Angouleme to the north was the center of commerce and trade, Nacostina prided itself on its cultural and political influence. The white marble facades that dotted the street would shimmer in the sunrise, and even now the city woke in the dark winter morning.

Winter.

It had been summer, before, and Victory wore a ribbed tank top with battered blue jeans. Not to mention the sword at her hip, which had fallen out of style decades before. Except for mercenaries. She patted her back pocket for the reassuring shape of her slim wallet. She carried her ID for the Mercenary Guild.

Orienting herself based on the phallic Governor-General's Monument, Victory dug through the recesses of her memory for the direction of the Guildhall, then straightened her shoulders and set off with purpose. Her predatory saunter didn't invite question or curiosity from humans, and even convinced other supernaturals they had better things to do than accost a vampire on a mission.

With luck, Toria had stayed in the city. She'd raised a smart kid. Toria would leave some sort of message for her with the Guild, they'd reunite, and they would find their way home.

BEFORE

Toria and Kane might look nothing alike, might enjoy different interests and hobbies, and might have occasional strong differences in opinion, but in most ways, they were a matched set. They were bonded through a combination of strong magic and the affection born of years of friendship. They shared compatible life goals and had built a mercenary partnership fast becoming famous on two continents. But in one major way, their lives differed.

She lived in a cozy apartment above the stable-turned-garage at Limani's mage school. Kane shared rooms in the main house with the head of the mage school, with whom he had been in a steadfast relationship for close to five years.

She dated on occasion, most often outside of Limani, with men more interested in her warrior-mage mystique—and other attributes—than her personality. Kane loved life on the road, but was always anxious to get home.

When Toria arrived home, it was to a cold bed.

Never much romance. Grab a beer, have some laughs, have a good time. A guy in every port, as it were, who didn't expect anything real from Toria. Whom she respected enough not to expect anything different, even though sometimes she longed for the closeness shared by Kane and Archer.

Toria and Kane loved each other, and Archer had bolstered their relationship rather than getting in the middle or trying to prevent it. But with them, she was the perpetual third wheel. No one had ever wooed her. She knew the excitement of lust, not the intimacy of romantic love.

She hadn't expected anyone like Liam to appear in her life, deconstructing her emotional barriers with the skill and patience born of his long years. A far cry from the college boys she tumbled with in Oxenafor or the socialites she partied with in New Angouleme.

It wasn't like in the books. No epic, romantic gestures. No declarations of undying devotion. Instead, a dinner here, a coffee there. A walk in the park, or a surprise visit to the cinema.

The caress of Liam's fingers across the palm of her hand, more erotic than a weekend spent naked in a Londinium penthouse.

They had even kissed once, a chaste moment on Hugh's front porch, both of them soaked from a late-night summer storm.

Toria might have dragged him to her room then and there. But an element of caution stopped her. Even though elven elders did not frown on elven-human relationships in this time, neither did they encourage them. She couldn't risk becoming so involved with the past.

Caution, even, that Liam might be manipulating her for his own ends.

Paranoia and anxiety, her constant companions since her first night in the past. A small voice in her head, whispering lies and exaggerations.

Liam left then, wishing her sweet dreams and pressing another kiss to the corner of her mouth.

He jogged to his car, through the final drops of the rain shower. She watched him from the porch, clutching the railing with bloodless fingers. When the car turned the corner at the end of the block, she crept into the house and trudged to her room. The voice whirled in her head as she wrung water out of her hair with a towel, undressed for bed, and slipped under the covers.

Liam expects sex in exchange for all he's done for you here. He's too much of a gentleman to ask for it.

So? He's sexy as hell and a kind man.

He thinks you're a product of the past. He'll lose all respect for you.

He wouldn't.

But what if? What if? Whatifwhatifwhatif?

Now, Toria waited in the lobby of the museum a few minutes before closing. Hank, the stuffed mammoth, loomed over her as she leaned against the base of his display, waiting for Liam to emerge from his office and escort her to a late dinner. She paid half her attention to Officer Brinkley urging a few stragglers out of the museum, but the rest of her shimmered with the taste of Liam's lips against hers the night before.

She prayed this encounter wouldn't be awkward. She tried to use her voiceless pleas to any deity to drown out the voice once again whispering vitriol.

He's barely going to look at you, much less touch you.

Shut up.

If he even shows up at all.

SHUT UP.

A touch to her shoulder jolted her out of the silent argument. She whirled around, aborting a reach for the sword she hadn't worn in weeks.

Liam cocked a grin at her surprise. "Sorry. Had to make a detour through the publicity office."

"It's fine." Toria willed her heartbeat to slow. The constant low-level strum of anxiety meant her fight-or-flight reflexes operated at a hair trigger these days. "Ready for dinner?"

"In a few. There's someone I wanted you to meet." Liam grasped her hand and tugged her close, tucking her arm into the crook of his elbow and leaning against Hank's display.

Not inclined to do anything about Liam trapping her—*Take that*, she shot at the voice in her skull—Toria leaned next to him. "Who are we waiting for?"

"Friend of mine in town for work." Liam stroked Toria's hand with his thumb where he caught it in his gentle grasp. "You told me a rather eccentric vampire raised you. I understand why you won't tell me who."

Gentle shivers raised the hair on Toria's bare arms, shifting from sexy to terror as her stomach dropped to the general area of her knees. "You didn't—But how could you—"

"No, no, calm down." Liam pulled her closer to his side and draped his arm over her shoulders. "I have no idea who your mother is and I respect your privacy enough not to go digging, to see whether she's still alive in this time period. But I do know another vampire I'd describe as eccentric, and I thought you might like to meet him."

Toria inhaled, held it, and released. At this rate, she was going to give herself an aneurysm. "Okay. Thank you." She swatted Liam in the chest. "Don't do that to a girl."

"Many apologies, your ladyship." Liam chuckled low in his throat.

He kept his arm wrapped around her, and his warmth did much to restore her equilibrium. "Apology accepted. Who's your friend?"

"A bit of a scholar, which is how we met. He does research here at the museum on occasion. Ah, there he is." Liam stepped away from Toria and lifted a hand in greeting as a tall man strolled through the entrance to the museum.

His tawny skin held the ashy undertone of a vampire who'd had darker skin in life. His riotous shock of midnight black hair gleamed with golden highlights under the hanging lamps.

The man was still too far away for Toria to see his eye color, but she already knew they were a shade lighter than his hair from the way the pupils drowned in his irises. According to the portrait in her mother's library, at least.

Toria hung back, giving Liam time to shake the man's hand and exchange the usual courtesies between two friends who hadn't seen each other for some time. The hooked nose cemented it. It hadn't healed well when Victory broke it, right before turning him into a vampire.

This was going to be so awkward.

"I'd love for you to meet someone." Liam tugged Toria forward before she could balk. "This is my friend, Toria Connor. Toria, this is Jarimis."

"A pleasure." Jarimis shook Toria's hand, giving a sort of half-bow more common in earlier centuries. Like the one Jarimis was from. He hesitated when Toria returned the handshake, then his eyes widened. "You didn't just want me to meet a random pretty face. Most people express much more surprise at my cold hands, but this one didn't even flinch."

"I knew you'd catch on!" Liam caught Toria's free hand with his own, entwining their fingers as if it was the most natural thing in the world.

He left Toria free to explain on her own, for which she didn't know whether to bless or curse him. As if meeting a true specter of her past wasn't awkward enough, though Liam couldn't have known Jarimis' relation to her.

"I'm familiar with vampires. It's a long story." The moment the words left her mouth, she knew she'd said the wrong thing. Jarimis would pounce on the mystery like a gleeful kitten. His eyes already gleamed with curiosity.

But what else was Toria supposed to say—*It's a pleasure to meet you, big brother? We've never met because you're dead in my future? Thanks for the awesome sword?*

Jarimis did not carry his rapier. Thankful for small favors, relief washed through her that she had stopped carrying hers.

If Jarimis noticed her attention on his waist, he likely dismissed it as the common issue of humans unable to meet a vampire's gaze. "You'll have to tell me about it at some point when we're both free. But I have work to do tonight, and I won't keep you any longer."

"Yes, I'm sure you're eager to tackle your latest project." Liam waved over Brinkley from where he lounged at the information desk.

Toria dropped back as the men worked out Jarimis' access to the museum's archives, and how he should alert security when he was ready to leave in a few hours. Based on their conversation, she surmised this was a standing procedure, and Jarimis had a history of performing some of his more obscure research here.

Even as she trailed one hand over the base of Hank's display, she stared at Jarimis' profile. It was one thing to be familiar with the portrait in Victory's library, and the other formal painting displayed in the Jarimis University campus center. To hear stories of his and Victory's adventures together as mercenaries.

But this was a man in a time between, after he and Victory stopped traveling together but before he convinced her to retire in Limani so he could establish a college. Even if he led the life of a scholar now, he still stood like a fighter, loose-limbed and aware of every inch of his surroundings.

She remembered he preferred knives as his chosen weapons, and the odd way his suit coat draped on his shoulders made sense. He carried at least two short blades, maybe more. Jarimis might no longer be a mercenary, but he'd been raised as a warrior and part of that would never leave him.

The men broke off their conversation, and after a final handshake with Liam, Jarimis followed Brinkley into the depths of the museum. He spared a look to Toria as they passed, and Toria twitched. She had blown this entire encounter, but to be fair, it was nothing she could have ever predicted. Now the trick would be avoiding Jarimis without making either him or Liam suspicious.

Liam returned to Toria, once again claiming her hand. "Ready for dinner? I made reservations for an outdoor table."

His physical ease with her made her want to stick a mental tongue out at the voice in her head, but her anxiety over the encounter with Jarimis overshadowed her ability to unpack the meaning behind Liam's actions.

"Yeah, that sounds great. It's nice outside." Toria didn't pull away from Liam as they left the museum. Bright lamps lined the street, illuminating locals and tourists alike who spilled out of the restaurants and bars tucked between government buildings. Everyone enjoyed the glorious summer evening thanks to the break in humidity brought by yesterday's storm.

Once they sat in a café that specialized in small dishes from Aragonia, Liam filled the space between them with the latest museum gossip. If he sensed that he had put Toria in an uncomfortable position with Jarimis, he didn't mention it.

Toria sipped her wine and nibbled at the offerings from the variety of plates Liam ordered. When his consideration ran out and he tired of her one-word answers, he pushed his empty wine glass to the side and leaned forward, elbows propped on the table and fingers steepled at his lips. "Something's the matter."

"I'm fine." The response was instinctual, but she knew she wasn't getting out of this one. She downed the last of her own sweet white wine and set the glass next to his on the edge of the table.

"After the way you'd discussed your mother and her daywalker, I assumed you'd be comfortable around other vampires." Liam toyed with his cloth napkin. "I apologize if I assumed wrong."

"You didn't assume wrong." Toria settled in her seat. "It's just—"

Liam stiffened, interrupting her. "Was he someone you knew?"

"No! No." Toria snagged his hand across the table before the anxious crease between his eyes deepened further. "I've never met him."

"Well, he does know about the artifact. I've asked him to look out for mentions of similar objects in other libraries and museums." Liam split the tiny amount of wine left in the bottom of the bottle between their glasses and waved for the waiter.

Toria sipped the last of the wine. "Has he found anything else?"

"Not to my knowledge. But I've never commissioned an active search. Just told him to keep an ear out." The waiter arrived with their check, and Liam busied himself with his wallet.

He offered to drive her home when they left the small courtyard behind the restaurant, but Toria declined. "I appreciate it, but I spent all afternoon staining floors with Hugh. I'd like to walk for a bit in the fresh air." Once again, their hands had found each other.

"Would you like company?" Liam smoothed the fabric at Toria's shoulder, a gesture both perfunctory and affectionate in its casualness.

"Would you mind if I said no?" She braced herself for his concern.

But as they had spent more time with each other, Liam's attitudes about propriety had slipped away one by one. "Not at all. Sometimes I need time to myself as well." He leaned over, and when she didn't pull away, tilted his head enough to touch a gentle kiss to her lips. "Dinner tomorrow night?"

"You don't have to keep taking me out, you know. I can cook for you, or something."

That had come out of nowhere. Toria could bake, for a special enough occasion, but at home she ate the majority of her meals in the mage school's dining hall for good reason. To distract herself from the funny lurch in her heart, Toria raised their linked hands and kissed his knuckles.

"I do enjoy Hugh's company, but I'm feeling this urge to keep you all to myself these days." Liam pecked her lips with a second kiss, then stepped away, almost as if he fought the same inclination toward public indecency. "Have a good evening, my dear."

"Same to you."

Liam strolled toward the museum, where he kept his car parked. Once he disappeared from sight around the block, Toria turned in the opposite direction.

She did want a walk to clear her head, but she hadn't mentioned a destination to Liam. If she happened to end up at the bar to have a drink with Lyra, he didn't need to know.

Toria rambled to where the streets narrowed and the architecture became less refined. As she left the downtown government district and entered the Mercenary Guildhall's neighborhood, her tailored trousers and silk sleeveless blouse marked her as out of place. She adopted an extra bit of swagger to put off sufficient "don't mess with me" vibes, and only one brave soul catcalled her from across the street. She flipped him off.

Her time in the past had changed her in ways she didn't always like. For one thing, her sword hadn't left Hugh's since her futile night at the Guildhall. She wore a slim knife in its ankle sheath when possible, a gift from Hugh, but women in this time period wore skirts an awful lot of the time. So Toria did as well, in her attempts to chameleon her way into societal invisibility.

But what if invisibility was no longer enough? A certain mop of tousled black hair over inquisitive eyes flashed in her mind like a beacon, for once overwhelming the nasty voice until it left off its near-constant diatribe of catastrophizing language. She had met Jarimis, of all people. Jarimis knew her name. What happened next?

When Asaron brought her to Victory as an infant, would Jarimis' future daywalker Allesandra side with Mikelos regarding her adoption because she recognized the name "Toria" from a story Jarimis once told her about the strange woman he met in Nacostina?

In another timeline, she might decide she was too old to chase after a toddler.

Layers upon layers upon layers of circumstances and odds and chance. Did she stay as far away from Jarimis as possible to avoid contaminating the timeline? Or did she make friends, as was Liam's preference, so when the time came, Allesandra remembered Toria's name and gave her the life she was meant to have?

Where did she draw the line?

She could give into temptation and connect with Jarimis. But what about all of the other things she wanted with a desperation born of homesickness and loneliness and rage?

Like smashing Rubin's face in instead of smiling and ducking behind Liam, perpetrating the image of harmless girl out of her depth in this terrifying future. Getting revenge for Syri, or even preventing the events that led to Syri's death in the first place.

Hell, warning everyone in Nacostina about its imminent destruction.

Either time was a closed circuit, and she destroyed her future: Syri lived, but Rubin never returned to Europa to orchestrate the world spell after the Last War. Or her warning to Nacostina prevented its destruction, but caused a ripple effect that prevented the Last War from happening at all.

Or things became even worse, and nuclear destruction spanned far beyond the New Continent. Rubin and his cronies wouldn't have the chance to set the world spell because they'd be dead, along with everyone else.

This was why Toria needed a drink.

She turned the final corner toward Lyra's bar and let her mind wander to more pleasant topics, such as the delicious blueberry beer on tap, or whether the local craft brewery had something else unique to offer.

When she pushed open the heavy wooden door and stepped into the bar, utter mayhem greeted her.

If someone took a swing at Toria, she fought back. A drunken brawl wasn't the way she'd prefer to exercise lax muscles and hone her combat instincts, but she blocked the punch, ducked under the flailing arms of another man, and dove her shoulder into her attacker.

Toria had no idea who instigated the brawl that enveloped the merc bar. She didn't care, and she didn't pick sides, instead throwing herself at the nearest combatants. She lost herself in a whirlwind of punches, jabs, and kicks, both longing for her sword and thankful her odds of killing someone lessened without it. Still, at least one man would walk funny after getting the thick heel of her fashionable shoes in an awkward place.

Lungs heaving, she spun for another enemy. But none came. She was the last one on her feet.

Kane would have approved.

Nacostina police, with perfect timing, tumbled into the door right as Toria had time to catch the burning breath in her ribcage. She raised her arms right away, but Lyra popped her head out from behind the bar and convinced the cops Toria didn't need to be arrested with the full batch of bored, drunk, and/or out-of-work mercenaries.

Toria's whisper of "I am a bored, out-of-work mercenary" to Lyra earned her a sharp elbow in already aching ribs, so she chose the better part of valor and remained silent for the rest of the proceedings.

As Lyra supervised the removal of the final miscreants, Toria peered in the mirror behind the bar to finger the cut at her hairline from someone's ring and evaluate her other injuries. Along with her face and ribs, bruises stained her knuckles. She peered at the ruins of her blouse. Tragedy.

She gripped the sliced fabric at her stomach. With a sharp tug, she pulled away a strip of silk, rolled it into a thick wad, and pressed it to her forehead.

"Oh, honey, you didn't have to do that." Lyra dropped a stack of clean clothes onto the bar next to where Toria slouched on a barstool. She pressed gentle fingers to Toria's cheek and gasped when Toria flinched away. "Is it broken?"

"No." Toria almost shook her head, but thought better of the action. "The cheekbone might be fractured, but I'd be in worse shape if I broke my jaw."

"You shouldn't have gotten involved." Lyra huffed in exasperation and moved out into the seating area littered with scattered tables and toppled chairs, shattered glass and drops of blood—not all of which belonged to Toria.

After she patched Toria's forehead to her satisfaction, Lyra poured each of them a shot of whiskey and settled onto the next stool. "Thanks for the help, by the way. You ended that faster than it would have, otherwise."

Toria shrugged, making note of another movement to avoid for the foreseeable future when a sharp pain lanced her side. "I promise that wasn't my intention."

"What, you walked into the bar, saw the fight, and thought it looked like fun?" Lyra tossed back her shot, flinched at the taste, and slammed the glass on the bar. "I'm going to need more alcohol for this."

Toria sipped her whiskey and relished the burn as it passed her throat. "I walked into the bar and dodged a punch. Though I won't deny the lack of physical excitement in my life may have contributed to me punching back instead of turning around." She refilled Lyra's glass from the bottle between them. "I'm glad you hid instead of joining the fun."

Lyra scoffed, ignoring the drink. "Kojo would never forgive me if I was hurt."

"I'm not sure I'd have forgiven myself if you'd been hurt. Another reason I stayed to clear the mess." Toria waved away the refill Lyra offered her.

Lyra made another aborted gesture toward Toria's face. "Are you sure you'll be okay?"

No, she wasn't okay, but if anything, the pain from her injuries was easier to handle than everything else on her plate at the moment. And if she drank with Lyra to drown out the noise in her head, at least she kept it here rather than at Hugh's house. That was healthy. Healthier, anyway. Healthier than what, Toria wasn't inclined to consider further. She changed the subject. "I suppose you called Kojo?"

"Right after the police. He said he'd be here when he got here."

"Isn't this his bar?" It had surprised Toria to learn Lyra wasn't the owner, but instead worked as head bartender for her boyfriend who had other real estate dealings. She figured out the code for "slum lord," but Toria wasn't in a position to judge. She wanted to keep the one real friend she'd made in Nacostina who treated her like a normal person, not a refugee from another world.

She'd run into Kojo twice at the bar since their first meeting. First, he'd scoffed at the idea of a female mercenary and then settled on facetious comments—how nice for Lyra to have a little friend to keep her company at work some nights.

"I should get to work on this mess." Lyra pressed a hand to Toria's shoulder before she rose. "Sit. Rest."

It wasn't in her nature to not pitch in with the cleanup, but Toria's ribcage seconded Lyra's instructions. She'd kill for some hardcore painkillers, but not after consuming alcohol. She'd muddle through.

Even better would be a dose of raw earth power from Kane. The cure-all worked for everything except hangovers (and sometimes she thought he was holding out on her for those).

Quiet enveloped the room, which seemed out of place when she was used to the thrum of conversation. As if sensing Toria's unease, Lyra flipped on a small radio, and an elegant string composition washed away the silence. Toria propped her head up with an elbow on the bar, holding her torso in the most pain-free position possible, and lost herself in the music.

For a brief moment, she wasn't in a trashed bar on the seedy side of Nacostina. She curled in the over-stuffed armchair in her father's music studio, at home in Limani. She closed her eyes as her father played, and the classical music caressed her skin and made the hair on her arms stand up.

The radio announcer's voice jarred her out of her reverie, thundering across the final strains of music. "And that was the striking duet of cellist Connor and violinist Mikelos, recorded live in Veneti, where they are this summer's featured performers...."

Toria let her head fall forward to thud on the bar. Obviously the music brought back good memories. It was her father playing it.

She'd always known her father weathered the Last War in Europa. He and Connor, the first vampire he'd bonded with, would return to their winter estate south of Roma after completing this summer tour.

But she knew where he was right now. For a moment, the temptation to make her way across the ocean and find him overwhelmed her.

Mikelos wouldn't even know her. Her surname's namesake, the vampire Connor, would never let the crazy mage near him. Because that's what Toria was, or was at least turning into. A crazy person. She raised her head and pulled the bottle of whiskey closer.

Lyra, teeth clenched, snatched the bottle out of her hand before she uncapped it. "Kojo wants to talk to you." The man in question loomed over her shoulder.

Kojo didn't acknowledge Lyra, who moved out of the way to return to sweeping up. He also didn't sit, instead leaning against the bar and studying Toria. His show of bravado and dominance made Toria's skin crawl, but she didn't stand up. She was shorter off the barstool, anyway. "Good evening, Kojo."

"I heard you helped out tonight." He pulled Lyra's abandoned glass and the whiskey bottle to himself and poured a drink. He didn't offer Toria a refill.

"I suppose you could call it that. Knocked a few heads, at least."

"A woman shouldn't be fighting."

"A woman should do what she's trained to do." Toria rubbed her hands on her thighs to keep them flat at his insult. "Of course, you think women shouldn't wear pants, either."

Kojo pressed his lips together, but didn't answer. He downed the rest of his whiskey, unable to hide his annoyance. "Lyra dresses appropriate to a woman of her station, as befits a woman who represents my business interests. No one knows what the hell you are."

"A customer who appreciates good beer." Tension knotted Toria's back, but she hid the twinge of pain from her ribs from appearing on her face. "And good company."

"Remember that you're a customer." Kojo slid the bottle and his empty glass to the other side of the bar, out of Toria's reach. "You don't belong here. And no one asked for your help."

Behind Kojo, Lyra swept the same section of clean floor over and over again. Her grip had tightened on the broom handle.

"Don't call it help," Toria said. "Call it… my getting wrapped into an awkward circumstance and doing what I felt best."

"What's best is relative." From inside his coat, Kojo withdrew a thick wad of cash held together with a shiny money clip. He peeled away three of the bills and placed them in front of Toria.

"What's this?" Toria didn't touch the money, which was more than she'd seen in one place the entire time she'd been in the past. This covered a week's worth of fancy dinners with Liam, or another half a wardrobe from Granny Tia. But she wanted Kojo to say it out loud.

"You're playing at being a mercenary, right? That's for protecting my establishment tonight."

His establishment. Not his girlfriend.

"I'm not playing at anything." Toria slid off the barstool and held herself straight. Pain thrummed through her bruised face, echoing her heartbeat, but she let none of it show in her demeanor. She left the cash where it lay and stalked out of the bar, picking her way through the remnants of the brawl.

Lyra's gaze burned between her shoulder blades, but she didn't dare turn around and go to the woman. Toria had seen this before, hired with Kane to protect a woman from her abusive ex-husband. The man had seen the client as his property, worth as much as her inheritance and family status brought him.

This was much the same, even if Kojo seemed to value Lyra as arm candy and a source of cheap labor to run the bar. Going to her friend now would force Kojo to see Toria as a threat to his control over Lyra. She would rather be disrespected and underestimated.

That meant she could come back again, and continue her friendship with Lyra undisturbed.

Toria aimed for a nicer area of town and got into the first cab willing to stop for the limping woman with a torn, bloody blouse. She ignored the driver's curious questions and gave Hugh's address, then curled inward, wrapping her arms around her ribs and biting her bottom lip against the pain. She had sacrificed more than one hit to the torso while slipping under a defense to defeat her opponent. Familiarity told her it was bruising, not a more serious crack, but knowledge didn't help with the pain.

She paid and staggered out of the car in front of the bed and breakfast. She waved off the driver's offer of a ride to the hospital. The house was dark. Hugh must still be at his card game. It wasn't at the bed and breakfast tonight, so at least she wouldn't walk into a cluster of chivalrous old men who last week had alternated between flirting with her and cursing her skill at cards.

Toria dug out the first aid kit Hugh kept in a kitchen cupboard. She used the reflection of the overhead light in the window above the sink to replace the patchy dressing on her forehead. She stripped off the unsalvageable blouse and wrapped her ribs with a long strip of bandage. Though she moved at a snail's pace, she cleaned away the supplies she'd used and replaced the kit, leaving no trace of her efforts.

She collected a glass from the kitchen and snagged a bottle from Hugh's liquor stash. Tucking both items under one arm, she hauled herself up the two flights of stairs, teeth gritted against the pain. Once ensconced in her cozy room, she donned a loose nightshirt and tucked herself in bed with a glass of port.

The specific action of bringing glass to lips was easier than thinking. The port warmed her belly the way the whiskey at the bar hadn't. Maybe she could ask Lyra to get some in stock.

If she ever returned to the bar. If Lyra let her in if she did go back. If her friend forgave her for walking out.

The interesting thing about spiral thinking was how it out-shouted the rational part of Toria's mind. Whether it was the stress of the evening, the pain in her battered body, or the alcohol, the anxious voice overwhelmed everything else until the rational mind seemed like the imposter. What place did rationality have in a world with no hope?

She could have used her magical ability to knock out every fighter in the bar without ending up with so much as a scratch. It might have resulted in a bad reaction headache, but a good night's sleep fixed that. Instead, she'd waded into the fray and courted worse injury.

She had been mistaken earlier. Kane would be so disappointed in her. In her mind, his eyes flashed under a furrowed brow, arms crossed over his chest. He was her voice of sanity, the rational one who countered her tendency toward the dramatic.

But Kane wasn't here, and without him, she was losing her mind.

The next morning, Hugh exclaimed over Toria's bruised face and the way she braced one arm around her ribcage. He tried to convince her to go to the hospital. She waved him off with the excuse she'd sustained far worse injuries over time, but promised to revisit the idea if her pain level worsened.

Their current project involved refinishing the floors of the sunroom off the kitchen. Toria kept Hugh company from a stool as he sanded the wooden floors by hand, and soon their banter devolved into a more serious discussion of what sort of patrons Hugh expected to target with his bed and breakfast.

In a way, she relished the pain. Though her sword languished in her bedroom, the previous night proved her muscle memory still provided the necessary combat skills.

Later, Hugh broke the companionable silence of their ploughman's lunch. "Meeting Liam again today?" He kept his tone neutral, but she didn't miss the teasing sparkle in his eyes.

"The idea had occurred to me." If anything, Liam's presence would serve as a distraction from her pain. Toria rose from the table to bring their empty plates to the sink.

"No, I'll take care of all this." Hugh shooed her out of the kitchen. "It's a gorgeous day. Go clean up and drag Liam away from his office for the afternoon."

Toria wasn't sure about the odds of Liam neglecting his work, but if nothing else, she could spend the afternoon walking along the sprawling areas of greenery downtown. She wanted to tour the gardens outside the museum, with a closer inspection of the decorative statuary. The objects d'art presented an intellectual curiosity to her metallurgy experience.

Long-disused welding techniques occupied her mind through her quick cleanup. Getting to the museum was old hat, by now—walk three blocks to a cluster of stores nearest Hugh's house, where she could either snag a taxi or hop on the trolley. The indirect trolley route ended with another four-block walk to the museum. Not a hardship in the bright summer afternoon. Enough humidity to curl the tips of her hair, but not drench her in sweat.

Even walking in thick shoes with low heels was second nature these days. She and Granny Tia had achieved a detente regarding her wardrobe. Toria put up with the shoes and ridiculous brassieres and bandeaus in exchange that Granny Tia never again suggest Toria wear a girdle.

Her stroll through the gardens occupied an hour, after which time Toria was more than ready to duck inside and rest her sore ribs. She climbed the stairs to Liam's office but found it empty. He often stepped out for meetings or conversations with other departments within the museum. Letting her feet wander, Toria continued through the museum, grateful the granite building remained cool despite the summer heat.

As often happened, Toria found herself in the exotic minerals exhibit in the east wing, in front of one particular display that burned with magical power. Even without her magesight active, Toria sensed its internal hum of power, a sharp chord out of sync with the surrounding power-neutral stones.

"Fascinating, isn't it, Ms. Connor?"

Toria jerked away from the case, where she'd been about to touch the palm of her hand to the spotless glass. She'd missed Rubin's approach in her overwhelming focus on the meteorite. Though she'd managed to avoid the curator since their first uncomfortable meeting, she should have known she wouldn't be able to put off the man forever.

Inside, her hackles raised and her right hand itched for her distant sword. But years of professionalism won out. "Yes, sir."

Rubin gave no indication he was aware his presence made Toria's skin crawl as he faced the display case next to her. "The deacons mentioned to me that you view this particular artifact almost every time you visit the museum."

He didn't phrase it as a question, so she stood in silence.

After a few uncomfortable beats, Rubin spoke again. "The smaller artifacts in permanent exhibits are often switched out to keep some elements fresh for returning visitors. I believe this one is slated for removal soon. Unhealthy fascination with artifacts is seen as something of a warning sign in certain circles."

Toria twitched in surprise, but resisted the urge to step away from the man. "I'm not sure I understand what you're implying, sir." She channeled her mother at Victory's most regal, insinuating a hint of offense into her tone.

Rubin waved a dismissive hand. "It makes Security jumpy."

When he turned to Toria, she stood her ground, though she ached to back away. Once again, she had no good response and elected for silence. In a sudden flash of double vision, a bullet hole appeared in his forehead and brain matter exploded from the back of his skull. But this image did nothing to comfort her.

He ignored the awkward pause. "Though I imagine you have become familiar with the various security members on site. Along with other members of my team." Disdain colored his last words, and now his insinuation was clear.

Despite her anxiety at facing this dead man walking, Toria had no desire to give Rubin the satisfaction of intimidating her. "Are you referring to my friendship with Liam, sir?"

"Is that what they're calling it these days?" Rubin clasped his hands behind his back and loomed over Toria.

She lifted her nose higher in the air and didn't allow him to use her shorter height against her. "Friendship is an accurate term no matter the era, I've found."

Toria had provided security for some of the most prestigious women in Britannia. While she always kept visual alert for external threats, she kept her ears open as well. Based on this exposure, to powerful ladies maneuvering men who almost always thought it the other way around, she could out-polite Rubin any day of the week and make it clear the entire time she would not be cowed.

"My deputy curator is not employed to be your friend. That is Mr. Ainsworth's position. Liamacorin was merely to function as a guide to this time period. Once I am certain he has fulfilled this duty, I will make sure his attentions are focused elsewhere." Rubin stepped out of Toria's personal space and treated her to a short, mocking bow. "And you might want to get the bruise on your face looked at. Good afternoon, Ms. Connor."

He turned on his heel and wended between the handful of other visitors at a brisk clip, leaving Toria to stare after his receding form. Sharp pain pierced her palms, and she forced her balled fists loose before her fingernails broke the skin. Even summoning another memory of Rubin's death brought no relief, and the full force of his words struck Toria like a battering ram, more crushing than even her bruised ribs.

Hugh was her friend because he was being paid. And her tentative—thing—whatever it was, whatever it might be, with Liam was over before it had a chance.

The deacon on duty spoke with a clump of visitors at the other end of the gallery, so Toria staggered to his vacant bench and collapsed. She curled forward as much as her ribs allowed and pressed her forehead to her palms. All attempts at meditative breathing failed, and her shoulders shook with the force of the sharp gasps for air.

The world blurred into darkness and white noise as Toria pulled inward.

Everything was a lie. Though he had been a steady rock since her first night in Nacostina, Toria reevaluated every word Hugh had ever spoken to her. Every action of comfort and support rippled through her mind like a slide show on high speed. She was aware of his financial compensation for her room and board, but not the precise amount. Was it so much money that all of it had been an act? Sufficient funds for meals and rent, but also a façade of friendship?

And Liam.

Was that a lie, too? His kind words, the trail of fingers down her bare arm, the press of warm lips? Liam's job had been to acclimate Toria to the time period, no more and no less. Anything beyond had to be a dream.

A shadow of Kane's voice in her ears. *You left me.*

It was an accident. This whole damned thing was an accident, but it was happening, and it was Toria's life. She didn't leave Kane, a stupid rock had ripped her away, and the wound in her soul was a jagged, missing limb. A sucking chest wound, like the way it hurt to breathe. She gasped around the suffocating panic and clawed at the fabric of her trousers, seeking anything to ground herself.

She wasn't a whole person without Kane. Liam could never be any sort of replacement, and she didn't deserve the happiness she might find with him.

Better she wise up now, before the pleasant dream of happily ever after exploded in her face. She would leave, now, tonight. Leave Hugh, leave Liam, leave this doomed city and make her way as half a person.

Hands stroked her arms, and she sobbed at the tempting memory.

But the smooth motion continued. Warm palms with long fingers, one of which had a tiny callous at a knuckle from years of holding a pen. She focused on the touch, narrowing her whole world to the connection with something outside herself. The roar in her ears dissipated, replaced by a low murmur. Her name, interspersed with soft words of how everything would be okay.

Nothing would ever be okay, but Toria lifted her head. The late afternoon sunlight streamed through the high windows. With a shaky hand, she wiped away tears as everything around her shifted into sharp relief. Motes of dust danced in the warm light, and the deacon whose seat she'd stolen occupied visitors who peered down the hall with concern on their faces. Concern for her.

Liam knelt before her. When Toria met his eyes, he smiled.

She was prepared not to believe him. That this was all an act, an effort to get the broken, crying woman out of public. But his eyes crinkled at the corners. This was real.

"There you are." Liam kept his tone light and words soothing. And he made no immediate effort to move Toria. Instead, he rose with a slight creak in his knees and settled next to her on the bench.

Toria snuggled into Liam's side when he draped an arm over her shoulders, and she clutched his other hand in both of hers. Her voice cracked when she tried to speak. She cleared the remnants of her tears from her throat and tried again. "You're going to get tired of finding me like this."

"A man never denies his desire to be the hero, though I will admit I hate to see you cry." Liam held her close. "Or see you in pain. What happened to your face?"

"There was an…altercation at Lyra's last night. I helped clean it up."

"A bar fight?" Liam's voice rose in pitch. His teeth clicked as he cut off further words. Liam tensed next to her, and she expected questions. But none came. "I'm glad you're alright."

His shoulders loosened and he seemed content to cuddle her in silence while her residual shivers tapered out.

The shadows in the hall lengthened. A few late afternoon visitors wandered through, but the deacon corralled them away from Toria and Liam. Had Liam requested it, or was the man that considerate?

When Toria's breathing smoothed, Liam spoke again. "One thing I do know for certain." He kept his voice low, as if sharing a secret with her.

"What's that?" Toria whispered in return, and the excitement of their flirtation was almost enough to chase away the remnants of her anxiety.

"If push came to shove, I have no doubt you'd be the one rescuing me."

"Is that so?"

"I am aware of my physical limitations." Liam untangled his hand from hers to flex his arm, and Toria poked a firm bicep. "I'm happy to be the brains of this operation."

She pulled away in mock offense. "And what does that make me?"

"You're the one who finishes bar fights. So, the brawn, the magic, and another good set of brains." Liam booped her nose with his index finger.

Toria laughed at the incongruous action, and the satisfaction across Liam's face warmed her inside.

Toria might be a little crazy these days, but she wasn't an idiot. She knew enough about human nature to recognize when someone was pulling the wool over her eyes, and Liam wasn't. Hugh wasn't either. She might be adrift in time, but these men were her friends.

Her stomach rumbled. Panic used calories. "Take me to dinner?"

Liam rose from the bench and bowed to her. His action was charming, in stark contrast to Rubin's mockery. "It would be my pleasure."

Time to be realistic. It wasn't "dinner with Liam." These were dates.

Toria wouldn't have it any other way. She'd never be able to go back to picking up guys in Oxenafor bars after this. With Kane, she knew what it felt like to be understood. Was this what it felt like to be wanted, even cherished? The pool of warmth in her stomach had nothing to do with arousal.

They shared a candle-lit meal at yet another cozy bistro, where Liam kept the conversation light and the air between them relaxed. He deferred to her anxiety attack and other injuries by foregoing the wine, instead requesting two waters from the waiter.

Toria knew she was in trouble when she found his concern for her hydration charming.

Well, trouble surrounded her in many forms, but this was the latest.

Liam offered to drive Toria home after dinner, but she declined. "I know you must have dropped everything when you found out about my little episode. Far be it from me to keep you from organizing your paperwork for tomorrow." She rose on her toes to peck a kiss to his lips.

Liam wrapped his arms around her waist and pulled her to his chest before she could escape, gentle in respect for her ribs. "If I was distracted at dinner, it was to keep myself from being lost in your eyes." Toria choked down a giggle. "Too much?"

"Perfect." She looped her arms around Liam's neck to kiss him again, and they stayed distracted until a waitress poked her head out the front door and cleared her throat in their direction.

They broke apart, with great reluctance and sharing embarrassed laughter. Rubin's words crawled through Toria's brain again, but she shoved them down. Liam was a man of this time, with uncommon public displays of affection. If he made out with her in the street, his feelings for her, whether simple friendship and lust or the chance for something more, were real.

Liam chased her final kiss with one of his own before stepping away. "I should get back and finish that report for Finance. I know you'll be okay getting home, but I don't want to leave if you're still feeling…unsure about anything."

"I promise I'll be fine. Some things just caught up to me." Toria patted his arm. "Trust me."

"I do."

The sincerity glowed in Liam's expression, until Toria realized it was the reflection of a streetlight catching the extra structures in elven eyes that allowed them to see better than humans in the dark. "Good night, hon."

"Good night, sweetheart." Liam kissed her cheek one more time before walking toward the museum, whistling out of tune with his hands shoved in his suit pockets.

Toria waited until he turned the corner before she set off in her own chosen direction. But not to the trolley stop or to snag a cab for home. Even as she resolved not to let Rubin's words haunt her, one of Liam's comments stuck in her head.

She was the brawn to his brains, even without dismissing her own intelligence. But these weeks in Nacostina had thrown her exercise habits out the window. If she craved someone to spar with, she'd also trade her left arm—or at least a pinky finger or two—for a decent pair of running shoes.

But cardio was yet another thing "not done" in this time period for well-bred young women. Toria wandered, and the fancy décor of Nacostina's downtown devolved into the row homes and corner shops becoming as familiar to her as Liam's swanky restaurants. Not everyone she knew in Nacostina was a well-bred young woman.

Lyra might have some suggestions for her, or maybe an idea how to make friends with some of the mercs who frequented the bar. Even if full Guild status was out of reach, there might be a way to gain access to the Guildhall and take advantage of the bored mercenaries.

To work out with them, of course.

Maintaining her proper fighting form included other benefits, as well. Mental health wasn't a significant health concern in this era, especially for women. The last thing she needed was a massive anxiety attack in a more public space and to get thrown in an asylum for hysteria, or some other such nonsense.

Either way, she needed an outlet for her energy beyond Hugh's renovation work. The chemical imbalances in her brain demanded it. Not to mention the waistline that enjoyed Liam's dinners and the accompanying wine.

At the very least, Lyra might have an idea for attire. A request for workout clothing that didn't involve the words "tennis" or "croquet" would scandalize Granny Tia.

As she passed the Guildhall toward the bar, the ring of steel against steel echoed out the front door.

Oh, hell. Not again. Her ribs made sprinting out of the question, so Toria lurched the final distance. She skidded to a halt at the bar's entrance, propped open for the evening breeze.

She ducked a flung beer bottle and dashed inside. Tactical surveillance revealed a bar fight smaller than the previous night's, but this time it involved weapons. Lyra was nowhere in sight, but Toria prayed she was out of harm's way behind the bar or in the stock room.

Two nights in a row of this nonsense was a little much. Toria shoved her way through the men who circled the four combatants, ignoring the curse of the man she elbowed and tuning out the shouts and cheers.

She had two options, but only one was feasible. Breaking up a fight between multiple men who out-massed her was a different beast than participating in a standard barroom brawl. And she couldn't injure her ribs further, risking a crack or outright break.

Magic, then.

She rubbed her palms together, and electricity crackled up her arms. The men to either side gasped and backed away, and as the bolts of lightning expanded to shimmer around her entire body, more of the attention turned from the fight to her.

To be honest, this wasn't her intended effect. But so much magic permeated the air. And she couldn't fall on her usual grounding trick—shoving the excess power through her link to Kane, where he could sink it in the earth without a thought. Instead, it crackled through her skin until her hair haloed her face with static electricity. Ozone overwhelmed even the worst bar scents.

Being a regular mage kind of sucked. There had to be a better way to do this.

An experiment for another day. Toria assigned mental targets to each fighter, even the two distracted by her light show. She flicked her arms, stretching her fingers out. The electric bolts slid down her limbs and shot across the space, zapping each of the men with almost fifty-thousand volts of power.

They dropped to the floor, unconscious. One of them twitched a bit, like a fallen marionette, before going still.

Stunned silence reigned for three heartbeats before the bar exploded into mayhem. In disparate groups, the gathered onlookers rushed for Toria to apprehend her, shoved away, or milled in stunned shock. None of them made any progress, and she had time to back away, keeping her line of exit to the door free.

Even knocking out the fighters hadn't used all the collected energy, so she dumped the rest into her combat shields, which she summoned to full strength. Anyone who grabbed for her would get a nasty surprise, scorched fingers or a complete blackout.

"Hey!"

A feminine shout snapped everyone, including Toria, to attention. Lyra stood on the bar and overlooked the crowd. With her arms crossed and hair corralled by her kerchief, she radiated a fierce energy that had nothing to do with magic and everything to do with sheer force of personality. "Bar's closed. Get out." Her lowered volume did nothing to diminish the authority behind her voice.

Despite a few muttered complaints, they all turned to the door as one. And stopped again, when they found Toria between them and their exit. She slid a few paces to the side and gestured to the door like an usher. Within moments, the bar had emptied, except for the four men still passed out, surrounded by shoved tables and toppled chairs.

Lyra had already hopped off the bar and held the telephone to her ear, summoning the police for the second night in a row. Toria released her combat shields and grounded the excess energy through a slow trickle into the wooden floor, where it dissipated in safety. She picked her way over to the men and checked for pulses. Four out of four strong heartbeats. She unclenched her teeth. The last thing she needed was to kill someone by accident. Even Liam would have had a hard time extricating her from such a mess of red tape.

"They good?"

Toria shot a double thumbs-up to Lyra, who relayed the information on the telephone.

When Toria retreated to the bar, Lyra caught her bottom lip between her teeth and eyed the telephone again.

Toria hopped onto a bar stool and sat sideways, watching for signs of stirring in the unconscious men. "You should probably call him."

Lyra's fingers tightened on the edge of the bar. "He's going to be upset."

"So, what?" The other coin dropped when Lyra shot Toria a pointed look. "Wait, how is he going to blame you for this?"

"This particular fight happened because Jordan made an inappropriate comment about me. Aviv is Kojo's cousin, and felt the need to defend my honor. Then their friends got involved." Lyra pointed to one of the men, who had darker skin than the rest and a family resemblance in the set of Kojo's jaw. "Kojo is going to think I need a bouncer in here if these fights keep happening."

Toria considered this new mess. "I can't say I disagree with him."

"It'll be someone who reports to Kojo every time a man flirts with me, or I'm too nice to a customer."

"Isn't that kind of your job?"

"It's complicated." The fear in Lyra's voice twisted something in Toria's chest, but she continued before Toria could speak up. "Kojo comes off as rough, but he's a delicate person. I don't want to hurt him."

Toria's turn to bite her lip before she said something she'd regret. All the bad vibes she'd gotten from Kojo fell into place, but she'd seen this pattern before. It would always be excuses upon excuses, and Toria wasn't sure it was worth risking this tentative friendship by speaking up now.

The boyfriend would win, every time.

No one had closed the bar's front door in the mass exodus after Toria shut down the fight, so Kojo's entrance was less dramatic than he might prefer. He swept in before Toria voiced any argument against him, though the delay in the expression of pleasure Lyra slapped on her face was yet another piece of evidence against the man.

He stepped over the prone bodies, lip curled in disgust. The weather today had been too warm for the dapper three-piece suite he wore, but in Kojo's world, appearance was more important than discomfort. He prodded his cousin with one polished loafer. "They dead?"

"No." Toria rested an elbow on the bar and made herself at home. She had even less interest in hopping to her feet and showing the man any deference than she had before, which had been zero. "Knocked out."

Kojo ignored the kiss Lyra pressed to his cheek. "Damned police aren't even here yet?"

"They didn't seem thrilled to hear from me so soon after yesterday." Lyra stepped toward the phone. "Should I try again?"

Kojo lifted his cap to ruck his hand through a stubble of hair. "Nah. I'll call. They'll listen to me."

Toria bristled at the insinuation that they hadn't believed Lyra, but the reminder of where—and when—she was rose its monstrous head once again.

Kojo stomped behind the bar and snagged the bottle of well scotch and a single glass. His priorities seemed to be in order. After he downed a shot and slammed the glass on the bar, he fixed his glare on Toria. "What the hell are you doing here?"

Lyra answered, not meeting Kojo's gaze as she righted an overturned chair. "She's the one who knocked them out. Stopped the fight before it got any worse, or pulled in the whole crowd."

"So, Lyra wasn't lying about the magic thing?" Kojo surveyed the bodies again and let out a low whistle.

"No." Toria left an intentional pause, as if determining how much to reveal to Kojo. But she already had an idea of how to play this, for her benefit and Lyra's. "I qualify as a master-level mage. It's why I thought the Mercenary Guild might accept me."

Kojo snorted. "Well, they weren't going to take you on the basis of that ridiculous sword. Lyra told me about your little pig-sticker."

She kept her peace, despite the insult to her beloved rapier. One of the men groaned and shifted. They'd wake soon. Toria hoped the cops arrived first. She pushed her knuckles on the bar, hiding her smirk when Kojo jumped at her cracking joints. "The bar fights here are becoming a trend. I know you serve a lot of mercs, but they'd rather get paid to fight."

Lyra's eyes widened across the room, but Toria flicked a finger at her. The woman resumed resetting the furniture, though Toria sensed her sharp attention on them.

"Business is slow everywhere in Nacostina for those folks." Kojo toyed with his empty glass. "Regardless of what they want, they're stuck here. Half the fights stem from competition over the available jobs."

"Have you thought about hiring one? Contributing to the local economy?"

Kojo snorted. "Why the hell would I want to employ one of those maniacs?"

"To break up situations like this before you end up with bodies on your floor?" Toria pointed a thumb over her shoulder. "They might not be unconscious next time."

Kojo's hand drifted toward his coat. "Is that a threat?"

"Oh, sheesh." Years of experience prevented Toria from rolling her eyes. "No. Consider it a job application."

"I don't even like you."

"I don't like you either, but your girlfriend is kind of cool, and I'd hate to see something happen to her." Toria straightened in her seat and pointed to the front door. "The cops still haven't even shown up. And it's through sheer luck I was here the last two nights."

"You want me to pay you to hang out in my establishment and drink my liquor and flirt with my girl? I don't see how that's a good business investment on my part." Kojo refilled his drink, but his sarcasm didn't hide all the hesitancy in his voice.

"Nah, I genuinely need a job. And think of it this way—I'm not a member of the Mercenary Guild. I'm a hell of a lot cheaper than any of those assholes, and I'm happy to accept payment under the table." She leaned forward on the bar, projecting innocent earnestness.

"She really knock those men out with magic?" Kojo asked Lyra.

"Didn't even snap her fingers." Lyra picked her way between the tables, giving the stirring men a wide berth. "The regulars have now seen her defeat them with fists and magic. Park her at the bar, and they might think twice about causing a stir. I know I'm tired of replacing furniture."

"I'm tired of paying for it." Kojo pressed his lips together. "Okay. But only because of your condition." He turned to Toria and pointed at her with his empty glass. "I'm not paying you full-time, I don't give a shit about schedules, and you don't get to set your rate. You park yourself at this bar at least four nights a week, and I'll make sure Lyra has a packet of cash for you on occasion. You don't get paid if you stop showing up, and if I don't pay you enough, you don't have to show up."

He slammed the glass on the bar and stormed away, snatching the telephone off the hook and dialing with all the ferocity possible with a rotary. Once the conversation engrossed him, Toria whirled on Lyra. "What the hell did he mean about your condition?"

Lyra pressed a hand to her abdomen, and Toria's stomach sank even before the response came. "We found out last week."

Toria smiled around gritted teeth. "Congratulations! I'm so happy for you!" She embraced Lyra.

"Thank you." Lyra released her and stepped back, but caught Toria's hands in hers in excitement. "I won't show for another few weeks. This is where people keep wanting to buy me a celebratory drink, but I should buy you one instead."

"Why would I buy you a drink for being pregnant? That's not—" Right. While she was much more familiar with the differences in tech levels between now and her own time, medical knowledge had also evolved. But the last thing she wanted right now was a fight over why Lyra shouldn't drink while pregnant when she had no way to support her position. "Why don't we call it even?"

"Sounds fair. How did you get Kojo to hire you like that?"

Toria couldn't respond with a quip about years of experience dealing with mercenary contracts and elitist male assholes. "I had a feeling."

"Well, it worked." Lyra dropped Toria's hands like fire as Kojo slammed the telephone home.

"Cops will be here in a few. They want the mage to stick around for questioning. I'm going to try to wake my damned fool cousin." Without waiting for a response, he stalked toward the men lying in the middle of the bar.

Lyra and Toria settled themselves on adjoining barstools while Kojo roused Aviv. Toria kept a weather eye on the men, though she wasn't sure who needed her protection.

It had grown late by the time the police arrived and finished questioning everyone, including noting Toria's contact information. They declined to arrest anyone, because Toria couldn't say who had instigated the fight, Kojo hadn't been present, and Lyra and the men clammed up. Fighting among themselves was one thing, but snitching to the establishment was on another level.

Since Toria made her living working around, and sometimes outside, the establishment herself, she couldn't disapprove.

Toria promised Lyra she would return the next evening for her first night of "work," and set off for the bed and breakfast. She couldn't decide whether to tell Liam about this venture. Hugh would be happy she found something to utilize her skill set, but Toria didn't want to push anything in her fledgling relationship.

When she stepped out of the cab in front of Hugh's house, she realized she'd never asked Lyra about suitable workout clothing.

She snuck past Hugh's bedroom, where he dozed in an armchair to the low sounds of his radio. If she broke up fights every other night, she might not need more exercise after all.

BETWEEN

As Victory stalked through the dark city, the impossible sank in. Her wild thought in the museum evolved into inescapable reality as long-forgotten memories stirred with every landmark she passed.

How would she find Toria in this mess? Nacostina in the time before the Last War was larger than any city on the New Continent in the future from which her daughter came.

She paused on a street corner a few blocks from where she remembered the Mercenary Guildhall and stared into the night sky. Unknown variables flitted through her mind. What year was it? Victory had never lived in Nacostina full-time, but for a span of years had passed through frequently. Was she in danger of running into her past self?

And how close in time was she to the bomb dropping? Though the winter air didn't affect her, she shivered.

The most important question was the time until dawn, and where she would find shelter from the coming day. Find shelter. Find Toria. Attainable goals.

Victory jogged the remaining distance, at a human speed designed not to attract unnecessary attention. She pulled open the Guildhall front door and paused when a brush of lukewarm air hit her instead of a blast of heat.

The battered lobby, lit by a single lamp at the empty front desk, told a story. This was a Mercenary Guild fallen upon hard times.

Such as it had been before the Last War.

A voice rang out. "Close the damned door!" An older man shuffled into view, leaning on a cane. Patchy facial hair covered pasty skin, and his build showed muscle given over to paunch after his mobility-hindering injury.

His scathing glare did little to intimidate Victory, though she followed his instruction. She approached the desk as he settled himself behind it. "Good morning. I'm here looking for someone."

The old merc scanned Victory, squinting. "You don't look like you're hiring. Do look like you should be cold, though."

Her bare arms were out of place, considering the season. "I appreciate the concern, but that's the least of my troubles tonight." Victory smiled wide enough to flash fang, all the explanation needed.

"Good. Our clothing stores are reserved for Guildmembers only."

Victory kept her ID in her wallet, because again, she had no idea whether the Guild might already have record of her in town. Another passing thought—the man wouldn't recognize her modern badge. Damn it. At least she had no memory of ever running into herself, but she also had no idea how time travel worked. The weird science and magic stuff was Toria's department. She steered the conversation back to the point. "As I said, I'm looking for someone. If she's in town, she'll have come through here looking for work." If the man had no record of Toria, either Toria wasn't here, or worse, hadn't appeared in this time period.

Squinty placed a hand on a stack of folders. "She? Vampire, too?"

"No. Human. Young woman in her mid-twenties. Carries a rapier." Victory paused, considering how much information to give away. But some details were such an inherent function of who her daughter was that she could never imagine Toria hiding them unless necessary. "Some magical ability."

Disappointment flared when the man didn't bother with the papers. Instead, he sat back in his seat and laughed. "You're not looking for a merc. You're looking for the kid who works security at the bar down the block. Rumor is she tried to join the Guild when she first showed up. Can you imagine? A lady merc?"

Victory placed a hand on the pommel of the bastard sword strapped to her waist. "How novel."

His winter-pale skin bloomed red in embarrassment. When Victory let the uncomfortable silence drag on, he heaved himself to his feet. "I don't know who you are or why you're searching for that girl, but you're not going anywhere now. Bar's closed, and dawn's coming soon. You need a place to stay?"

The merc's matter-of-fact tone broke through Victory's immediate instinct of denial. "I didn't mean to be caught out so late. I'd appreciate the help, if it's not a bother." She weighed cover stories in her head and decided the less information she provided, the less chance of it biting her ass later. "My membership lapsed, though."

"Lady, you and half the other mercs in the world." He snagged his cane and gestured for Victory to follow. One light of every three sconces lit the hall. "We've got rooms to spare right now."

Victory trailed him through halls she remembered from better days. But he led her where she expected, an interior bedroom with no windows to risk exposure to sunlight. Before she closed the door, she touched the old merc's arm. "Thank you."

"Don't think I'd have let a human get away with this." The gruffness in his voice eased. "I'd have scrounged up a coat before I tossed you out, though."

The next evening, Victory stripped the sheets and bundled them at the foot of the bed. Leaving no other evidence of her stay, she swept past the unfamiliar face at the front desk and exited the building. He didn't bother to call after her.

Thanks to cooling relations between the British and the Romans even before the Last War, Nacostina had had no Master of the City for decades. The good news: no vampire to whom Victory must report her presence in the city.

The bad news: none of the perks. No one to provide asylum, and no established, civilized blood supply. Victory hesitated to count on the Guild's charity for a second day unless she was desperate.

The surrounding area showed the same signs of passive neglect as the Guildhall, and the locals didn't stroll the streets so much as scurry to their destinations, bundled against the cold in secondhand clothing.

Victory added a coat to her list of priorities, so she wouldn't seem out of place.

Every Mercenary Guildhall the world over had a bar within spitting distance, and she found this one quickly. She slipped in behind two men and paused inside the entrance as the door swung closed behind her. The long room boasted a handful of customers.

She snagged a passing waitress, who looked at her askance. "Was told someone a friend works here. Toria Connor?"

The young woman pushed her thick glasses up her nose. "Yeah! Lyra's friend." She pointed to the pregnant bartender, who shined glasses behind the bar. "I don't think she's supposed to be in tonight, though."

"Any idea where she's staying?"

The waitress crossed her arms and eyed Victory with a hint of suspicion. "And why should I tell you?"

Victory could feign innocence when necessary. "We're friends from home, but I got into town earlier than expected. We were supposed to meet here, but if she's not working tonight…." She let the sentence trail off with an eloquent shrug.

Her wariness easing, the waitress jabbed a thumb behind her. "I'll go check her contact info in the back." She darted between the tables, dodging one drinker who tried to pinch her rear.

Lurking by the entrance might be conspicuous, but no one paid Victory a second glance in the bar's atmosphere of solitary drinking. Even the bartender had disappeared on some errand or another.

The waitress soon returned and pressed a scrap of paper into Victory's hand. "Here. Swanky neighborhood across town, but we haven't had to deal with a single fight since Toria started working, so I stopped complaining about her slumming."

"Thanks." Ignoring the waitress's unnecessary commentary, Victory committed the address to memory and shoved the paper into her pocket.

"My pleasure!" The woman beamed at her, and she now appeared to place Victory in the "friend" category. "Come by the next time Toria is working and have a drink."

Victory smiled back, mindful of her teeth. "I will."

Winter wind gusted as Victory left the bar. She oriented herself and set off. She had no cash for a taxi, but she got directions from a couple who staggered out of a restaurant. They reeked of wine, too tipsy to note her half-dressed state.

She caught the scent of werewolf once, but she ducked into an alleyway without bothering to search for the source, thankful to be downwind.

She maintained a human walking pace to conserve strength. If Toria had been transported to the city much earlier than Victory, maybe she would have an idea of where to acquire sustenance for her mother.

Victory should have interrogated the waitress further. How long had Toria been in the past?

BEFORE

Life settled into routine. Work with Hugh on the house in the morning, listening to the radio for reports of escalating skirmishes out west. Meet Liam for lunch or dinner, depending on his schedule for the day. Make out like teenagers in the refinished front parlor at the bed and breakfast if they met for dinner on a night she didn't work.

Dating in the past was a different beast than to which she was accustomed. She'd have dragged Liam to her room ages ago, but he pulled away the one time she pressed his hand to her breast.

Apparently, he worried he was moving too fast for *her*.

She'd bitten her tongue so hard she tasted blood, but mind won out over body.

On the nights she worked, she kept watch from her seat at the end of the bar, nursing a beer or cocktail and chatting with Lyra when the bartender was free. Word had spread of the way she knocked out over a dozen men with the power of magic alone. She didn't correct the facts, and the bar had not seen an incident since. The money Kojo left wasn't consistent, but he valued her time at least as much as he valued not replacing furniture and glassware at the bar, so a tidy emergency fund accumulated in the corner of her bottom dresser drawer.

Hugh knew about her job at the bar, and left a sandwich or other snack in the kitchen for her every night when she got home. Asaron, a two-thousand-year-old vampire mercenary, was the only grandfather she'd ever known. She imagined this might be like having a human one.

Liam, however, did not know about the job at the bar. At least, not the whole truth. He thought she helped Lyra bartend. He wasn't keen on the location in the seedier part of Nacostina, but he'd been pleased she'd acclimated enough to make a friend who was neither him nor Hugh.

He also never asked why Toria stopped visiting the museum. She wasn't sure of her answer. *I can't handle coming face to face with the man I was raised on stories of. Or the man who killed my best friend.* Jarimis remained in town on his extended research trip. He often accessed the museum's archives.

Rubin, of course, wasn't going anywhere. At least he'd never requested another audience with her. If he'd ever made good on his threat to order Liam to stay away from her, Liam never said.

In this lazy manner, summer turned and the weather cooled toward winter. Granny Tia outfitted Toria with a second, weather-appropriate wardrobe. This time, she caved on the necessity of pairing a girdle with stockings. Liam kept their courtship, or whatever this was, to a torturous snail's pace. Toria had seen his apartment once, a quick peek in the front door while Liam retrieved a book, but he preferred spending time at the bed and breakfast, under Hugh's chaperonage.

Of course, he'd also never complained when Hugh tended to disappear the evenings he came over. Toria apologized to Hugh for forcing him out of his own house, but he'd laughed, assuring her spending the evening at his own neighborhood pub had been a habit on hold until she'd settled in.

The majority of the bed and breakfast's renovations finished in time for the weather to turn cold. It saddened Toria that she would never see it filled with guests. Like the rest of the city, the house would be gone soon.

But for now, Hugh enjoyed his weekend card game while Liam and Toria shared a bottle of wine in front of the fireplace. Though she spent hours agonizing over how to convince Liam and Hugh to leave Nacostina for no apparent reason, she tried not to let the obsessive thoughts consume her when she wasn't alone.

"Working tonight?" Liam dragged gentle fingers through Toria's hair as she draped herself half over him on the sofa in the parlor. Wind creaked the front porch outside, but the fire and a wool blanket kept them cozy.

"Not tonight." She raised her head from where it rested on his chest. "Why? Have better plans?" With one arm curled beneath her, she tucked the index finger of the other into a belt loop of his trousers. It helped her avoid temptation, and she didn't want the cuddles to end as Liam dashed to the other end of the sofa out of misplaced decorum.

Her head rose with the heave of his chest. "You're trouble, you know that?"

Toria tilted her head in invitation until Liam pressed forward with a kiss. She deepened it until their tongues touched, and she melted into the spiciness of his taste. She had kissed an elf before, though under much different circumstances, and had no idea whether the spicy undertones were an elven thing or unique to Liam alone. He did drink cinnamon tea like water. She responded after they broke apart for air. "I'm the best kind of trouble."

"That you are." Liam wound his fingers in her hair and kissed her again.

Toria tightened her fingers on Liam's beltloop. This was dangerous, but she'd rather be frustrated than go too far and chase him away. She could take care of herself after he left. Though she didn't want to lose the closeness with Liam's body, sacrifices must be made. "More wine?"

At least the tension in Liam's body indicated his own struggle. "Not sure that's a wise idea right now. Water would be nice, though." He tried to sit up, but Toria pressed her hand on his chest.

"Relax. I'll get it." She rose from the couch and snagged the empty bottle. Glancing over her shoulder on the way out was a mistake. Liam draped over the sofa, clothes disheveled and lips swollen, was another assault on her self-control.

As she filled two glasses from the water pitcher in the kitchen, she entertained herself with thoughts of marching into the living room, straddling his lap, and having her way with him. A fantasy for another world, another life.

Instead, when she returned to the parlor, she handed Liam his glass and curled on the opposite corner of the couch, tucking her feet beneath her and pulling the blanket over her lap. Liam had straightened his clothing, and they sipped water accompanied by the crackle of fire.

Liam finished first. He set his glass on the low table and propped his elbows on his knees, hunched forward. The reflected flames lit his eyes gold. "I've been putting this off, but now is as good a time as any."

Toria's fingers clenched around her empty glass. Those words out of a man's mouth were never a good sign, but everything had been normal less than five minutes ago. "What's wrong, hon?" She set her glass down as well, doing her best to keep the tension out of her movement and her voice light.

"You already know I don't like you working at that bar." Liam stared into the fireplace. "I've found you a job at a restaurant near Hugh's pub. Or you're welcome to work at the museum's café. Cammy's been asking after you."

Considering and dismissing a dozen thoughts, Toria pressed her lips together until she settled on a response that viewed Liam's words in the best possible light. "That's generous of you, but I'm happy where I am."

"But you have to see it's a little ridiculous." Now Liam faced her, settling sideways on the couch.

Any other time, Toria might have laughed at his earnestness. "And how is that?"

Liam saw the trap and chose his next words with care. She appreciated that much. "I recognize your skill in the arts of magic. But it's not a good neighborhood, and I'm concerned for your safety. I understand this bar is frequented by out-of-work mercenaries, and they can be an unpredictable lot."

Oh, the irony. "Are you concerned for my safety, or are you still on that kick where you think it's inappropriate for me to have a job at all?" When his eyes darted to the side, she crossed her arms and snorted. "Yeah, I figured. What, were you going to keep finding me better and better jobs until you decided I had one you could live with?"

"It's not like that at all." Liam toyed with the blanket fringe. "Being concerned for your safety is a reason I thought you would accept." He stared her down, his brow furrowed. "I can't figure out why you need this job at all. You're getting paid, right?"

"I am getting paid. But I'm saving it all."

"Why? For what?"

"Have you figured out nothing about me?" Toria threw up her hands. "What made you think I would be happy with charity for my needs?"

"Is that what you're worried about? We might cut you off and throw you out on the street? What did I ever do to make you think *that*?"

"Well, it's pretty obvious from this conversation that you don't trust me." Toria shoved the blanket aside and paced the floor before the fireplace, the slap of her bare feet loud on the warm wood.

Liam remained seated, but he'd crossed his arms. "I don't trust you? You're the one accusing me of abandoning you at any moment."

She spun on him, jabbing a finger. "You're the one who keeps forgetting the most important thing I ever told you."

"And what's that?"

"I am a master-level mage. I can protect myself." She snagged the metal poker from next to the fireplace and gripped it like a blade. "Hell, I've never seen you do a lick of magic. Bet I could take you."

Liam rose to face off across the low table between them. "You mentioned once that the other bartender there had traces of earth magic. Is that what this is about? You miss being with your own kind?"

His words slammed Toria in the gut, too close to the truth "Sure. That's as good a reason as any." She let the poker tip drop.

"Elven magic is different. It's not parlor tricks."

"I'm aware." Calling him on his elitism would do nothing more than derail the conversation. "Your magic is as part of you as mine is of me. But you keep acting like mine isn't real. Have you even looked at me?"

She couldn't force Liam to use the elven equivalent of magesight, but perhaps she could goad him into it. Toria snapped the dazzling ambient magic into view. With a mental twist, she summoned combat-level shields. Layers of prismatic power enveloped her in every shade of violet. Liam's own passive shields spun around him, a rainbow sheen of bronze and copper plates.

The beautiful sight stunned her for a beat. She set her own shields to spin at the same frequency. Their power echoed in counterpoint through the room. If Liam saw her now, he'd have no excuse to doubt her.

"Stop!" He turned away.

"You can't ignore what I am."

He whirled on her, and his eyes flashed gold again. Not the reflection of flame, but from the internal fire of his own magic. His voice roared across the space between them. "I can't see you dying like this!"

That stopped Toria short, and she collapsed her combat shields, leaving the lightest framework of energy to pulse in time with his. "What?"

Liam's chest heaved, his arms stiff at his side. "Every time…every time I look at you with magic, all I see is pieces of you draining away into nothing." He half turned away from her, as if reaching his limit. "It was never about your safety, or money. I can't bear you risking what little time we have left together."

His words hit her like a punch in the gut, but she found nothing out of the ordinary. If anything, her shields, even in their passive state, were more powerful than ever before. "Help me see what you see." Toria released the hold on both her magesight and the power she manipulated, and the room dulled to reality. She stepped around the table and touched Liam's elbow.

He jerked away from her as if burned, and she snatched her hand back. But at least he looked at her again. "I can't explain it. It must be outside the plane of human magesight, else you'd have seen it ages ago."

"Please try." Nothing felt out of place to Toria, comfortable and at ease with her own magic. Two decades of experience, and nothing Liam said made sense to her right now.

Liam gestured to her left side, encompassing empty space. "It's like watching pieces of you…your magic, but also skin and bone and hair…leech away, sucked into nothingness. I can't see you like this and do nothing about it. So sometimes it's easier to pretend it's not happening. Try to hold you close. Even if it suffocates you."

"Why didn't you tell me?" Toria waved her hand in the area Liam indicated but found nothing amiss.

"I spoke to Rubin—"

"What?" Toria's turn to lash out. "What did you say to him?" The last thing Toria needed was to remind him of her presence.

"He's my boss!" Liam's confusion reminded Toria he had no idea why she hated-feared-reviled the man. "He has experience with someone like you, someone jerked out of their time by the artifact."

Steadying herself, Toria tried a second time to touch Liam. He didn't resist when she interlocked their fingers. "What did he say?"

"He's seen this before." Liam squeezed her hand, almost to the point of pain. "According to the records, everyone who has been displaced in time has died within a few years. They get weak almost right away, then waste away to nothing if illness doesn't claim them first."

"That's why the museum can afford to support the victims. You never planned to support me the rest of my life. Just keep me comfortable as long as I lasted."

"But you haven't shown the expected symptoms." Liam tugged her into his embrace. She tucked her face into his neck, and he spoke into her hair. "I got curious, then I got close to you. I thought you would be okay, because of your magic. But every time I look, I can't deny what I see."

Toria wrapped her arms around Liam's waist. "We'll fix this."

"I don't know if we can." Liam's voice cracked. "I never meant for this to happen. I'm sorry."

"What are you apologizing for? Caring about me?"

Liam's throat bobbed with his swallow. "I should have kept my distance."

"Because I'm going to die?"

"Because you're human."

She jerked out of his arms. "Are you fucking kidding me?" He flinched at her language. "You tell me I'm going to die, but all you can think about is how you screwed up by falling for me?"

"I don't want to lose you."

"Let me get this straight. You tell me you don't know why I'm going to die or how to stop it. But you're not apologizing for not telling me. You're apologizing for the fact you won't outlive me when I die from old age, but when I waste away for no damned good reason." Toria's laughter felt like shards of glass in her throat. "Fucking elves. It's nice to know some things don't change. You all think you know what's best for the world, even as you're in the midst of destroying it."

Liam furrowed his brow. "Destroying? What are you talking about?"

No point to making up an explanation for her runaway words. He wouldn't listen to her anyway. "What's more important to you? Finding a way to save me? Or protecting yourself?"

Liam wouldn't meet her eyes, and that was all the answer she needed.

96

"Get the hell out." Toria pointed to the front door.

He reached for her, but she slammed up combat shields and electricity snapped through the room. Liam yanked away his hand, shaking out his fingers as blisters formed on his skin. He hissed in pain, but Toria held fast against the betrayal in his eyes.

Liam curled his wounded hand against his chest and retreated one step, and another, until he stood in the foyer. "I'm sorry."

Toria held her ground. "I know."

In silence, he shoved his feet into his shoes and snagged his overcoat from the coatrack, not bothering to don it before escaping out the front door.

The door's slam echoed through the house, and Toria had no reason to hide her flinch at the noise. It broke her self-control, and she collapsed onto the couch. The throw pillow smelled like Liam, and she buried her face into it as she cried.

He'd lied to her.

She was dying, cut off from her life in the past with no one but him. And he hadn't even had the balls to tell her. He was willing to let her die because the alternative was too hard.

Fucking elves. Fucking men.

She wanted to go home. She wanted Kane.

Spasms ripped Toria's body. She screamed into the pillow, but there was no one to hear her. And no one to care.

She didn't deserve to live with any sort of happiness, like the small bit she'd found with Liam.

Thunder cracked around the house. She'd lost control of her power in the midst of her breakdown, summoning the fury of a storm to match what she felt within. Anathema to everything she knew about using her ability.

She didn't care. The world crumbled around her, and she saw no reason to stop it.

The front door banged open, and over the continuous rumble outside, her mother's voice called her name.

That was it. She'd lost her power, and she might be losing her body, and now she'd lost her mind.

"*Toria!*"

A hand gripped her arm, so cold it burned, pulling her up. Embers in the fireplace glowed in the dim light. Victory knelt before her, water streaming down her face and wet hair draped over her shoulder in a heavy tail.

"Mama?"

"I'm here."

NOW

As far as she could tell, Victory still had a few blocks to travel before she arrived at the address she'd gotten at the bar. A car sped by, traveling too fast for the quiet neighborhood, but all else was still in the brisk evening air. The night sky was clear enough to see a handful of stars despite the urban lighting.

In an instant, everything changed.

Wind tore down the street as clouds billowed from nothing. The heavy scent of ozone caught in her nose, and the skies opened up.

In moments, lashing rain drenched her to the skin.

This was no freak storm. This was pure magic.

Pure *storm* magic.

Victory broke into a sprint, almost wiping out in a puddle. Even over the howling gale, her sensitive hearing picked out a woman's scream.

She knew that voice. She knew that heartbeat.

Victory pounded the pavement, following the trail of her daughter's sobs to an imposing house set back from the street. Towering trees over the front garden did nothing to protect her from the rain. She slowed at the front porch, and the doorknob turned in her hand.

Beyond the foyer sat a dark room, lit by embers and lightning. Her daughter curled on the couch, her shoulders heaving as she buried her cries into a pillow. Victory dashed across the room and dropped to her knees at Toria's side, hauling her to a sitting position.

Her heart broke at her daughter's wrenching anguish.

"Mama?" Shock penetrated Toria's expression, and she gripped Victory's hands in her own.

"I'm here." Victory sat next to Toria and wrapped her daughter in her arms. "I'm with you."

Toria held her tight, but Victory's appearance seemed to have startled her out of her devastation. "Where did you—How did you find me?"

Victory pulled away and cupped her hands around Toria's face. "You know I'd always find you."

Toria wiped tear streaks from her cheeks. "I know, but where have you been?"

"What do you mean? I found you as soon as I could." Victory released Toria and scanned the room, furnished in a style both old and familiar. "I know we're in Nacostina before the Last War, but where are we? Whose house is this?"

"I live here." Toria grabbed Victory's hand again and held it tight, as if her mother was a dream who might disappear at any moment. "Mom, I've been here for six months."

Shock jolted through Victory. Toria bared her teeth in a hiss of pain, and Victory released her hand. Six months? But she'd touched the object on the ground mere moments after Toria disappeared.

She observed the woman who sat before her anew and saw the truth in Toria's words right away. Her daughter was paler than when Victory had last seen her. Months was long enough for a summer tan to fade.

She reached for Toria's hair, but Toria caught the tie holding it first. It fell forward, sweeping across her face, inches longer than before. "Short hair on women stands out here, so I've been letting it grow."

She noted more differences. Toria had lost muscle in her arms and shoulders, unconscionable weakness for a woman who made her living through both her magical and physical prowess.

Except if this was Nacostina before the Last War, Toria couldn't be a mercenary here. This was the time in which women were prohibited from the Guild, except for supernaturals like Victory.

She grasped Toria's hands again. "Calm the storm outside. Then tell me everything."

After she wrested control of the weather to dissipate the unnatural storm cell and found dry clothing for her mother, Toria prepared tea in the kitchen. Victory puttered around the room. She opened and closed the refrigerator a few times, and continued to survey the space as if she searched for something.

"You're looking for the dishwasher."

Victory stopped in her tracks and touched a finger to her nose. "You're right. That's what I was missing."

"You have no idea how much I've missed having one." Toria left the strainer in the sink and carried the two cups to the trestle table, where Victory joined her. "Along with things like private telephone lines and decent underwear."

"I don't romanticize the past like most of my kind, so I'm with you there, kid." Victory wore an old set of Hugh's pajamas, having scoffed at Toria's nightgowns. "So. Six months."

Toria rolled hot liquid in her mouth. It wasn't Liam's cinnamon tea. She'd avoided the brand he favored when she'd offered a selection to Victory. "Something like that. I got here right before summer. Now it's late fall."

"How close are we to…the day?"

Even her mother had trouble articulating the city's eventual devastation. "A little over two weeks."

Victory released an exhale, a sure sign her thoughts were whirling. "Fuck."

"Pretty much."

"What was your plan?"

"Save some cash and bolt a few days beforehand." That Victory took for granted Toria had thought through the variables warmed her in places the tea didn't reach. "Try to take a few people with me, though I'm not sure how I'm going to convince them to pick up and leave."

"And where were you thinking?"

"South. Roman territory. Set up shop somewhere off the coast. Find a town in the islands of the Grand Strand in need of a blacksmith, maybe use my magic for supplemental income."

"Then what?"

"Live out the rest of my life, I guess. Try not to change the timeline and mess up the future we know."

Victory twisted her mug on the wooden table. "Why bother, if you don't think we'll make it back to see it?"

"Because the life I left was pretty damned good, Mom!" Toria sprang from her seat. She placed her empty cup in the sink and braced both hands on the counter. "Kane and I were happy. We had lives and careers and a home." Tears prickled again, but she forced them down through sheer will. She'd already cried enough, and she couldn't risk losing control and mucking with the weather patterns a second time.

Victory brought her own cup to the sink and placed her cool hand atop Toria's. To her, cool skin meant support and love. "Why aren't you trying to get back?"

"Because there's no way to figure out how." Toria found the courage to face her mother again. Careful probing had forced Liam to reveal that not much research existed into the meteorite's history, so the archives held no useful information. And now, well, she'd be lucky to ever step foot inside the museum to examine the artifact ever again. "An artifact of unknown magical origin transported us here. This isn't the first time it's happened, and no one has ever been able to go back." Liam's earlier words rang through her memory. "And that's not the worst of it."

Victory's bark of laughter held no humor. "I'm standing in a doomed city wearing the pajamas of a man I don't know. We have no idea what has happened to your partner and my daywalker. I'm not sure how this could get any worse."

"The people who get sent through time don't live long afterward. Something must get…caught…in the space between time." Toria's imagination filled in what Liam described when he saw her with elven magesight. She specialized in chemistry and metallurgy, but a certain amount of basic physics knowledge accompanied those skills, and her mind supplied potential possibilities. "I don't think we exist in the same temporal reality as everything and everyone else around us right now. The universe likes things a certain way. Even magic operates under strict rules at the levels of matter and energy. We're not where we're supposed to be, and the natural order of things is trying to correct itself."

Toria lived a life based on evidence, and she found nothing to support Liam's claims. But despite everything, she trusted him. Trusted him to tell the truth, even truth of her coming death. The dichotomy tore at her soul, until she no longer knew what to believe. Moisture collected in the corners of her eyes.

Her mother cupped her other hand to Toria's cheeks. "I could live another eight hundred years and still never be as smart as you."

Heat flushed Toria's skin, and she batted Victory's hand away. "I'm just a nerd, Mom."

Out of nowhere, Victory swiveled her entire body in the direction of the front door, and her hand made an aborted grasp for the bastard sword still upstairs with Toria's rapier. The front door clicked open.

"I'm home!" Hugh's shout echoed through the house, and he appeared in the kitchen doorway a moment later. He took in the sight of Victory standing with Toria, but when he spoke, he sounded curious rather than suspicious. "Good evening, Toria. Why is a vampire wearing my pajamas standing in my kitchen?"

"Good evening, Hugh." Toria wanted to cross her fingers for luck. "I'd like you to meet my mother, Victory."

Victory kept her posture loose and unthreatening, arms at her sides. After a second's hesitation, Hugh crossed the space between them and extended a hand. "Good evening, ma'am. Hugh Ainsworth."

She shook his hand. "A pleasure. Thank you for the temporary loan of your clothing."

"Glad to help. I imagine you got caught in that storm earlier?"

"Indeed." Victory's damp hair straggled over her shoulders.

"Hugh, the water is still warm if you'd like tea." Toria lifted the kettle in query.

"I think I'd better," Hugh said in a wondrous tone. He sat at the table.

As Toria fixed a cup the way Hugh liked, Victory sat across from him and clasped her hands in front of her. The silence wore on Toria until she placed the cup before Hugh and sank next to her mother. "Okay. I'm guessing you'd like an explanation."

"That would be useful."

One of these days, Toria would find something capable of surprising the man. Today was not that day. Or maybe it was. She glanced at Victory, who gave an almost imperceptible nod. "I haven't been entirely…honest about my past."

To her mingled shock and relief, Hugh threw back his head and guffawed. "Sweetheart, I've known you weren't telling me the whole truth about yourself since the first moment I met you. But you've always been up-front with the things that mattered, and it's been nice having someone else around the house, so I made my peace with it."

Toria curled her fingers in the fabric of Victory's robe under the table. "I'm a mage and a mercenary. I am from Limani. Everything I've told you about me as a person is true. But I'm not from last century. I'm from the next."

Hugh blinked once and looked at Victory. Instead of denying the joke, she sat in silence. "You're from the future," he said.

"Yeah." Toria's chest tightened.

"Huh." Hugh paused to sip his tea. "That explains that."

She almost gasped as relief washed over her. "Explains what?"

"Liam thanked me for teaching you how to use the telephone." Hugh smirked at Toria. "I never showed you how to use it."

This time, Victory joined his chuckling, giving Toria a gentle nudge with her elbow. "You need to do better than that if you and Kane ever want to get into wetwork jobs."

"I was in shock over the whole situation, okay?" But her grumbling was half-hearted at best. "What did you assume?"

"You might not be from the past, but something crazy had happened to you," Hugh said, grasping Toria's hand. "So, I figured I'd be here for you and let you tell me things in your own time."

"I can't tell you how much I appreciate you watching out for her, Mr. Ainsworth." Victory caught Toria's other hand under the table, and Toria leeched emotional strength from both connections.

"Call me Hugh, please. And your girl is more than capable of watching out for herself." He released Toria and stood with his empty mug. "I'm happy to help however I can. Goes for you, too."

"Thanks, Hugh." How had Toria gotten so lucky? She threw the craziest wrench at Hugh's head, and he didn't bat an eye. Most people would have been shocked, at least until they started in on questions about the future. Things Toria couldn't—and wouldn't—be able to answer.

"I hate to abandon you, ladies, but I'm beat. How's the green room looking, Toria?"

"It'll be perfect." Another load she hadn't recognized lifted from Toria's shoulders. Hugh was willing to shelter her mother the same way he did her. "I haven't gotten around to hanging the curtain rod over the window, so it'll be easier to tack up a few layers of drop cloths to keep out the sun. Just need to get some linens for the bed."

"I'll make sure to dig some out and leave them in the room before I hit the sack." A flicker of uncertainty crossed Hugh's face, and his next words came slower. "Unfortunately, that's all I can do for you. I would say you're the first official guest of my bed and breakfast, but I'm not sure how I'd manage the breakfast part."

Victory waved away his concerns. "I'll be fine for another day or so, until Toria and I can figure something out. You've done more than enough already."

"My pleasure. I'll leave you two to talk. I'm sure you've got a lot to catch up on." Hugh paused in the kitchen doorway on his way out of the kitchen. "I'm honored, Toria. You'll tell me this truth, but not that boy of yours?"

Victory's razor-sharp focus narrowed on Toria. "What boy?"

Toria groaned and dropped her forehead to the table.

The two women talked late into the night, first in the kitchen before switching to plush armchairs in the sunroom off the kitchen. Victory imagined an airy room with sun streaming through the large glass windows during daylight. She pried the story of Liamacorin, elven deputy curator, out of her daughter before packing an exhausted Toria off to bed.

She sat up for another few hours, staring into the shadowy trees at the house's rear, before slipping upstairs herself. After checking the blankets pinned over the window, she curled under fresh-scented bedclothes and passed the day in sleep.

When she woke after sunset, verified by the lack of light around the edges of the blocked window, one heartbeat echoed through the large house. Toria hummed while she cooked, a habit since childhood, but Victory heard it as if she stood in the kitchen next to her. A collection of clothing sat outside the bedroom door, wrapped in packaging branded with the name of a half-remembered department store.

When she stepped into the kitchen adorned in trousers and a tucked blouse, she found Toria in similar garments as she sat at the kitchen table and flipped through a newspaper. An empty mug of tea and a plate with crumbs sat abandoned at her elbow.

Toria nodded in satisfaction at her entrance. "I hoped I'd gotten the sizes correct. How are the shoes?"

"Serviceable." They didn't pinch anywhere important, so the loafers would do for now. Victory sat across the table and twitched her shoulders, attempting to settle the brassiere better around her breasts and torso.

Toria's gaze was knowing. "I know, it's the worst. Sometimes I'm tempted to bind my breasts every day, but I know it's not healthy in the long run." She paused, worrying her bottom lip between her teeth. "I'm still not sure what to do about the blood situation. I can keep a supply maintained with magic once we have it, but it's the acquisition part where I'm drawing a blank."

"I've been considering that." Victory traced the grain of the wooden tabletop with one finger. "There's no Master of the City to orchestrate a supply. But I have—options—in the short term."

"Yeah, the short term we have before Nacostina is toast." Toria flipped another page of the newspaper.

Victory tugged it away. "No, the short term we have until we find a way home."

Her daughter's attention settled somewhere over Victory's shoulder. "I don't want to talk about that right now, Mom."

"We have to talk about it sometime." The headline screamed from the front page of the newspaper, in huge, impossible-to-miss font. *TALKS WITH QIN EMPIRE STALL AGAIN.* Victory stabbed a finger on the text. "You know as well as I do that we can't do anything about this. And I don't accept your solution of fleeing."

Toria slapped the flat of her hand on the table and jolted to her feet. The bench skidded across the tiled floor. "I've been here for months. You just got here. You have no idea what's going on." Her voice rose in pitch, and the quickening of her heartbeat rang in Victory's ears.

Victory kept her voice level, not echoing Toria's near hysterical tone. "I hoped you'd be more willing to help me work through it instead of telling me it can't be done. You told me about the artifact—a meteorite?—but that you haven't been given access to it."

Instead of responding, Toria brought her dishes to the sink.

The daughter Victory raised would have abandoned the dishes as irrelevant minutia in the face of this challenge, rising to the task of finding their way home.

Instead, Toria washed mug and saucer with jerky, robotic movements and slipped them into the drying rack where they rattled against the metal. Toria's hands shook, along with her racing heartbeat. This reaction was out of proportion to their conversation.

What the hell was wrong? What had happened to her bright, brave, confident girl?

She remembered Toria's words from the night before. According to that elf, she was dying. Victory had no ability to see the way Toria's, and now her own, life force might be draining away. But the pallor in Toria's cheeks had nothing to do with a faded summer tan. And a gaping hole existed at Toria's side where Kane should have stood.

Perhaps it was a matter of time before Victory experienced these same effects of panic and hopelessness. After all, Mikelos should have been at her side as well.

Victory tried a different tack. "You're going to the bar tonight? May I walk you?"

Toria's jaw tightened. "I'm not sure that's a good idea. The more you walk around the city, the greater the chance of running into a werewolf noble. We have no way to explain your presence here, and we've started the prolonged period of standoffishness with the Roman Empire at this point."

Before Victory retorted that she knew the history because she'd *lived* it, the other implication of Toria's response hit her.

We've started.

Toria might want to make it back to Limani and Kane and her own time, but on some level, she'd acclimated. Nacostina, and the life she'd built here, had become home.

If anything, anxiety rolled off Toria in waves as a direct response to the war of desires raging in her subconscious. Victory took a deliberate mental step backward. Because Toria was right. Her daughter had lived this life for months. She was ahead of Victory in terms of possible options in the immediate and long-term. "You're right. I'll be careful if I go out later."

A fraction of the tension in Toria's shoulders deflated, replaced by a more familiar spark in her eyes as she approached the table. "I left a note for Hugh to snag a newspaper this morning so I could check the local crime blotter. Do you remember how to get to the riverfront?"

"I'm pretty sure I can figure it out. Why?" Victory preferred that spark over Toria's previous levels of distress, even if it meant trouble.

Toria flipped open the newspaper to an interior page. "Two reports of muggings last night. Both victims were young human women, and one reported that her assailant seemed like he might try for more if she hadn't given up her purse and run."

"You know, I hadn't trolled for rapists as a meal source even a hundred years before this." But Victory scanned the column Toria pointed out, noting the reported locations and few identifiable features the women had been able to relate about their attacker.

"I'm not saying to kill the guy, Mom!"

"No, no. I wouldn't. But I can have a snack and scare the hell out of him."

"I'm not sure a reported vampire attack would be any better than you running into a werewolf on the street."

"That would mean the man had to recognize he'd been attacked by a vampire. I have my ways." With Toria once again within arm's length, Victory risked a gamble. She caught Toria's hand, gratified when her daughter did not jerk away. "Trust me."

"I do. Just—be careful." Toria returned her reassuring grip. "I have to go to work. I'll see you when I get home tonight." She left Victory in the kitchen, donning shoes and coat by the front door and disappearing into the night.

Be careful? Since when was it Toria's responsibility to keep Victory safe? For a quarter of a century, it had been the other way around.

Now they were in the past, and everything was out of whack. Her daughter, who'd never been on her own since bonding with Kane almost twenty years ago, had survived alone for months.

Victory had some thinking to do, if she wanted to avoid another uncomfortable confrontation with Toria.

But first, blood called.

Being in a city without a Master didn't imbue Victory with a sense of freedom or personal empowerment. It kind of stressed her the hell out.

Or she was projecting. Easier to think about where her next meal came from than the imminent destruction of the city or the current mental state of her daughter.

She found a brand-new coat in her size near the front door. The thick black wool was unnecessary for her warmth, but in combination with the other clothing Toria procured, it allowed her to pass through the city unremarked. Now she was a lady of class and means on a stroll toward an evening engagement instead of a wild woman wearing too little clothing and too much sword.

Victory came full circle, returning to Nacostina's central district. She kept her senses open for werewolf signs, but luck was in her favor as she traveled the wide avenue along the grassy park in the center of the district.

She stopped for a moment along the sidewalk and stared into one particular area of the park, where Mikelos and Kane set up camp in the future, and allowed herself one minute to ache for Mikelos. She could afford no more and give no less.

She turned toward the river, and soon meandered amidst the trunks and bare branches of the cherry trees. She'd missed seeing them bloom in her final year of diplomatic missions to Nacostina.

The fact that she had this second chance in Nacostina and still missed the cherry blossoms caused her heart to ache almost as much as it did for Mikelos. She chased away memories of the petals floating in the night breeze, picking them out of her and Jarimis' hair as they stumbled through the park after all the bars had closed for the night. This time, the piercing pain had nothing to do with Mikelos. Of course being in this city again summoned memories of her lost progeny. He had spent almost as much time here on academic research as she had on courier missions.

Time to re-center, before she lost herself in a whirlwind of memory. No one was in view, so she planted her feet on the path. Sight: the glimmer of moonglow on river water between the trees. Sound: the rustle of the breeze whipping bare branches against each other. Touch: the uneven gravel of the pathway below the leather soles of her shoes. Smell: Fresh mulch on the ground between the tree trunks, preparing the flowerbeds for winter. Taste: the barest hint of smoke from a fireplace past the edge of the park.

Now she could focus on the present. Such as it was.

A flash of movement caught her attention. When she whipped around, she expected a shadow to detach itself from amidst the trees and drift across her field of view. But no—a squirrel ran up the tree trunk and disappeared. No shadows, this time.

She resumed her stroll through the trees, as if it was nothing out of the ordinary for a woman to walk alone at night. With her hands tucked into her pockets, her unbuttoned coat flared behind her like a cloak of old. The first claws of hunger scraped within her body. A single heartbeat floated on the wind, but she kept her pace steady. Might be nothing more than another lone soul out for a midnight walk.

In an empty park in the cold night. Sure.

Footsteps on the gravel echoed in counterpoint to the heartbeat ahead of her. The person rustled through the remnants of fallen leaves as they left the main pathway to pass alongside her. Not suspicious at all.

One foot in front of the other, and she kept her shoulders loose, relaxed. Her fingers ached from the lack of blood flow as her reservoirs diminished. Hunting was so easy when she played bait instead.

Now, the footsteps crackled behind her, back on the path. Her shoulder blades twitched under the attention, but she resisted the urge to check behind her. The footsteps crept too quiet for human ears for another minute or two as the man—it was always a man—scoped her out. To make herself even more tempting a target, Victory wandered off the path and toward the river, away from the lampposts along the walkway. Away from where any passersby might hear a woman's cries.

She paused at the edge of the grass, against a railing that protected pedestrians from tumbling into the water below. Victory removed her hands from her pockets and wrapped them around the cold iron. She tracked the man as he darted between the trees, following his path with hearing alone as he centered himself behind her.

A little closer, buddy.

With a grunt, he burst from the minimal cover of the tree trunks and sprinted toward her. But the element of surprise was not on his side. Victory whirled, one arm outstretched. She caught the man around the throat with vice-like fingers and used his forward momentum to swing against the railing. Pressing so he bent backward at the waist, she pinned him with her second hand around his neck and her hip against his lower half.

His cry of alarm strangled and died beneath her grip. The man clawed at the lapels of Victory's coat until lack of air turned scrabbling fingers against her hands.

Victory leaned over him, her gaze boring into his eyes. They bulged in fear. If he knew she was a vampire, he might have closed his eyes in defense. But she had the upper hand, and he soon caved beneath her attention.

"Stop. Just stop." Victory preferred a physical fight to pushing mental power behind her words. But she was hungry, this guy was a jerk who attacked defenseless women, and she was in no mood to make things more difficult for herself.

She eased her grip on his throat before he suffocated. Caught in her thrall, the man made no move against her, his body slack. Unblinking eyes, black against pallid skin in the moonlight, never left hers. Victory grabbed the man's shoulder and pulled him upright, with one cautious step backward. He swayed on his feet, arms limp at his sides and mouth agape. Though his eyes still locked on hers, he didn't see her. No one was home.

"Hey. Buddy." Victory snapped her fingers before his nose, and a semblance of consciousness emerged. His mouth snapped shut. "What did you think you were going to do to me?"

Maybe he feared she might fall into the river and rushed to her aid? A long shot, but taking advantage of the man without verification didn't sit well.

His words slurred, either from intoxication or her mental control. "Steal your cash. Your jewelry." His throat worked as he swallowed. "Fuck you."

A threat, not an insult.

Victory snagged the man's wrist and held it up, shoving up his coat cuff. A few day's growth of beard covered sallow cheeks, but while his clothing was old and worn, everything about him was on the clean side. Further proof his designs on Victory's person and belongings were born of malice.

She drew a short knife from the sheath she'd tucked at her waist. Keeping one hand locked around the man's wrist, she flipped her grip on the blade and drew its edge inside his forearm.

Blood welled from the wound. Her stomach tightened in longing at the rich, coppery scent. She ached to suck him dry, but she had to do this right to conceal her presence.

"Don't. Move. An inch." She impressed the order with as much intent as possible before breaking the lock between their eyes. After a moment's test, during which the man remained stock-still as instructed, Victory ducked her head and licked a long strip along his forearm, capturing all the released blood before it fell to the grass.

This was the slowest, most inefficient method of feeding in all of existence, but it got the job done. Energy tingled in Victory's extremities and borrowed warmth flowed through her veins.

She couldn't lose herself in the blood. Victory kept her senses open for any sign of unexpected company.

But no one else had the crazy idea for a moonlit stroll, and Victory slowed her feeding before the man got low on blood. Vampires were an evolved species, after all, and didn't leave dead bodies in their wake.

She licked her lips clean and pulled a fresh handkerchief from her pocket. After binding the man's arm, she captured his attention once again with a finger snap. "Hey, buddy. Listen up."

His gaze was glossier than before, but he swayed little. He'd be fine.

"You were overcome with remorse over your poor decisions and tried to kill yourself out here in the park. But you came to your senses, bound your wound, and decided to turn yourself in to the police instead. Go."

He stumbled away. Victory kept him in sight long enough to ensure that he lurched toward the buildings. The last thing she needed was for him to make a wrong turn and drown.

Her mental commands would last long enough for him to find the police, though it would all wear off by sunrise. The physical evidence of his injury would contradict him by the time he came to his senses and denied everything. Two problems solved in one fell swoop.

Victory allowed her mind to turn to other pressing matters as she trekked toward her temporary home.

If only fixing Toria was as easy as telling her to snap out of it. But her daughter's issues would not be so easy to banish, be they anxiety, depression, post-traumatic stress disorder, or all of the above. The time before the Last War was the era of buck up your chin and get over it. Psychotherapy or medication wouldn't be an option until they got home.

No matter how close Toria had become to the people here in Nacostina, they didn't hold a candle to the importance her daughter held for her. Victory would save her daughter, even if it meant saving her from herself.

Victory held her head high as she jogged to the bed and breakfast. She had a mission. Now she needed a plan.

The bar patrons kept quiet tonight. If all Toria had to do was slouch in her corner and nurse a cider or two for a few hours, she'd call it a win. She had no time for the drama of intoxicated, unemployed mercs taking their frustrations out on the nearest waitress.

A crew of men tromped into the bar, perking her attention. After they settled themselves at tables and called for a round of drinks, she relegated them to her passive awareness and focused on her own bottle.

Which appeared to be empty. *When had that happened?*

Lyra set another bottle in front of Toria and claimed the old. "You're putting them away tonight."

"Not intentionally." Though she followed her words with a large swig.

"Something going on?" Lyra rested her forearms atop her expanding stomach. She'd stopped wearing an apron while she worked, embracing maternity clothing after popping a blouse button in the middle of mixing drinks.

"I'm okay. It's just… life." Toria injected as much optimism into her voice as possible, but couldn't hide the disapproval in her expression when Lyra picked up a wine glass.

"Don't start." Lyra brandished the glass at Toria. "It's supposed to be good for the baby."

"I still find your research sources questionable." Between Kojo's insistence and an article Lyra found in a magazine, Toria knew her argument of "that's not how it's done in Limani" held little weight. "But I will refrain from the topic tonight."

"I appreciate that."

Toria activated her magesight and did what little she could: checked on Lyra's baby her own way. The sparkling motes of earth magic Toria had seen gathered around Lyra at their first meeting had increased in intensity. These days, the energy centered on Lyra's womb.

Based on the secondary aura around her friend, Toria knew Lyra was going to have a boy, and that the boy would be an earth mage of decent power. Until she noted obvious signs of distress, she would manage to keep her future-inspired concerns low-key.

They shared their drinks in companionable silence, overlooking the bar. Business had increased with the coming of the colder weather, but Lyra reported that cheaper drinks in smaller quantities were the order of the day. Kojo had stopped ordering the fancier varieties of small-batch beer, and Toria refrained from hard liquor while working, but at least cider was still popular enough.

The dam burst, and the words spilled out. "I had a fight with Liam." *Now where the hell had that come from?*

"Oh, honey, I'm so sorry." Lyra set her wineglass down and passed around the bar to give Toria a sideways hug. "No wonder you're all out of sorts."

She kept her arm tucked around Toria's back, and Toria allowed herself a comforting moment to rest her head upon Lyra's shoulder. Her friend's maternalistic instincts had kicked into hardcore mode the past few weeks. At times it was annoying, like when she'd demanded to know Liam's marriage intentions toward Toria and expressed her concerns about the viability of children in a mixed-race marriage. But right now, with Toria's mind an even thicker maelstrom of emotions than usual, she would take it.

A man perched down the bar waved for a drink, but Lyra directed her waitress to serve him. "Is there anything you want to talk about?"

Toria lifted her head. "No, I'm okay. We had a dumb argument. Thanks for the hug." After all, she couldn't tell Lyra the full story, as much as it pained her to keep secrets from her friend.

What was she supposed to say? *I'm from the future and I've lied to you this whole time?*

I might be dying, and I can't explain how or why?

No, better to keep it all inside than risk spilling too much.

Lyra pecked a kiss to Toria's temple. "I'm always here to listen if you need it."

"Thanks, hon. But it could always be worse, like you and—" Toria snapped her mouth shut, but she'd done the damage.

Lyra stiffened and pulled away. "What's that supposed to mean?" The comfort in her voice vanished, replaced by suspicion.

Oh, hell. Toria kept the important things inside, and the other stuff she'd bottled up for so long slipped out instead. "Nothing. Sorry. I wasn't thinking." Maybe she could blame it on the alcohol? But Lyra had seen her put away more than a handful of beers and still retain most of her sobriety. That wouldn't fly.

"I see. You think that since you and Liam are having problems, you can criticize my relationship instead?" Irritation clipped Lyra's words, and she retreated to the far side of the bar.

"You know that's not what I meant." Toria gripped the edge of her barstool to ground herself. It might not be a result of the alcohol, but the roar in her ears grew louder as her anxiety spiked. This was where she should drown Lyra in platitudes, with admiration for the strong relationship she shared with Kojo and how they would be fantastic parents.

The words wouldn't come.

Kojo was an asshole who neglected Lyra except when it suited him. Despite her concerns about Liam's marriage suitability, Lyra's ring finger remained empty. As her pregnancy progressed, Toria knew he spent fewer nights at the apartment the two shared. Lyra passed it off as him not wanting to disturb her rest with his unpredictable schedule.

Toria tried again. "I only meant our situations are so different. You and Kojo have been together so long, whereas Liam and I are just starting out."

The frostiness thawed, but Lyra still held herself distant. "You're right. Our relationships are nothing alike." She paused, as if about to say more, then turned away.

Toria spent another hour at her post, but Lyra busied herself with serving customers and spot cleaning behind the bar. A refill never came once she finished her cider, so Toria toyed with the empty bottle until she'd shredded the label into a pile next to her.

At least Toria knew Lyra hadn't experienced physical abuse at Kojo's hands. The words rang hollow in her head no matter how many times she repeated the mantra. Abuse was abuse, whether physical or emotional. And Toria could do nothing about it.

A quick glance showed the usual card players in the back. Two men at the bar, seated apart and determined to put away cheap beer like it was their job.

Three other small clusters of friends. The group who appeared to be celebrating someone's promotion at work. A mellow undercurrent flowed through the room. These people had more interest in staying out of the cold than in taking their life's frustrations out on other bar patrons.

Fuck it. No reason for Toria to stick around. She shoved the empty bottle and pile of scraps away and sauntered out of the bar without her usual goodbye to Lyra.

She never made it home that night. Toria huddled into her coat and journeyed the streets of Nacostina for hours, letting the cold clear away the fears and frustrations that cluttered her mind. Hunger won out before exhaustion, and she found herself in a twenty-four-hour diner to watch the sunrise.

As a mug of coffee warmed her insides, Toria attempted to contain the anxiety. It threatened to bubble over without the focus of placing one foot in front of the other. She ordered scrambled eggs and toast from the waitress and requested a pen and scrap of paper.

"Will this work instead?" The waitress's wrinkled hands drew a stub of pencil and second pad of paper from her apron.

"Perfect, thank you."

"I'll get breakfast for you in two shakes." The waitress topped off Toria's coffee before leaving the quiet of the corner booth.

Soon, she filled the top page of the notepad with chemical equations and doodles of molecules. Toria couldn't afford to let her fears overwhelm her. If she distracted part of her brain with things free of emotion, maybe the rest of it wouldn't leave her sobbing into her eggs.

Hugh would be concerned she hadn't come home last night, but she could apologize later for making him worry. Victory probably wouldn't give a shit.

Her pencil skittered over the edge of the paper. That wasn't fair. Her mother had followed her into the past and searched the city for her. Toria's frustration stemmed from the way Victory didn't trust her analysis of the situation. Victory was a smart woman, but this time travel thing was so far out of both of their realms of experience.

So why the hell couldn't Victory follow the lead of the person who'd been here longer, gotten the scope of the land? It wasn't a happy solution, and Toria knew Victory facing the prospect of losing Mikelos was as difficult as the journey Toria faced without Kane.

Thoughts crashed into thoughts as Toria sketched out the mechanics of the chemical formula for the steel/silver alloy that coated her rapier. She had two ways to face life without Kane, after all. She could survive without Kane. Or she could live without Kane.

The last few months had been a mess, but while she couldn't claim to be thriving in Nacostina, Toria at least thought she'd moved on to living. An echo of Liam's touch caressed her face, and she shivered.

The waitress slid Toria's breakfast across the table to her, jerking Toria out of the memory. "Let me know if you need anything else. Fresh coffee's brewing before the morning rush, so I can get you a refill in a bit. Here's some water instead."

"Thank—" Toria's voice cracked, and she swallowed. "Thank you. This looks delicious. I can wait on the coffee."

"Looks fancy. What're you working on?" The waitress craned her head to examine Toria's scribblings.

"Um. Doodling some math. Nothing important."

"My Edward had all the brains in the family." The waitress patted Toria's shoulder. "Watch out you don't scare the boys away from your pretty face. Men don't like a girl smarter than them." After her sage advice, she moved to her next table.

The effort not to roll her eyes made Toria feel like she'd strained a muscle. She devoured her breakfast and left without waiting for her coffee refill, leaving cash on the table.

No place to go but home. She peeked inside Victory's room, but her mother was already a lump under her light blanket.

Toria tried to sleep the day away, but tossed and turned until she dragged herself out of bed hours before sunset. If it was cheating to leave the house so early, leaving her mother behind, Toria felt no guilt. At least this time, she had a firm destination in mind.

Because even if she had to live in the past for the rest of her life, she didn't have to spend it alone.

Liam lived in a trendy district near the museum, a mere two stops farther by trolley.

As she climbed the three flights of stairs to Liam's apartment, Toria kept one hand braced on the stair rail and the other buried deep in her coat pocket. If she didn't acknowledge it, she could ignore the way her hands shook. It was harder to avoid the way her heart battered her chest and her breathing came in shorter gasps than her current level of exertion warranted.

Outside Liam's door, she knocked. No answer, and no sounds of life within the apartment. He wasn't home yet. He could be working late, or already had dinner plans. Toria leaned against the wall next to his door and slid down. She wrapped her arms around her knees and settled in to wait. If she left now, she wasn't sure she'd ever make it back.

This was still easier than facing Victory's disappointment.

She jumped to her feet at the first set of footsteps on the stairs, but they stopped on the floor below. Toria resettled herself on the carpet and didn't move again, which is how Liam found her huddled on the ground when he turned the bend in the hallway.

He broke into a jog the final few feet between them and crouched before her. "Toria." He paused before touching her.

She didn't give him a chance to draw away. Toria grabbed his hand and pulled it to her lips, pressing a kiss against his knuckles.

The motion unbalanced him, and they laughed together, banishing a bit of the tension.

"I wasn't expecting to see you here." Heedless of his suit, Liam leaned against the wall, close enough for their shoulders to touch. He allowed her to keep his hand. At some point, he must've had the blisters where her shields repelled him healed by magic. "I missed you."

"I missed you, too." The giggles had freed other emotions, and Toria wiped the corner of her eye where a tear threatened to fall. "Sorry for showing up on your doorstep."

"As if I would ever complain about seeing you."

They stared at each other, and Toria could drown in his blue eyes. "I owe you an apology."

Liam's head shook so hard his hair threatened to escape its queue. "Not at all. I'm the one who screwed up. Your reaction was understandable, and I needed to give you time."

In moments like these, Toria had difficulty believing Liam was real. "Do you still…regret me?" Regret being with her, regret loving her?

A corner of Liam's lips twitched upward. "Sweetheart, you're all I thought about today. Which is a trick, considering all that's been happening at the museum."

"Oh?" Toria feigned surprise. Victory had reported appearing out of thin air in the middle of a gallery, just as she had six months earlier. "What's going on?"

Liam's head dropped against the wall. "We had some sort of break-in the other night, and work has been overwhelming with the upcoming gala. Now I have inventory control, supervising the press release, organizing a security review."

"Wow. Anything stolen?"

"Not that we can tell so far. The woman didn't seem to leave the same way she came in, and it all makes for a strange situation."

"Was anyone hurt?" She hoped Liam didn't recognize her more than idle interest in the answer.

"No. The intruder knocked Jasper around a bit, but no permanent injury."

"Good." Toria's heart skipped a beat. Victory had confessed her worry that she'd killed the man by accident, and she would be so relieved to hear otherwise. "Are there any leads?"

"None so far. Jasper reported a female intruder, but not many other details. There's some suspicion she might be supernatural based on the scuffle, but even humans have shown extraordinary abilities under stress," Liam said. "No clues there, and without knowing why she was there, we have no motive. All I can do is listen to Officer Comstock complain about how this is all due to his limited budget."

Toria relaxed. She had listened to many rants by Liam about the frequent demands of the museum's head of security.

Liam patted Toria's knee with his free hand. "Enough about my woes. We shouldn't sit in the hallway for the rest of the evening. May I escort you to dinner, my dear?"

"Your apartment is right here, you know. We could always eat in."

The grip on Toria's knee tightened, as if Liam's hand had experienced some sort of spasm. "That's a bit of a temptation, isn't it?"

If Toria had her way, she'd push him through the front door and rip his fashionable suit from his body. She was tired, and stressed out, and a little bit in love, and wanted to get laid. Instead, she said, "Probably. How long do you think the wait is at the Aragonian place?"

Instead of answering, Liam leaned forward and captured Toria's lips with his own in a deep kiss. "We're okay?" His pupils were blown. At least she knew she had some sort of effect on the man.

"We're okay."

They left so much unspoken. But for tonight, Toria would be content to recapture what they had.

Toria was gone, again, when Victory woke.

She stared at the darkened ceiling until she couldn't put it off any longer. After she washed and dressed in another set of old-fashioned clothing, she descended the stairs and met Hugh in the kitchen.

He greeted her over his newspaper, the cheer in his voice allaying much of Victory's initial hesitance. "Good evening! Or is it good morning, for you?"

"Either works." Victory gestured to the stove. "Do you mind if I make tea?"

"Please, help yourself. I'd fancy a mug, myself." He returned to his paper, sweater sleeves pushed up to avoid ink stains.

The man's nonchalance at a vampire in his kitchen explained much of Toria's fondness for Hugh. Victory put on the kettle and surveyed the tea selection. "Dare I ask how you have a tin of spiced tea I've never seen outside an elven tea house?"

"That seems to be Liam's favorite tea blend, so I never questioned how it appeared in my stock. Chamomile for me, please."

Once she prepared the tea, Victory brought the steaming mugs to the table. "Anything interesting in the news?"

"Now that you mention it…." Hugh slid a section of newspaper toward her. "Toria asked me to fetch a copy on my errands. She pulled this out for you."

Toria had circled the police blotter column in thick pen, and Victory laughed aloud when she skimmed the contents. A suspect in multiple attempted robberies had turned himself into the police the night before and been identified by one of his previous victims. The article included no mention of any wounds, self-inflicted or otherwise.

"You fed well last night?" Hugh cradled his mug in his hands.

"It will suffice for a few days. And I'm always happy to provide a public service."

"If you have no other plans for the evening, you're welcome to accompany me to the cinema. Otherwise, please continue to make yourself at home here."

"You're too kind." The offer tempted Victory more than expected, but such a trip down memory lane would do nothing more than remind her of all she'd lost since the Last War. "But I might stay in. Is Toria at work tonight?"

"I'm not sure where she is. The fellows at the museum expected me to be a bit of a father-figure for her, but I knew from the second I met the girl I wouldn't stand a chance against whatever she put her mind to."

"You're more similar to her father than you know."

Hugh must have heard the catch in Victory's voice. "I'd love to hear about him. She told me you raised her with your daywalker?"

She had to be careful what she said, considering Mikelos' current fame. "I can do one better. I have all sorts of embarrassing stories from Toria's childhood."

Hugh clapped his hands. "Now we're talking! I've got an hour before I need to leave for the film. Give me all you've got!"

Victory filled the time with tales that would have Toria blushing and running from the room, such as the hijinks she got up to with her burgeoning magical abilities at age seven to her disastrous first date in middle school. After she waved Hugh out the door for his movie, she made another cup of tea and perused the rest of the newspaper. She puttered around the bed and breakfast, cleaning up the kitchen and admiring the renovations Hugh and Toria had spent the previous months on.

She stood in the entryway to the front parlor and considered building a fire to accompany a book from the overflowing shelves. Instead, she plucked her coat off the rack and left the front door, locking it with the key Hugh had pressed on her before he left.

More memories of the city had dredged themselves up. Instead of walking miles to the main district, Victory found the nearest trolley stop and rode in comfort, out of the wind.

Soon, she stood before the "scene of the crime." The Museum of New Continental History had another hour until closing, based on the posted entrance times. According to the newspaper article, the police had no solid leads about the break-in earlier in the week. Since this was long before the era of security cameras, Victory felt confident in the safety of her actions.

If Toria wasn't going to investigate options for returning to their proper time, Victory could take steps instead. She would begin by finding the meteorite in question.

She climbed the museum's steps and entered the building, greeted by a blast of heated air. Bright light illuminated the rotunda and highlighted the stuffed mammoth, which dominated the space. Beelining for the geological gallery would invite suspicion, so Victory wandered toward the large display and read the descriptions of how Hank had been one of the few remaining in the northern stretches of the New Continent.

The background noise of other museum patrons settled into a low buzz while Victory browsed the exhibit, until one voice cut through the crowd and sent a shock up her spine.

"Yes, I'm sorry, I know I'm later than expected. Did Dr. Duvall leave the archives key for me?"

Don't turn around. Don't turn around.

But she was desperate to see the face that lived in memory and scant photographs. Jarimis, her progeny, the closest thing Victory ever had to a son before Kane.

"Thanks, chaps. I'll drop them off here when I'm done."

Victory locked her knees and gripped the lip of the stuffed mammoth's information placard. As Jarimis left the security desk and passed through the rotunda, his coldness brushed the edge of her senses. She didn't move, frozen in place by longing and fear. Longing to see him one more time, hale and whole. Fear, now, of Toria's warnings. What effect would their meeting have on the timeline?

The wood beneath her hand shifted, and Victory jerked away from the exhibit. The edge of the placard had cracked under her fingers.

She fled the museum, muttering an absent apology to the man she pushed past toward the doors. Buildings and streets sped by in a blur. The urge to return to the museum, hunt down Jarimis, and sweep him into her arms burned within her. Instead, she raced in the opposite direction until she heard sobs, and realized they came from her.

Heedless of everything around her, Victory halted in her tracks. She collapsed on the front steps of an apartment building and buried her face in her hands.

If she returned for Jarimis now, she would never let him go. And if she never let him go, how much else would she be tempted to change? Jarimis had survived the Last War, but so many others hadn't.

At least she'd gotten to hear his voice one last time.

Her mother stepped onto the trolley at the stop nearest the museum. She sucked air between clenched teeth, then faced the inevitable and patted the empty seat next to her, an invitation for Victory to sit. "Good evening, Mom."

"Good evening, love."

They rode in awkward silence past the next stop, until Toria bit the bullet first. "Where were you tonight?"

"Out. You?"

"Out. With a friend." The conversation lapsed again, but Toria knew her mother wouldn't be able to resist the bait. Her mental timer made it to forty-seven seconds.

"With Liam?"

"Yes."

"You know, you used to tell me about all the boys you dated."

"This is kind of different, Mom."

"It's a guy, whom you like, whom you regularly see. I fail to see how this is different."

Toria slumped on the bench, crossing her arms and staring straight ahead. She didn't want to talk about Liam. She didn't want to think about Liam, because that way lay frustration and madness. "You are impossible."

"You're used to it by now."

She leaned in until her shoulder connected with her mother's, and they spent the rest of the trip in silence, but less charged with tension.

After they disembarked the trolley at Hugh's stop, Victory linked her arm with Toria's for the walk, and she didn't resist the closeness. Until her mother dropped a bombshell on her.

"I saw Jarimis today."

Toria pulled away, halting in the middle of the sidewalk. "Holy crap, Mom. You didn't."

In a pool of light from a streetlamp, darkness shadowed Victory's face. "Didn't what?"

"Talk to him." Toria imagined no quicker way to corrupt the timeline than for Jarimis to figure out Victory wasn't the same Victory he knew. Hell, she hadn't trusted herself not to slip in front of the man, which was why she'd feigned discomfort with the idea of making friends. Liam had never pushed the issue, dropping the dinner plans he'd made. And she'd never even met Jarimis, dead decades before she was born.

"No, I didn't talk to him." Victory snagged her by the arm and all but dragged her down the street. "I don't know why you suddenly think I'm an idiot, by the way."

"I don't think you're an idiot." Even if it was always a daughter's prerogative to think her mother was an idiot, and vice versa. "You've experienced a large shock and haven't adapted to the situation yet." They clambered onto the porch, and Toria dug in her coat pocket for her housekeys.

Victory waited to resume the conversation until they had divested themselves of coats and shoes inside the house. "Maybe I'd have adapted better if you hadn't thrown a temper tantrum and disappeared on me for two days."

Toria ignored the jab, and instead called into the house. "Hugh! I'm home!"

"He's not here. He invited me to a movie with him, but I declined."

Toria followed Victory into the kitchen, stuttering to a halt again when the implications of Victory's earlier words hit her. "Wait, how did you run into Jarimis. Did you go to the *museum*?"

"Yes. Wanted to scope out the artifact that sent us here, but never made it that far. Overheard Jarimis talking to the security desk and left after he was out of sight." Victory opened the refrigerator, made a sound of frustration, and shut it again. "I'm going to be tired of tea soon."

Her mother's glibness was like an actual, physical pain. "Are you fucking insane? You are. You have lost your mind."

Victory slammed a hand on the counter and faced Toria. "No, but I think you have."

"You have to stay away from the museum. You have to stay away from Jarimis. You can't be a vampire walking around a British city pre-Last War and not expect to attract the wrong sort of attention." The volume of her voice rose in a steady arc until the last shouted words rang through the kitchen.

"Well, what the hell am I supposed to do, Toria?" Victory snarled, showing fang. "You're not doing a damned thing to find your way home, so should I spend the rest of eternity hiding in this house, leaving to prowl the streets for my next meal from the dregs of society? Except it won't be eternity, because we're going to die in a few short weeks when the city is wiped off the map."

"You know I'm getting out beforehand. I'm not suicidal." Toria knew her brain was fucked up these days, but she'd never let Hugh and Liam die.

"And what's your plan, exactly?" Victory leaned against the counter. "The Toria I knew a week ago would have plans upon plans, and she'd have gotten as far away from the combat zones as possible once she'd decided all hope was lost of getting home."

Toria balled her hands at her sides. The urge to storm away and hide in her bedroom was strong, but she wasn't a child anymore. "It hasn't been a week for me."

"Which is it? Either we're going to die with everyone else. Or you haven't given up hope, and you still think we can find a way home." Victory crossed the kitchen and stopped short in front of Toria. "Hope or fear?"

She didn't have an answer. Instead, she stepped forward and hugged her mother tight. "I love you, Mama."

Victory wrapped her arms around Toria and clung back. "I love you, too."

Toria pulled out of Victory's embrace. Without another word, she left the kitchen and climbed the stairs to her tiny room.

At least this time, her daughter left Victory a note that she would be at work for the evening. Hugh wasn't home either, so Victory dressed and left the house. The trolley ride to the central district passed without incident, but Victory needed more preparation before she entered the museum.

She ordered tea at a café across the street, selecting a seat where she could see the museum's entrance through the large plate-glass window.

She'd finished the first cup out of the pot the waitress left on the table when Jarimis strode up the street outside. He bounded up the museum steps and disappeared inside. No luck tonight.

One of these evenings, her progeny wouldn't be at the museum on whatever research fascinated him at the moment. Victory settled in to finish her tea while surveying the interesting mix of patrons who surrounded her instead. She'd return to the bed and breakfast afterward.

The bell above the door tinkled, which Victory ignored. But the chilly air brought an undercurrent of something more, and she straightened in time for Jarimis to drop into the seat across from her.

He spoke without preamble. "I thought I spotted you when I came by, and I knew I wouldn't be able to focus on my work unless I knew for sure. This is such a pleasant surprise! I thought you weren't planning to be in Nacostina for weeks."

If she'd been human, Victory's heart would have stopped. Since she wasn't a human, she gaped at Jarimis until she found her voice. "Ah, change of plans."

Jarimis stole a sip of her tea. "Delicious, though you take yours too sweet, as always. Let me ask for a refill, and we can catch up." He bounced up and wended his way through the crowded café.

She should leave. That was the right decision, and she heard Toria screaming in her mind's ear. Disappear right now, before Jarimis returned, and stay as far from the museum as possible.

Except her progeny knew she was here, and he would tear the city apart to find her.

Victory kept her hands clasped on her lap to keep them from shaking as Jarimis returned with a second teacup and tiny pitcher of milk. She waited until he finished doctoring his tea. "What are you doing here, Jarimis?"

"Didn't you get my letter? I'm investigating a collection of jewelry for an investor in Parisii, trying to figure out whether a similar item he inherited from his grandmother might hail from the original set. Dull work, but it paid for access to the archives here for my own research. You know, the surrealist project."

"Right. The surrealist project." She didn't remember it, but to be fair, she hadn't often kept track of Jarimis' pet projects even when they'd shared living space.

"But what are you doing here? I thought the contract in Wan City wouldn't have you back until next year, at the earliest."

"Like I said, change of plans." That wasn't too far off, either. The contacts Victory had maintained in Qin court warned her about the escalating violence between the empires, and she'd boarded the first train east as soon as possible, missing the firebombing in Wan City by days. In fact, her past self was due in Nacostina soon.

She should mention that to Toria, though it would be another detail for her daughter to panic over.

"Seeing you is a pleasant surprise, either way. You're staying at the Baugher Hotel, as usual?"

If she said yes, Victory would have to rush over and register a room tonight. Perhaps she could draw on her past self's line of credit? Except past Victory would be sure to notice, even though she didn't remember any such thing years ago.

Was she remembering correctly? Had the timelines diverged, and no matter what they did now, it would have no bearing on their future? But what if she was wrong?

Except…a simpler solution existed. "I'm staying elsewhere. Can we meet for dinner tomorrow night? There's someone I'd like you to meet."

Puzzlement clouded Jarimis' expression. "Absolutely. I always fancy the wine at Devi's if your friend won't mind Indus fare."

"She'll be fine with that. Thanks." If Toria didn't kill Victory before she had a chance to eat.

They coordinated times, and Jarimis finished the last of his tea. "Work is calling, since security will kick me out of the archives at midnight." He rose to his feet and crossed to Victory's side of the small table. She tilted her head in long-forgotten habit to accept the kiss he brushed against her cheek. "Having you back early is fantastic. Love you, Mum."

"Love you too, Zvi." The nickname rolled off her tongue as if decades hadn't passed since Victory last used it.

Something in her voice must have given her away. Jarimis pulled away, his thick eyebrows furling over narrowed eyes.

Victory's mouth dried. "Something wrong?"

"No, no." Jarimis ran a hand through his already mussed hair. "I'm imagining things. See you tomorrow."

She tracked him as he left the café and dashed across the street. Once he entered the museum, Victory slumped in her seat. She was almost one thousand years old and not much frightened her anymore, but how Toria would react to this crazy plan spawned an empty pit in her stomach.

Toria was civil when she returned home from work to find Victory staring into the cold fireplace in the front parlor. Her daughter settled a small log in the hearth and lit it with a wave of her fingers, then fetched two glasses of port. She even curled against Victory's side while they sipped the drinks and stared into the flames together.

Victory could almost pretend everything was okay. That they were home at the manor in Limani, sharing a quiet night.

As long as neither of them spoke. Victory broke the silence first. "Are you working tomorrow night?"

Toria kept her stare on the fire before them. "I don't have to be. Why?"

"I'd like to take you to a restaurant I remember."

Now her daughter tilted her face toward Victory. "Why?"

"Because I have good memories of it, and I've been given this crazy chance to share it with you."

Silence reigned for a few beats, and some of the tension bled from Toria's body. "Sure. That'd be fun."

They managed to speak of inconsequential topics until the fire ran down, and Toria yawned and hauled herself to her feet. "Love you, Mama." She kissed Victory's cheek and disappeared upstairs.

Once alone in the parlor, Victory raised a hand to her face. How similar her two children were, without ever having met.

Some of Toria's stoniness returned the next evening, but she sat with Hugh in the day room off the kitchen, waiting for Victory to be ready for dinner. Part of Victory had expected Toria to be gone by sunset once again, so she approached the evening with forced optimism over this stroke of luck.

Victory turned toward the trolley stop when they left the bed and breakfast, but Toria pulled her in the opposite direction. "It'll be faster to catch a taxi this way."

"I don't mind the trolley, you know." Victory allowed herself to be led along.

"Sure, because you won't mind walking five blocks from the trolley stop to the restaurant. I will freeze in these stockings before we get there." Toria cleaned up nice, in a royal blue dress under her black coat instead of trousers. Her daughter caught the appraisal. "I've been to this restaurant already."

"Oh." Victory tried to ignore the stab of disappointment. This wasn't something new to share with her daughter after all.

"Liam took me for my birthday a few weeks ago."

Right! If Toria had been here for months, she was no longer twenty-four. "You're catching up to Kane at this rate."

Toria pressed her lips together as she waved for a passing cab. "I try not to think about that, thanks."

Silence fell again on the way to the restaurant, but Toria followed her into the dim room without protest. Victory inhaled the comforting scent of wine and rich spices of the Indus region and greeted the maître d'. "Good evening. I called last night to make a reservation for—"

"Your party is waiting, ma'am." The man straightened his suit and gestured for another staff member to take their coats. "Your usual table will suffice?"

"Perfect." Victory couldn't remember the man's name, but he remembered her, or Jarimis. He gestured for them to accompany a host standing to the side.

They followed the host to a table set behind a partial curtain and away from the main dining room. Jarimis waited for them already. Victory settled into the seat he held out for her and accepted a kiss pressed to her cheek in greeting.

The waiter attempted to help Toria into her seat, but she brushed him aside. She gripped her chairback and waited for the man to deposit their menus on the table and step away. "What the hell is he doing here?"

"Toria!" Victory snapped at the same low volume. At least she'd taught her daughter where it was inappropriate to make a scene, even if she lacked the rest of her manners at the moment. "Sit down."

Through this, Jarimis sat without a word, his hands placed flat on the table in front of him. Finally, Toria sat. She leaned forward, ignoring Jarimis and glaring daggers at Victory. "This is a terrible idea. What the hell are you thinking?"

For now, she ignored her daughter's rudeness. "Toria, I'd like you to meet my progeny Jarimis."

Jarimis inclined his head in greeting. "We've met. But you seemed uncomfortable in my presence, so I persuaded Liam not to pressure a further acquaintance on our part."

"Because at least someone in my family has some sense."

"Something you want to tell me, Mum?" Jarimis asked. "Adopted another stray?"

Victory had to tread this conversational landmine with care. "Jarimis, I would like you to meet my adopted daughter, Toria Connor."

"But you're not…." Jarimis trailed off, wheels in his head turning. As if prompted to interrupt at the worst possible moment, a waiter arrived for their drink orders. Jarimis rattled off a request for a bottle of wine and sent him on his way. He looked from Victory, to Toria, and back again. "May I please see the tattoo on your wrist, Toria?"

She hesitated, but held her hand out. He examined the ink, turning her hand one way and the other with delicate fingers.

125

The waiter returned with their bottle of wine. After Jarimis approved his taste, the man poured three glasses of the burgundy liquid and vanished again. With her reclaimed hand, Toria clutched her wine glass and gulped like a drowning woman.

Jarimis sipped his drink with more sedation. "Here's my conclusion so far. Liam explained Toria's situation, that she was from a century in the past. Except one hundred years ago, Victory and I spent a decade in Rus, then worked together another few years in Parisii." He tilted his wine glass toward Victory. "At no time were we ever apart enough for you to adopt a child, and I'm certain you'd have told me about it if she disappeared off the face of the earth. Correct?"

"That's not information I would have kept from you. And even if I had, I'd have recruited you to help tear the world apart while I looked for her."

"Exactly. I know you too well, Mum. So. Toria cannot be from the past. But you're not lying about your relationship with this girl. There's also the tattoo."

"What about it?" Toria's glare over her wineglass had softened, but not by much.

"Language changes over the years. By virtue of my many professions, I recognize that dialect of elven. That's not how those names would have been structured a century ago." Jarimis drained the last of his wine and set down his glass. "However, due to the nature of the evolution of language, it's how the names might be structured, say, a century or so in the future. Ergo, Toria is not from the past. She is from the future."

Toria toasted him with her glass. "Damn."

Jarimis pointed at Toria. "Also, the way you speak. Like a certain other uneducated mercenary I know."

Taking the jab with the love in which he intended, Victory didn't put too much heat in her glare toward Jarimis. "I'm plenty educated, thank you. Asaron would have something to say about that."

"And where is Asaron these days, Mum?"

Victory had no answer. Memory was a fickle thing, and her sire's location at this particular point in time escaped her. The satisfaction on Jarimis' face said it all. His trap had caught her. "I'm sure you'll tell me."

"It's not important. I got the answer I needed." Jarimis patted Victory's hand. "This is why I've always encouraged you to keep a journal like I do."

"So that you'll know every detail of your life if you ever get transported to the past?" Toria cracked a grin as the shock crossed Jarimis' face. "You're right. But you didn't want to be right, did you?"

Her children stared at each other across the table. Should this be where she panicked?

"Not particularly, but here we are," Jarimis said. "Are you going to share the wine or hoard it for yourself?" He held out his wineglass. Toria lifted the bottle and refilled both their glasses. "Another thing that sets you apart. I'm shocked Liam has not picked up on this."

"Liam sees…what he wants to see." Toria set the empty wine bottle at the edge of the table for the waiter to collect. "And I will admit to being much more careful around him."

"He won't thank you for lying to him."

Toria locked eyes with Jarimis, and pride swelled in Victory at how long her daughter was able to meet her progeny's gaze. "Are you going to tell him?"

"Probably not. But why confide in me, instead?" This time, Jarimis looked to Victory for the answer.

Victory raised a hand before Toria protested. "I have faith that you will keep this knowledge to yourself," Victory said. "Toria has done her best to explain the logic of timelines to me, but I know she's worried how our actions here will affect both the past and our future. But I know you, and I believe that between the two of you, an answer to this situation is possible."

Victory's past and present and future boiled down to this single instance in time. If Toria's worries about paradox were true, this was where they all winked out of existence. Or worse.

Nothing happened. Time continued to flow. The waiter returned, and Toria ordered her meal and requested a second bottle of the same wine for the table.

Once he was gone, Jarimis leaned over to Toria. "Tell me everything you know so far."

And to Victory's immense relief, Toria began her tale.

After the meal, Jarimis squabbled with Victory over which of them would pay the check, and for a moment, no time had passed at all. Until Toria heaved an over-dramatic sigh and placed cash on the table to cover the entire bill.

As she rose to her feet and accepted the coat the waiter handed to her, she pointed to Jarimis and Victory in turn. "Face it, Jarimis, you're a poor academic. And you've been living off me since the second you got here, Mom." She thanked the waiter, and he faded into the background once again. "Enjoy the rest of the wine. The night is still young, so I'm going over to work to make sure the kids are behaving themselves."

She stooped to kiss her mother's cheek in farewell and, to Victory's immense surprise, did the same for Jarimis with a muttered word in his ear. She swept from the restaurant, leaving both vampires to stare after her.

Jarimis shook himself free of his astonishment first, and split the remainder of the wine between their glasses. "She called me 'brother.'"

"That she did."

"She doesn't work with children, does she?"

"She's been moonlighting as a bouncer at a bar catering to the crowd near the Mercenary Guildhall."

"And how old is she?"

"Twenty-four—no, twenty-five going on five hundred."

Jarimis tilted his head in laughter. "Her resilience is amazing."

Her daughter had managed to keep herself in check past the initial panic at who they met at the restaurant. "She's been through a lot over the years. Being my daughter is not always a benefit."

"But being your son has always been a privilege, and I doubt that has changed in however many years it's been for you." Jarimis drained his wine and motioned for the passing waiter to fetch their coats as well. "We must be off."

"We? Where to?" Victory also finished her drink, and they stood as the waiter returned.

Jarimis flashed a wicked grin, showing the slightest hint of fang. "Another thing that I imagine has not changed is your aversion to problems you can't beat into submission with your sword alone, but for now, we have research to do."

Once outside the restaurant, Jarimis hailed a cab and directed the driver to the Museum of New Continental History. The sinking feeling in Victory's chest intensified as he led her past the front desk, greeting the security officers like old friends, and into the depths of the museum. Jarimis escorted her inside the museum's archives, a room lined with bookshelves, with a flourish.

"Research?" Victory asked.

"Of course!"

She leaned a hip against one of the tables and crossed her arms. "You're way too excited about this."

"This is a challenge worthy of my skill." Jarimis paused in pulling books from shelves and piling them onto a table. "Besides, it's either focus on this or pepper you with questions about the future that I know you wouldn't answer."

"Fair enough." She accepted the two tomes Jarimis handed her and settled into a seat while he finished his initial collection. "What do you need me to look for?"

"Your two books have information on the history of various meteors collected by the museum and its sister institutions. I need you to find information on the one that sent you and Toria here. Since the full provenance has been lost, see if any of the others listed might be the original source discovery." Jarimis sat across from her and dug paper and pens out of the battered satchel that had looked incongruous with his tailored suits even when Victory purchased it for him new. "I will be researching other items with temporal properties. What was it about the meteor that sent you here? A spell? From what school of magic? Or perhaps it was something about its physical makeup instead." He flipped open his first book and furled his brow. "I wish I knew more about geology, but I do know that most meteors have significant metallic properties."

Victory's head jolted up from where she skimmed her first book's index. "You need Toria."

"Oh?" Jarimis glanced up. "She said she was a warrior-mage and a mercenary."

"She is a warrior-mage and a mercenary." Despite her stress and the newfound urgency of the situation due to Jarimis' frenetic energy, pride forced a smile to Victory's lips. "But before she left home, she studied chemistry and metallurgy in college."

"Excellent information. I'll direct any questions to her." They resumed work, but Jarimis offered another aside. "Those are the sorts of things you have to be careful about saying, Mum. You revealed to me that Limani will have its own university one day."

Victory forced her hands steady, keeping her face tilted toward her book. He was right, but even more than he knew. Was this how paradoxes happened? Did Jarimis go on to found the college in Limani after they settled there because the Victory of his future planted the idea in his head here and now?

They worked in companionable silence, broken by the flipping of pages and scratch of pens on paper, until the telephone on the wall next to the door shattered the quiet with a sharp ring.

Victory and Jarimis exchanged glances, but she gestured for him to answer the call. He was the one registered to be in the archives, after all. He bounded across the room and snatched the handset off the hook. "Hello?"

Despite the crackling connection, she heard the words as well as if the speaker sat next to her. "Mr. Jarimis? There's a woman here at the information desk asking to see you. But the museum is about to close in a few minutes."

"Thank you for giving me a call. Did she say who she was?" Jarimis shrugged at Victory, who shrugged back.

Both of them froze at the answer. "Gave her name as Victory."

Jarimis kept his tone calm, even as Victory shoved herself to her feet. "Thank you. I'll be there in a moment." He replaced the handset. "I don't know what's going on. It's like when I saw you. You were not expected back."

Even as he spoke, the memories crashed down. "I remember now." She grabbed her coat from across the next table. "But there's nothing I can tell you without the risk of giving you information you shouldn't have." Damn it, why did her kids all have to be so *intelligent*?

"I understand. We have to get you out of here without you crossing paths with my Victory." Jarimis shuffled the books on the table so it appeared he used all of them, and Victory shoved her notes into the side pocket of his bag. He pointed to what Victory had thought a closet. "In there."

He escorted her across the room and pulled the door open. Instead of a closet, he revealed the antechamber to a clean room where delicate volumes could be examined with care, beyond another door with an inset window. Jarimis enclosed Victory within the small space, which had enough room for her to sink to her crossed legs. At least the glass in the opposite door prevented claustrophobia.

Jarimis' steps echoed across the library floor and faded into silence. Victory settled in to wait, arranging her limbs and clothing into a position she could maintain without moving for a long period of time. She wasn't the sort to meditate, but so much of mercenary life boiled down to "hurry up and wait." The headspace of calm expectation was a familiar friend.

She approximated fifteen minutes until the library door opened again. Victory tensed, but a single set of footsteps entered the room. They aimed for her hiding spot, not stopping along the way.

When the door opened, Jarimis alone stood above her. "We're okay. I convinced her I'd give her a tour later. Come on out." He let Victory grasp his wrist as leverage to haul herself to her feet.

"What can you tell me about why she was here?"

"I can tell you all I want. My Victory—past Victory has returned to Nacostina at the behest of her contacts in the Qin diplomatic corps. She delivered a packet of documents to officials here in the city and needs to stay here until she receives new orders." Jarimis sank into his seat and dug his fingers into his hair. "Mum, were you a spy?"

"You quit being a mercenary because you didn't like the sort of jobs Asaron and I took."

"No, I quit being a mercenary because I hated how I was raised to be a killer, and I never resigned myself to being one after you turned me into a vampire." Jarimis flipped a page in the open book closest to him. "Let's get to work. We have an hour left tonight, and I need to compile questions for Toria."

Victory tugged her assigned books toward her and leaned over the open pages. Her mind, however, was a million miles away from the artifact lists in front of her.

She remembered why her previous self returned to Nacostina early. Certain elements within the Qin royal court had protested the use of such extreme force against the encroaching British colonies and smuggled Victory information. Not a spy so much as a sympathetic, neutral third party.

British intelligence had thanked her for the information and sent her on her way, but not before asking her to deliver another packet south to the capital of the Roman colonial cities. British forces firebombed Wan City soon after.

War was coming.

If Lyra wanted to pretend their spat never occurred, well, Toria was not about to argue with the pregnant woman. Instead, Lyra cooed over her fancy clothes and asked point-blank whether Liam had popped the question, as if that was a rational response to Toria's fight with him.

Not like Liam would propose to Toria anyway, even if they were a regular couple and all of the time travel nonsense was out of the picture. Elves didn't marry. At this point, Toria held out as much hope for a ring as she did for sex.

"Not tonight, sorry." Toria accepted the glass of wine Lyra poured her, after the other woman insisted she dressed too nice to swill cheap beer. "We'll keep hoping, shall we?"

"We shall." Lyra beamed at her, before turning to her work.

With Toria's life so entwined with Kane's, she'd never seen herself as the marrying type. So why should this make her wistful?

Perhaps because without Kane, she missed the sense of a permanent link to another person. She didn't want to face a future alone, even if no ring was involved.

The bar was more crowded than usual tonight. Good for Toria's income, but bad for the men who surrounded her. Winter approached, and winter meant less work and even fewer jobs to go around for too many mercs.

Due to the number of unfamiliar faces, Toria remained at the bar until closing. She offered to escort Lyra home, but the other woman waved her off. "If you walk me home, I'll feel obliged to ask you in for coffee, and the place is a mess."

Toria laughed. "Fair enough. Get some rest, hon." She waited at the entrance to the bar until Lyra turned the corner toward her apartment. When she turned around for the long, cold walk to where she might hail a taxi, she jumped out of her skin when a man ghosted out of the shadows toward her.

"Good evening." Jarimis resettled his battered bag across his shoulder.

Toria pressed a hand to her chest. "Bloody hell. Don't do that to a girl. You're lucky I'm not armed."

Contrition crossed his face, and Jarimis offered her a short bow. "Many apologies. I recognize that you've had a long night, but maybe I can tempt you with breakfast?" He dug a scrap of paper out of his coat pocket and held it up. "I have questions about things I have been reliably informed you can answer."

It had been a long night, and she'd woken before noon. What the hell. If she had only one chance to spend time with the man who'd given her so much even after he'd died, she'd regret missing it.

It didn't reduce the awkwardness when he linked their arms for their taxi search. He was the same height and general build as Kane, and longing coursed through her. This man was her brother, but not the brother she still feared she would never see again.

If this was the trade life had forced her to make, it was a crappy one.

Jarimis directed the driver to an all-night diner near the museum, where the coffee was fresh and the waitress didn't blink at Toria's order of pancakes and bacon. Toria braced herself when Jarimis spoke after the waitress left, but his question surprised her.

"Human women of your apparent class are not able to perform activities beneficial to their health, yet they are expected to maintain stick-thin physiques." Jarimis pushed the sugar and cream across the table to Toria and eyed with suspicion the amount of both with which she doctored her coffee. "You have no such qualms?"

"I'd give my left arm for a decent spar with someone who knows what they're doing." Toria dumped cream in her mug, sipped the coffee, and added a bit more. "By my standards, I'm ridiculously out of shape. But there's a reason you never see a fat mage. Even if I use no other magic in the course of the day, the act of filtering ambient power and maintaining shields sucks up so much energy that I can still eat like this. Muscle tone is a different matter." She offered Jarimis the cream and sugar, but he curled his hands around his mug.

"Fascinating. I've met mages, obviously, but—" Jarimis cut himself off. "Pardon me. I didn't ask you here to interrogate you about the mechanics of magical energy. Though I have no doubt you could provide me with all the information I desire in that regard."

"I could. I am kind of a big nerd. Not as big as Kane, but pretty up there."

"Victory said you are a warrior-mage. Kane is your partner, whom you left behind?"

Toria bristled, and her coffee cup clattered against its saucer. "Not *intentionally.*"

Jarimis lifted both hands. "Forgive me. That was not an accusation. A few hundred years speaking Loquella, and I still say the wrong thing on occasion."

She repressed the surge of irritation, at this point almost indistinguishable from the anxiety that was her near-constant companion. "It's fine. You had other questions."

"This outlines the main areas with which I have queries." Jarimis dug a page of notepaper out of his bag and slid it across the table to Toria. "I'm not sure whether any of these have simple answers."

Toria skimmed the list of questions. "I can give you some of this in layman's terms pretty easily, such as ionic bonds, but the rest I'd have to brush up on myself. School was a few years ago."

"Are you perhaps willing to join me for a spot of research?"

He made it sound like asking Toria to afternoon tea, but his optimism chased away the snide response Toria might have made. "Sure," she said. "At the least, I can figure out what information is available in this time period and point you toward what's real and what's not."

"Thank you. That would be most appreciated."

The waitress approached their table and slid Toria's breakfast in front of her. "Careful, plate's hot." Without checking to see whether they needed anything else, she bustled away to another set of patrons across the diner.

Toria glanced at Jarimis, but he cradled his coffee and leaned back in the booth. "Please, don't mind me."

The grease and carbs did much to settle her, though she could not have said for sure whether nerves or the cheap wine Lyra had pressed on her caused the roiling in her stomach. At least Jarimis' silence wasn't awkward, and she ate in peace while he stared out the diner window at the early-risers who passed outside.

Until he stiffened in his seat and set his coffee cup down so hard it sloshed brown liquid onto the saucer. "Follow my lead."

"What?" Toria paused with her fork halfway to her mouth.

Jarimis snatched the list of questions from the table and shoved it into his coat pocket. The bell above the diner entrance jangled, and he waved to the new entrant. Toria peered over her shoulder and dropped her fork into her scrambled eggs. Victory surveyed the interior of the room and waved to Jarimis before striding between tables and booths toward them.

But the woman who slid next to Jarimis wasn't Victory. Wasn't Toria's Victory, at least. Though they appeared identical, Toria found the differences striking. This woman wore contemporary clothing with a naturalness her mother had not yet achieved. And while her mother displayed a fierce sharpness Toria had always found secure, this woman evoked a more brittle façade. An obsidian blade, to her mother's tempered steel.

This Victory accepted the kiss Jarimis pressed to her cheek in greeting as if her due. "You weren't at the hotel, so I thought I'd find you here. Introduce me to your friend."

"Peggy is an assistant at the museum who's been helping me with the jewelry project. Peg, this is my sire Victory."

Victory didn't extend a hand in greeting, so Toria kept her own clasped in her lap below the table. It was fascinating, however, how this woman who was not her mother dismissed her upon Jarimis' explanation that she was a mere underling at the museum. Instead, Victory turned her attention on Jarimis.

"I wanted to track you down rather than leave a message at that decrepit building you call a hotel. I'm leaving town again tonight."

Jarimis didn't feign the disappointment on his face, but Toria gave an internal cheer. The last thing they needed was this complication. Meeting Jarimis was intriguing, a fascinating look into a part of Victory's life known through story alone. Meeting this past version of her mother raised the hair on Toria's neck.

"That's unfortunate." Jarimis sipped his coffee. "What takes you off so soon?"

Victory glanced over the table at Toria, who dropped her eyes to her plate and continued eating. "The Foreign Office commissioned me to courier a message to Fort Caroline." It seemed "Peggy the assistant" was inconsequential enough to overhear this information.

"Be careful passing through Newport Hill. I'm not sure the Master has forgiven you for that card game." Jarimis and Victory exchanged the same sort of knowing expression Toria had seen so many times between Victory and Mikelos, of a shared memory long since forgotten by the rest of the world.

"Daniel can acknowledge that I cheat better than he does and get over it." Victory stole a sip of Jarimis' coffee, wrinkling her nose at the taste. "I must be off to check into the Baugher. You know you're always welcome to stay there under my credit line."

"That's kind of you. Safe travels, Mum."

Victory accepted another kiss from Jarimis and slid out of the booth, heels clicking on the tile floor as she left the diner. She had made no further acknowledgment of Toria.

"That was strange." Jarimis finished his coffee. "I apologize, because I'm sure it was even more awkward for you."

Toria placed her silverware on her empty plate and propped her elbows on the table, leaning toward Jarimis as if sharing a secret. "Was our mother really that much of a bitch back then? Now? However you want to call it."

Jarimis' eyebrows raised toward his hairline. "That's disrespectful."

"Oh, please." Toria pushed her empty plate to the edge of the table and cradled her coffee cup between her hands. "That wasn't weird, that was rude. So, tell me. Was it because I'm human? Or the cover story you gave me?"

"A combination of both." Jarimis peered out the diner window and checked his wristwatch. "I must be off to beat the dawn. You'll meet with me soon to go over my research questions?"

"Yeah, I can do that." She accepted a pen from Jarimis and jotted the bed and breakfast's four-digit telephone number on a napkin. He pulled a billfold out of his coat, but Toria waved him away. "I can cover my own breakfast."

"Unacceptable. I asked you to accompany me." He selected the money and laid it on the table, as if daring Toria to argue.

She didn't feel like making the effort. Her bed called, and with the nights lengthening, her waking hours were sure to increase with the introduction of vampires to her current life. Toria settled on politeness. "Thank you."

She also didn't feel like arguing when Jarimis insisted on waiting with her on the curb in front of the diner until she was safe inside a cab. A peek outside the rearview window as the car drove away showed him ambling down the sidewalk, hands shoved in his coat pocket, portraying the bumbling academic for the world.

Some of the stories on which Victory raised Toria included tales of Jarimis the assassin and knife-fighter, who'd never joined the Mercenary Guild because it impeded his access to the best jobs. But she'd just seen how much a vampire could change her personality. At this point, Jarimis was almost four hundred years old.

Sometimes, she was glad mercenaries didn't often see late middle age.

The moment the sun set, Victory launched into a race against time.

Neither Hugh nor Toria were at the bed and breakfast—Hugh had his card game, and Toria had already left for dinner with Liam, with plans to meet Jarimis at the museum afterward for research. Her daughter still seemed to treat it as a pointless lark, but at least she humored Victory. That was all she could ask of her daughter at this point.

Victory had arranged for a taxi at sunset. Asking the driver to "step on it" felt a bit silly, but the young man poured on the speed with a whoop of delight.

When he slid to a halt in front of the Baugher Hotel, Victory tipped him well and stepped out of the vehicle. A flood of memory washed over her as she pushed through the rotating doors to the lobby, and instinct almost led her to the front desk for her key. Instead, she returned the doorman's familiar greeting, another person lost to the seas of time in her mind, and detoured toward the lobby's far side.

She'd never spent much time at the hotel bar. This would be to her benefit now as she positioned herself to watch for her doppelganger's passing.

Victory perched on a plush-covered stool as the bartender approached her. "Red wine, please." She slipped money across the counter so she could be ready to leave instantly.

Drink in hand, she could be any woman in a hundred, killing time in a hotel bar for a million reasons. Waiting for a date, or recovering from a poor one. A woman prowling for a man, or a woman scorned.

She settled on a variation of that last one as she arranged her limbs and set her facial expression. One leg draped over the other, though she didn't show much skin wearing trousers. One arm leaned on the bar, while the other cradled her glass of wine. Expression of polite dismissal for the world in general.

One man in a posh suit made to join her, but a disdainful curl of her lip sent him scurrying to the other end of the bar for easier prey.

Halfway through her drink, a familiar silhouette caught her attention. Not that she'd ever seen herself from this angle. Did she swagger so much?

Her past self stalked through the lobby. She wore a flowing coat buttoned over slacks and low heels, dressed for travel with her hair bound in a braid pinned to her head. Her fabric-bound sword peeked from the top of the rucksack thrown over one shoulder.

Present Victory had not bothered to bring her sword.

She left her wine glass on the polished bar and slipped out of the hotel behind her target. The other woman's destination was the train station. Victory kept half a block between them.

The streets were empty except for the occasional office drone working late. Despite its class, the Baugher Hotel bordered a more industrial section of the city and catered to traveling employees instead of Nacostina's tourists.

Choosing her moment would be tricky, but she had over a hundred years of experience on the other woman. Most of her additional experience involved soothing ruffled feathers in Limani's city council chambers, but age had to count for something.

There. If other-Victory stayed on this side of the street for another block, she would pass a vacant lot bordered by empty office buildings. Even better, the lamps lined the opposite side of the street, offering the cover of darkness for her ambush.

She dashed forward, heels clicking on the sidewalk. The wind changed, and her scent beat her to other-Victory. The woman half turned as Victory slammed into her. They tumbled through the brush and overgrown weeds, into the shadows and away from prying eyes.

Other-Victory shoved away, scrambling to her feet first. She lunged for her dropped bag, but Victory snatched it while still on her knees. Dark locks of her loose hair fell across her face, shielding her identity.

The other woman snarled, startling Victory with its viciousness. "What the hell?" Other-Victory dropped into a fighting stance.

Victory clutched the bag to her chest as she climbed to her feet. She masked her voice with a raspy whisper. "I'm not here to kill you."

With a hiss of rage, other-Victory leapt forward. Victory dodged to the side, blocking with the bag. She considered going for the sword but dismissed the idea in a fraction of a second. This would be a fight from the core of her training. Asaron's first lessons before she touched a blade. How to trust her body, honing it as her finest and most reliable weapon.

She ducked under other-Victory's second punch and shoved her shoulder into the woman's stomach. Her double grunted in pain, and recovered to do what Victory would have done—tangle her fingers in Victory's loose hair and yank, hard.

An uncivilized move, but while there might be rules in war, there were none in combat.

Victory compartmentalized the pain, freeing one hand and raking her nails down other-Victory's cheek. After drawing blood, she jabbed the woman in the throat. Cartilage around other-Victory's trachea popped and shifted, prompting a cry of pain.

Her double released Victory's hair and staggered away, clasping her hands around her throat. The injury would heal after a good meal, but hurt like hell in the meantime.

Victory tossed the rucksack to the side and darted forward. She clutched the other woman by her upper-arms and forced her still, though other-Victory's eyes rolled in pain. Shaking her hair out of the way, she locked gazes with a familiar set of eyes.

Other-Victory's whimpers of pain faded, and her body slid into unconsciousness. As she had hoped, one hundred extra years of age and experience won out as Victory dominated her doppelganger's mind.

"Forget." The order rang out in the empty lot. "Sleep."

The other woman's eyes rolled up. Her head tilted, and her body sagged as deadweight. Victory eased her to the ground among the dirt and weeds. Still on her knees, she snagged the discarded bag and rifled through its contents until she found the diplomatic pouch. In the partial moonlight, she flipped through the pages.

...RUMINT sources agree major attack on British colonies imminent... method unknown...suggested targets include New Angouleme, Lenapenn, Nacostina... request foreign aid from Roman colonial government should such an attack occur....

Victory settled on her heels, and the pages fell from numb fingers.

The British government had known about the attack, and they had done nothing.

Rumors were a different beast from solid intelligence, but this proved the hydrogen bomb was not as much of a surprise as the history books presented. The pages crumpled in her hands as she retrieved them, shoving them in the pouch and back into her double's bag.

She staggered to her feet and stepped away from other-Victory's limp form. The woman would wake in an hour with little memory of the assault itself. Well before sunrise, with time to catch the pre-dawn train. Victory brushed dirt and dried leaves from her clothing as she left the empty lot.

After a pause to check that darkness hid the body, she continued toward the trolley. The words she'd read had burned themselves into her brain.

They had known, and done nothing.

Victory hid in the rear of the trolley, away from eyes that would view her dirt-stained clothing with disapproval. She would meet Jarimis and Toria at the museum after stopping at the bed and breakfast to change clothing and pin up her hair.

But when she let herself into the house, both of her children huddled around the kitchen table.

They broke off their conversation when Victory stepped into the kitchen. "What's going on?"

Toria ignored her question. "What the hell happened to you? Are you okay?"

"I'm fine." Victory shoved a tangle of hair behind her ear. "It's a long story."

"Alas, ours is not." Anger darkened Jarimis' face. "I have been banned from the museum."

"What?" Victory held up her hand. "Hold that thought. I need to get out of these clothes."

By the time she returned to the kitchen, one of them had put the kettle on. Victory prepared a mug of cinnamon spice tea and joined them at the table. "Let's start from the beginning. What did I miss that you have been barred from your place of work?"

Toria muttered under her breath. "Fucking Rubin." Shaking her head, she continued louder. "It's my fault. I met Jarimis at the lobby to the museum and the head curator was speaking with the security officers."

Jarimis broke in. "How is it not my fault? It was not until I said you would be aiding my research that he revoked my access."

"Trust me, you're not the one he has a problem with." Toria rearranged two pieces of notepaper. "Either way, we've lost our best resource. I can do what I can at the library during the day, but I'll be ferrying information to Jarimis instead of working with him."

Victory pressed the inside of her wrist to her mug, but the tea was still too hot to drink. "I don't understand why this Rubin—" She snapped her fingers. "Rubin. Is it the same man who…?"

"Yes, he is. Or will be." Ice dripped from Toria's words.

"I don't understand," Jarimis said.

Toria pursed her lips. "And I can't tell you. Future stuff." He inclined his head in acceptance of her explanation.

But Victory couldn't let this go, because it tied into her own issues of the evening. "When you met Rubin before, did he recognize you?"

"I have no idea." Her daughter stared into her tea, shoulders hunched and stiff. "That was… a strange time. We met him once, and the second time he tried to kill us. But no, he never said, 'Hey, you look like this time traveler I knew.'"

"Perhaps because from his perspective, he never had met you before." Victory snagged a pen and blank sheet of paper, but she had no idea how to visualize her words. She shoved the items to Toria. "I did something tonight neither of you are going to like."

Toria rolled her eyes. "Color me shocked." She doodled a spiral. "Go on."

"I mugged myself."

Jarimis stiffened, while Toria's hand jerked and the pen shot across the table. Jarimis snatched it before it hit the floor. "Mum. That is absurd."

"I'd say it's fucking ridiculous." Toria ignored Jarimis' disgruntled expression at her language. "What the hell, Mom?"

"I remembered that I—she?—had information regarding something important that might happen soon. I also remembered something odd that happened. I put the pieces together, and figured I was the one who was supposed to do the attacking. Toria, you weren't sure whether our actions now would have an impact on our futures. But you've had enough interaction with Rubin that he's sure to have recognized you in Parisii."

But Toria started shaking her head even before Victory finished. "It's more complicated than that." She sketched out a few lines on the notepaper, then crumpled it. "I can't present four dimensions in two. All we know for sure is that your memories didn't change. Tell me everything that happened between you and past you."

Victory related the events of her entire evening, from lying in wait at the hotel bar to leaving other-Victory in the empty lot. Her report concluded, she watched in fascination as Toria and Jarimis conducted a conversation through facial expressions alone.

Toria appeared to win the silent debate. "At least that settled something else important. You came into physical contact with your past self and the universe didn't implode."

"Was that a concern?" Victory's hand tightened on her teacup.

"I don't know enough about the most recent research into string theory," Toria said. "Technically, both of you are made of the same mass, but I suppose cellular degradation has to be accounted for, so maybe it was enough of not quite the same mass."

"I'm guessing the nature of sentient consciousness is still a mystery in your time?" Jarimis directed the question to Toria.

Victory might have felt offense, but he was correct to assume such knowledge was not in her purview.

In response, Toria shared a look of commiseration with her brother. "Yeah, still a bit beyond us."

An understatement to Victory, but she kept her peace. "So, our actions here are not changing our own pasts. Does that mean what we do here also won't change our future? Because we would remember a different past?"

"But the past has already changed, if what you remember occurring is different from the events you experienced on this end." Jarimis furrowed his brow. "This conversation is becoming circuitous."

Toria toyed with her ball of paper. "This conversation is becoming a pain in the ass. We still know nothing for sure. Where do we go from here?"

Victory's response was immediate. "I still want to get home. And you're coming with me."

Toria stilled. "Okay. Okay. Because I can imagine what you'd do if I disagreed at this point."

"Tie you up and drag you kicking and screaming. Admit you'd do the same if you were in my place."

"Well, there'd be a gag involved, so I didn't have to listen to so much screaming." At least Toria's wry tone meant less hard feelings. "But I also feel the need to play defense. What do we do if we can't make it home? I had my backup plans. I know it's not a fate you want to contemplate, but what would you do, Mom?"

Victory glanced at Jarimis

"Don't look at me. I'm an historian, not a physicist."

Toria leaned forward. "Neither am I, but it's still something we have to consider. We have two options."

"More than two, I'd think." Victory scoffed at the notion of so limited a future. "The world is a big place, and I could manage to avoid myself."

"Those weren't the options," Toria said. "What happens to *you*? Will there always be two of you, so you have to spend the rest of both of your lives avoiding yourself? Or at some point, perhaps the moment when you disappear from the future, do you merge into one person again? And if that happens, which one of you stays?"

The kitchen collapsed into silence, broken by the ticking clock above the window.

"I know that no matter what happens in the far future," Victory said, "I will stay with you for the rest of your life."

"Easy promise to make when it might not last long."

She resisted the urge to shake some sense into the girl. "Don't mock me when I'm being affectionate."

Jarimis broke in before Toria could retort. "I know I'm not supposed to ask anything about the future. But there are some things I've managed to put together out of what hasn't been said. I said I'm not going to ask!" He held up a finger when both women opened their mouths. "But I would stay—"

Toria gasped, interrupting Jarimis' declaration and flinching over the table. She clenched hard on Victory's hand, but she rode through the pain. When her daughter straightened, all the blood had drained from her face and the whites around her eyes showed. She released Victory and shot to her feet, staggering away from the table.

"I have to go." Toria's voice rasped on the words, called over her shoulder as she already made her way to the front door.

"Wait, Toria—!" But the door slammed on Victory's voice.

Jarimis' bewildered look matched what she felt. "Does, ah, this happen often?"

"No." Victory stared down the empty hallway. "A lot of this has never happened before."

Toria tugged on her coat as she sprinted. The lance of magic reverberated within her skin. Half pain, half pleasure, and an all-consuming need to be where the source of the magic called her. The clash of mountains screamed in her skull, and the loamy taste of sod clogged her throat.

One of her usual cabs idled by the corner outside Hugh's pub, and Toria dove inside. Christopher boggled at her from the front seat. "Late for work?"

Toria had no idea where she needed to be, just that she needed to be there *now*. She gasped for breath. "Hold on. I have to think."

She pressed fingers to her temples and sifted through the immense outpouring of power that surged through her. Through the pounding, she narrowed in on the sense of the energy. Earth energy, so familiar it made her chest ache.

Earth energy. Earth magic.

She knew of a single other person in this crazy past connected to the earth.

Lyra had delivered her baby.

Toria opened her eyes. "What's the nearest hospital to the bar where I work?"

Christopher furrowed his brow. "Probably Freeman Community Hospital. But if you're hurt, there's a closer clinic, and—"

"No. We have to go to Freeman. That's where my friend will be." Another heave of power filled her. Tendrils of energy crawled through her limbs, leaving her aching all over. She curled in her seat as Christopher pulled the taxi away from the curb and sped through the city.

The trip passed in a blur, as Toria dug fingernails into her palms and tried not to hyperventilate. She shoved her fare to Christopher as she lunged out of the taxi the moment he drew to a stop, ages or mere moments later.

Forcing herself to pause for a beat at the front entrance, Toria drew herself straight. The summons thrummed through her, stronger than ever.

Though every fiber in her being urged her to hurtle through the building until she found Lyra and the child, this had to be done right. Her feet tingled with each step as she entered the hospital and approached the front desk. An attendant greeted her when she gripped the counter.

"I'm so sorry, I know it's late." Toria heard her voice as if from a distance. "I think a friend delivered her baby here today." She did her best to exude politeness and normality, glad of the coat that hid her over-large sweater, snagged from Hugh, and the counter that hid her black cotton lounge-pants, with feet shoved into hiking boots from the future.

The woman leaned forward in her crisp white uniform to survey the paperwork spread before her. "Name?"

"Lyra Brownlee."

The attendant slid one finger down a page. "Yes, we admitted Ms. Brownlee earlier this afternoon. I can send a page up to see whether she's accepting visitors."

"Yes. Please."

The attendant rang for a young man to deliver a message to the labor and delivery ward. Unable to sit, Toria paced the waiting area. Time stretched into a meaningless river as the demand in her skull grew stronger and stronger. She whirled when a hand touched her shoulder.

"Sorry, miss." The messenger stepped back in haste. "Your friend said you were welcome to see her. If you'll come with me?"

Toria followed him through endless hallways and up three flights of stairs until they emerged into a bright ward painted in calming pastels. Medicinal herbal scents warred with harsh cleaning chemicals, but now she walked on a cloud, pushing past the messenger toward the room that called the loudest.

Lyra, reclined in a hospital bed, raised her head from studying the bundle of tiny human latched to her breast. Her face lit up, more beautiful than Toria had ever seen her, despite her hair tucked under a scarf and the lack of makeup. "Toria! What are you doing here?"

The messenger retreated, his work done, and Toria stepped into the hospital room. "I didn't realize you were due so soon. Are you okay?" Now that she was here, the forceful pull of magic receded. As if all it had wanted was for Toria to be in the same room with the infant, and now it was satisfied. With the compulsion gone, Toria wasn't sure what to do, so she hovered in the doorway.

"He's a few weeks early, but we're both fine. Just need to put some meat on his bones." Lyra extended her free hand. "Come closer."

Toria approached the side of the bed and leaned over mother and baby. "It's a boy?" The baby was tiny, with a miniature fist he might fit around Toria's pinky finger. But he nursed with ferocity, and Lyra emanated exhausted contentment.

"Yes. Though he's early enough Kojo and I had yet to settle on a name." Lyra's laughter pealed through the room. "And because I know you're aching to, you have my permission to look at him with magesight."

Toria gasped as power spun into view. The vibrant green hues of pure earthen elemental magic swirled around and through the infant. This child would be a mage, a powerful one.

The familiar ache in Toria's chest returned tenfold. His earth magic was her earth. The summoning sensation had been her soul calling for its missing half.

This child was Kane's ancestor.

A hand tugged Toria's arm, and she dismissed the magesight when Lyra called her name, her delight replaced with frantic worry. "Why did you make that sound? What did you see?"

"No, it's okay." Toria pressed her palms to her face in an attempt to clear the threatened tears. "He's perfect. Your son—"

"What the fuck is she doing here?"

Toria lurched away from Lyra's bed. Kojo filled the doorway, the glower on his face darkening the room. She could have returned Kojo's rudeness in kind, but Lyra didn't deserve that. "I came to congratulate you both."

Kojo stalked across the room, claiming the position nearest to the bed and forcing Toria out of his way. "How did you even know she'd given birth?" Suspicion dripped from his words.

Lyra broke in before Toria had to figure out an answer. "She's a mage, Kojo. They know things like this about their friends." The pleading tone in her voice could be heard through the exhaustion. "Toria says our child will be okay. Isn't that wonderful?"

Under the weight of Kojo's glare, Toria nodded her head in a short, jerky burst. "It's true. Perfect health." Now that she'd seen the baby, the power settled within her, a gentle, contented purr. "I should, ah, get to work. Leave you two to get to know your son."

"That won't be necessary." Kojo flicked one hand. "You were hired to watch out for Lyra. Now that she will not be working, your services are no longer needed."

Lyra gaped at him. "Kojo—" The baby squirmed in her grip, distracting her as she settled him against her other breast.

Toria didn't want to square off against Kojo above Lyra and her newborn. "I understand." She ignored Lyra's look of devastation behind Kojo.

He stepped forward, crowding Toria toward the door. "I'm sure the most recent payment covered the balance of your work." His tone brooked no argument.

144

Despite her wish not to cause trouble, sarcasm colored her words. "Yes, sir." Toria locked eyes with Lyra. "You know how to reach me if you need me."

Kojo slid between them before Lyra responded. "She needs to rest, now." He turned his back on Toria.

Toria studied the scene for a final second before slipping through the hospital halls toward the exit. Rather than the image of a loving family, the way Kojo stood over Lyra and his son reminded Toria more of a man inspecting acquired treasures. It left her with a cold lump in the pit of her stomach.

Toria wandered the neighborhood around the hospital, trying to settle her anger and fear. Anger at Kojo for separating her from one of her few friends in this crazy world. Fear for Lyra and her son. The city's destruction was soon, and Toria had no idea how to save them.

The original half-formed plan had been to scoop up Lyra, Hugh, and Liam the day before the attack and stick them on a train leaving the city.

But now Victory and Jarimis were set on finding a way to return them to the future, and she had no idea how to rescue her friends if she wasn't still here.

It was an impossible choice—go home to the life she'd lost or save her friends. This was Kane's department.

And where did that leave Kane? If she made it home, but Lyra and her son died in Nacostina, would she even have a Kane to come home to? His ancestor's existence proved the mystery of how Toria was alive. The magic of the other half of her bond was out there in the world, sustaining her through the tiny link she'd found within her. If the baby died here, what was the point of going home to a life without Kane, where her death was certain?

The evening chill penetrated her coat to the point where she could no longer ignore it. She hailed a passing taxi, meaning to return to the bed and breakfast, but found herself giving the driver Liam's address instead.

In front of his building, Toria paid the driver and wondered what she was thinking. As much as she wanted to wrap herself in the arms of the man she loved—and she could no longer avoid the fact that she had fallen hopelessly, ridiculously in love with Liam—she was a mess. She was going to take one look at him and spill everything.

Maybe that wasn't such a terrible idea. The world was ending anyway. She might as well hurry along her part of it.

She climbed the steps to Liam's apartment and knocked on the door.

And knocked again, when no answer came.

Of all the damned luck. He wasn't even home—

The deadbolt slid, and the door swung open. Liam stood before her, bundled in a dressing gown with bare feet. Wet hair dripped onto his shoulders. "Toria? What are you doing here?"

"Can I come in?"

Liam hesitated, and Toria knew her wind-straggled hair and coat wrapped around anachronistic clothing made a sight. "I'm not sure that's a good idea."

Toria didn't have time for his chivalry. "I'm coming in anyway."

He didn't resist when she shouldered her way past him. She made it a few feet into the apartment, then stopped to inspect the unfamiliar surroundings. Despite its size, the sitting room seemed cozy instead of cramped, and every item in the room screamed "Liam" and "home" and "safe," from the wall of shelves crammed with books and curios to the mismatched furniture chosen for comfort over style.

In another few steps, she tossed her coat over an armchair and collapsed onto the sofa, burying her face in her hands. Liam's feet shuffled on the hardwood floor as he closed and locked the door. She expected him to return to his room to dress, but he surprised her. The sofa dipped with his weight when he settled next to her and snaked an arm around her shoulders.

Toria leaned against him and forced her breath into evenness. This wasn't like her regular panic attacks. This was real anxiety about real problems and real events. "I don't know what to do anymore. I thought I had a plan. I thought I knew what I was doing here." She tried to keep calm, but the words ran away, coming faster and faster. "But Victory showed up, and dragged Jarimis into everything, and I don't know how to save Lyra's baby, who is so important, you have no idea—"

Liam clasped Toria's cheeks and made her meet his eyes, hooded with concern. "Toria. Stop. Breathe." He waited for a full inhale and exhale. "Start over. Who is Victory? And what does Jarimis have to do with this? I didn't think you wanted anything to do with him."

She forced another breath before speaking again. "I didn't. It's complicated."

Liam released Toria's face. "Am I going to need tea for this?"

"If I don't get this all out now, I'm not sure I'll ever be able to." Toria snagged Liam's hand and entwined their fingers. If he reacted in anger or shock to this confession, it might be the last time she held his hand.

Liam paused, searching her face. "Go ahead."

"I've been lying to you." As expected, he tried to jerk his hand away. She didn't let go. "Let me finish, please. There was one big lie, right from the beginning, because I didn't know what else to do. Everything else built on it."

A muscle jumped in Liam's clenched jaw. But he left his hand.

"I'm not from the past. I'm from the future."

Liam opened his mouth. Shut it again. Studied Toria's face, as if expecting her to confess a joke. Finally, "I'm listening."

"I don't know how or why, but the artifact in the museum didn't pluck me from the past to bring me here. I was in Nacostina, in the future. Almost a hundred years." A jolt twinged through her back, and Toria forced herself to relax tightened shoulder muscles. "Do you understand? I don't know what happened, but I couldn't risk the future. I couldn't risk changing the world I left, so I went along with it when you explained I was from the past. It seemed easier."

They stared at each other in silence.

Liam broke first. "I'm hurt you lied to me, but as a scientist and historian, I understand why." He released her hand, but to brush damp hair off his forehead, not from anger or aversion. "And you didn't know me. You had no reason to trust me."

"But I trust you now. And things are happening, and I couldn't keep this up any longer." Toria's voice cracked, but Liam wasn't furious. He wasn't kicking her out of his apartment. She still had a chance to save him.

"Start from the beginning. What does Jarimis have to do with this?"

That startled a laugh from Toria, though it was half gasp. "That's not the beginning. It's not even close." With halting sentences, she did her best. Why she shied away from Jarimis because of his link to her past. How Victory stumbled back in time, on Toria's heels and months apart, and dragged her progeny into the mix. "Between the two of them, they convinced me maybe we could get home. I was going to help Jarimis research the meteor, but Rubin blocked us from the archives."

Liam's expression darkened. "Why?" As Toria had spoken, she'd sat cross-legged on Liam's sofa, facing him as he attempted to maintain dignity in his dressing gown. But over the course of her tale, he'd relaxed into her words, leaning forward in interest.

"We have no idea. He banned us tonight."

"But…." Liam's brow furled in concern. "Not that I hated the surprise, but what brought you to my doorstep now?"

"Lyra had her baby."

Liam sat straighter, joy sparkling in the way of elves speaking of children the world over. "That's fantastic news! How are they?"

"They're fine… for now." She knew she failed at keeping the pain from her voice.

"There's still something you're not telling me."

In silence, Toria worried at her bottom lip with her teeth.

"About Lyra and the baby?" When she didn't respond, Liam guessed again. "About me?"

Toria spread her hands in helplessness.

"About the city?"

The words burst forth in a ragged whisper. "About the entire damned world." This was already too much, but Toria could no longer face this without him.

He hadn't rejected her earlier, and he surprised her once more, cupping her cheek and pressing a chaste kiss to her lips. "But there was a world for you to leave and come to me, so it can't be all bad."

She had no way to explain that the world she'd left was the best she knew, that this polluted city with its etiquette and hierarchy and unfortunate underclothing was the place she wanted to leave. Even if it meant leaving him.

This time, the pain within her chest was all internal and tears welled up.

"No, stop that." Liam brushed the moisture away with the pad of his thumb. "Everything will work out, you'll see." This time, the kiss between them was deeper.

Toria could have drowned in his taste as she snaked her arms around Liam's neck and pulled him closer, combing her fingers into his hair. She groaned when he pulled away, even as she tried to follow his lips with her own.

"This isn't a good idea." Liam's voice was ragged.

She opened her eyes to find his dressing robe had slipped off one shoulder, exposing smooth, bare skin. More of Liam than she'd ever seen, always dressed in his impeccable shirts and tailored slacks. Her mouth dried at the uninterrupted line of his neck. "No, this is a brilliant idea." Toria licked her lips and pushed herself to her knees.

"Toria—"

She pressed a finger to his mouth. "No. Not this time." In one smooth motion, she straddled his lap and braced her hands on the top of the couch. The too-thin clothing layers between them proved Liam's interest in the proceedings, and he moaned as she ground herself against him.

His palm slid under her sweater, and the warmth of his fingers splayed against her bare skin melted her to the core. Liam's other hand clutched her neck and drew her in for another kiss. His mouth opened at the twist of her hips. She slipped her tongue against his and lost herself in the heated spice of his taste.

She shoved the dressing gown farther off his shoulder, passing her hand over his skin. It burned under her fingers, and Toria brushed the edge of her thumbnail over his exposed nipple.

Gasping into her mouth, Liam arched his back and pressed his erection against her. With a full-body shudder, he grasped her shoulders. She mewled in disappointment when he broke off the kiss, but she stilled at his beseeching look. "I've fought against this for so long. It's just not the way things are done."

Toria shook her head hard, hair whipping across her face. "I don't care how things are done. You can't treat me like glass."

"But this—"

"No, Liam." Her fierceness cut him off, as she pressed both palms against his chest. "I'm not from the past. I'm not some meek human woman from *this* past, that you have to treat with chivalry and deference. I'm a mercenary, and a warrior-mage, and I can damned well promise you I'm not some blushing virgin." The words came in a rush, and she lifted her hands, sagging away from him.

This was where he would push her away. Because maybe he did want a proper relationship for this day and age, and all she'd done was dump more complications in his lap.

Instead, he released her shoulders, tucking his hands against her bare waist. His touch made her shiver from something other than the apartment's temperature. "That's not it at all." His voice had dropped half an octave. "I never wanted to hurt you."

In a move she later blamed on mixed stubbornness and arousal, Toria pressed her hand to Liam's chest and pulled forth a tiny bit of power. "Trust me. I will never let you hurt me." This time, when she brushed Liam's skin, electricity rippled between them. His back arched, fingers digging into her skin as he rode the crest of pleasure.

Liam tugged the sweater over her head, tossing it to his living room floor. She hadn't bothered with the hated brassiere under such a bulky top, and Liam cupped her exposed breasts.

He didn't resort to dirty magical tricks, instead leaning forward to pull one nipple into his mouth. She gasped under the onslaught of liquid warmth, and she tangled her fingers through his hair in silent encouragement.

This time, worry didn't surge through her when Liam pulled away. His hands, fingers calloused by pens, slid to her back and dragged blunted fingernails down the length of her spine. "We're not doing this here."

"Never been a fan of couch sex, myself." Toria darted her tongue across his swollen lips.

Elven strength relied as much on supernatural ability as on muscle bulk, so Toria was prepared when Liam slid his hands under her rear, teasing her with an unnecessary squeeze. She looped her arms around his neck when he stood, carrying her with him. His dressing gown, belt loosened from their movements, flowed open as he rose. Toria pressed herself to his bare chest as he secured her in his grip, and with their combined heat, she was the warmest she'd been in months.

Liam pressed his forehead to hers, his whisper sharing breath with her while she held him close. "You still sure about this?"

"Sure as I've ever been in my life, love." And if this was the rest of her life, in the past with him, she'd take it.

Sunlight glared into Toria's closed eyelids as a single finger traced patterns on the skin of her bare back. She burrowed her face into the pillow clutched to her chest and groaned. "Too early."

Liam's warm chuckle chased away the last vestiges of sleep. His gentle caress continued. "You know, if you hadn't told me the truth of where you come from last night, I'd have figured it out this morning."

Toria forced her eyes open and surveyed the bedroom she'd been too preoccupied to study the night before. "How so?" It was as neat as the parlor, if less cluttered with books and other historical detritus. Instead, colorful tapestries softened the walls, surrounding the bed that dominated the space. The bed they had put to effective use.

"This tattoo is more detailed than any I've seen." Liam traced the crossed swords between her shoulder blades. "Granny Tia thought it was created magically because of the detail, but it's not, is it?"

Toria rolled to face Liam, who lay with his head propped on an elbow. Sleep had mussed his hair, and she traced a pattern of her own across his bare chest. "Tattoo gun. No magic involved. That's a dying art, later. I've only ever met one person with magical ink, and I wasn't in a position to learn from him at the time."

Liam shivered under her touch and grasped her hand. "Stop that, minx. Is that a story I can ask about?" He hauled Toria against his chest, and she draped herself over him, nestling into his warm embrace.

She could stay in this bed, in his arms, all day. "Not the full story. The mage in question was on the opposite side." Poised to activate what remained of a nuclear warhead and destroy Limani. A dirty variant of the same weapon that would soon reduce Nacostina to rubble and ashes. Toria nuzzled her face into the crook of Liam's neck and tried to use his comforting scent to chase away the memories of the Roman mage. Kane shooting him in the stomach. Slicing the tattooed skin from his leg to break his connection with the weapon.

"Hey, it's fine. Forget I asked." Liam held her close with one arm and combed his fingers through her tangled hair. "We should get up, though. If I'm hungry, I know you're hungry. And some of us have offices to get to."

Toria licked a stripe up Liam's neck in response. A certain part of his anatomy stirred in interest between her legs, but Liam pecked a kiss to the top of her head and shuffled out from underneath of her before she could make a dirty crack about what to have for breakfast. He tucked his winter-weight quilt over her shoulders and pressed another lingering kiss to her lips. She dozed to the homey sounds of Liam's shower.

And jolted awake again when Liam ripped away the blankets with a blast of cool air. "Wake up, sleepy." Toria stretched under Liam's appreciative gaze. He'd gathered her scattered clothing from the parlor and offered a knit cap when finger-combing her hair did nothing to tame it.

She should have taken a separate cab home, but instead accompanied Liam to work, cuddled to his side on the bench seat while he drove as if any space between them was too much. They snuck into the museum through a side entrance, and once in Liam's office, she put on the electric kettle while Liam ducked out to the café for pastries.

Toria lounged in a guest chair, hiking boots propped on the edge of his desk as a mug of spiced tea warmed her hands, when Liam's footsteps made their way down the hall. He'd pushed open his office door when Rubin called his name.

Liam and Toria stared at each other for a heartbeat. Toria waved for him to turn around and meet his boss. He dropped the pastry bag on the credenza inside his office door and stepped into the hallway to meet Rubin, leaving the door ajar behind him. Toria strained to eavesdrop.

"Good morning, sir. I thought I wouldn't see you until our meeting about the Midlands exhibit later."

"Gracious, man, don't bring up that nightmare before I have to deal with it. I was wondering if you'd seen this morning's paper?"

"Can't say that I have. Overslept this morning and didn't have a chance to purchase my usual copy on the way in." They'd made it out Liam's front door with seconds to spare, after he kept placing distracting kisses on Toria's bare skin while she dressed.

"It appears there are reports of warships entering the harbor in Wan City. I need you to contact our dig sites in northern Pacifica today and make sure they are up to date on their permits. Make sure they have adequate security as well."

"Yes, sir."

"These humans, eh? Gone are the days when we never had to worry about such power."

"I remember, sir."

Toria placed her empty mug on Liam's desk before it could drop from nerveless fingers.

"Well, I suppose the dragons pull the strings in Qin lands, but considering fewer dragons exist than our own lupine nobility, many more humans occupy positions of power in their government."

"I imagine so, sir."

Toria leaned a few inches to the right, catching Liam's profile, his face in neutral, through the cracked office door. His boneless relaxation in bed had vanished, replaced by a stiff spine. It seemed Rubin's anti-human bias had deep roots, and it was comforting to know the man she loved did not share his boss' opinions.

"Speaking of humans, Liam. I wanted you to know I saw our displaced ward here last night and requested she leave. There's no reason for her to be hanging about the place, distracting employees from their work."

Even Toria heard the unspoken message loud and clear, though she found it interesting when Rubin didn't also inform Liam he'd barred Jarimis from the premises as well.

"Ah, yes, sir. Should I reach out to Hugh Ainsworth and see whether he needs anything else for her care?"

"I don't think it will be necessary for you to have further contact with them. Hugh knows how to contact us in the event of—well, you know what to expect as well as I do."

Liam rolled his shoulders. "Do you think it will happen soon this time?"

"One can never tell with these things. Better not to dwell. I'm sure you have other work to do this morning, so I won't keep you any longer. See you at the meeting later."

"Have a good morning, sir." Liam waited until Rubin's footsteps retreated before slipping into his office. He shut the door and leaned against it, tipping his head.

Toria drummed nervous fingers on her thigh. "I know he's your boss or mentor or whatever, but I don't like the man."

Liam raised his head and grabbed the abandoned bag of pastries. He settled into the second guest chair, and Toria pushed his cup of lukewarm tea to him. He drained it without his usual wince of distaste when his tea did not live up to his exacting standards. "He has been my mentor for many years, but I am not unaware of his faults. I'm sorry you had to hear that prejudice from him."

Once again, Rubin's messy death flashed in Toria's mind. "Not your fault, and it's not the worst thing I've ever heard. Prejudice is still alive and well where I'm from." In a weird way, it was almost a relief to know the Last War wasn't the sole prompt of the world spell that caused so many problems in the future Toria had left. Though it probably hadn't helped.

"That's a shame." Liam contemplated the muffin in his hand as if it held the secrets of the universe. "One likes to think the world to come will be a better place than the one we leave behind."

"It's not better or worse. Just different."

Liam placed his breakfast on his desk, heedless of scattered crumbs, and braced his elbows on his knees. This could have been six months ago, when he'd first brought a bewildered Toria to his office after her surprise appearance in his museum. But this was now, and his expression held a different sort of warmth. "I want to help you go back to that world."

As if he were a powerful vampire, Toria couldn't match the burning emotions in his gaze. "A girl might think you're trying to get rid of her."

Liam reached for her hand. "You know that's not what I meant at all. You think I want to lose you when I've only just found you?"

Toria gathered strength from his touch. "I know. And trust me, I hate what feels like an impossible choice."

"Maybe it's not so impossible."

"I'm not sure what you mean."

Liam pushed a small notebook and pen from the corner of his desk to Toria. "Tell me where to find you in your own time. I'll seal it in an envelope and follow whatever directions you need to feel safe about the timeline."

"This is insane." But even as she spoke, Toria flipped open the notebook. "Why would you wait for me?"

"It's not waiting. It's taking the long way around." Liam skimmed his fingertips along Toria's jawline. "Besides, I'd rather wait a thousand years than watch you die in five."

"That shouldn't sound romantic, you know." Toria started writing without waiting for his response.

"I already know you're not that type of girl." Liam swallowed the last of his muffin and rose from his seat. "You write. I'll find an envelope."

153

"Find, like, ten envelopes. This is going to get complicated."

As he puttered around his office, Toria filled page after page with her scrawl. She ripped them out in multiple piles, slipping them in separate envelopes and labeling each with a year. Here is when Liam should avoid areas of conflict in the upcoming war. Here is when it would be safe to return to the New Continent. And above all else, he should stay away from Rubin. She left further details unwritten, hoping Liam would avoid being drawn into the man's madness regarding the world spell.

Either Liam wouldn't let his curiosity get the better of him, and she'd find him in Limani once she got home. Or she'd never make it back, and they'd live in this world together.

She refused to consider the third option. That she might make it home to learn Liam didn't survive the Last War.

She was a scientist, and this rebelled against everything she thought safe. But there had to be a line between pragmatism and living, and she supposed she'd found it.

Leaving Liam at work with his stack of sealed envelopes, the first labeled for him to open twenty-four hours before the city's final day, Toria ducked out the staff entrance and caught a cab to the bed and breakfast. After a shower and change of clothes, she spent the rest of the day working on another guest room with Hugh.

Her mother woke with the sunset. Hugh retreated to his pub for the evening, giving the women privacy. Toria appreciated it. The time was long past for a rational heart-to-heart with her mother, instead of the ricochet of emotions they'd experienced since Victory tumbled into this world.

They settled in the front parlor, where Toria built a fire before joining Victory on the couch. "I'm sorry for rushing out last night."

"I was just relieved to find you here when I woke up." Victory leaned to the side until her shoulder pressed against Toria's.

Sitting close, with their feet propped on the coffee table, it could have been any number of moments from Toria's childhood. But this time, the stakes were much higher. "My friend had her baby, and his magic drew me to him. He's Kane's ancestor."

Victory cursed, low-voiced and in a language Toria didn't recognize. "I won't ask how you know or whether you're sure. But this is a wrinkle we don't need."

"Trust me, I know. But the good news is that Liam is on our side. He'll help Jarimis and I complete any research we need to find a way home."

"I gather he knows more now than he did yesterday?"

154

"Not everything. But enough. Including the truth about where we're from." Toria let her head drop onto Victory's shoulder. "I think I love him, Mama."

"Sweetheart, I could tell from the first night I found you here that you loved him. Otherwise you wouldn't hurt so much."

"This all sucks."

"I know."

"And I think I'm really messed up."

"I think I knew that as well."

"I've been having panic attacks. Where I can't breathe, and the world crushes me in its grip." Even vocalizing it was a pale reflection of the true experience. Liam had seen her through some of the worst of it, but how would expressing such weakness change Victory's opinion of her? Her mother was centuries old and didn't know the meaning of helpless.

"Yeah. Been there, too." Victory rested her cheek atop Toria's head. "It sucks."

"You're joking."

"Of course not. I've been terrified for my life more times than I can count. You know by now it's an occupational hazard. But I do remember every time I've felt despair. Which is what you've been experiencing, and I don't envy it." Victory rubbed her thumb on the back of Toria's hand. "I have no idea what I'd have done if I were the one to be sent here first. You kept your head, where I'd have mucked things up beyond repair by now."

"You did give a guard a minor concussion and cause a security breach."

Victory waved away the debate before it could start

Toria snatched her hand. "Mom, you're shaking." She held tight when Victory tried to pull away.

"I'm fine."

"No, you're cold, too. I mean, more cold than usual." Toria peered into Victory's face. "When was the last time you ate?" Even by the flickering firelight, Victory's stark pallor struck her.

"When I stopped that mugger the other night. I told you that I'm fine."

"Don't be dumb." Toria stood up, anxious to move, to help. "Where's Jarimis tonight? Can he help?"

"His supply in Nacostina is complicated. I already asked, and there's nothing he can do."

"This is something we can fix, at least." Toria crouched by the fireplace and lifted her hands. She built a miniature shield around the logs and flames and suppressed the air within. After a short *whoomph*, the room plunged into darkness. But when she rose, Victory hadn't moved from the couch. "What are you waiting for?"

"What are you talking about?"

"You can feed from me."

"You don't know what you're offering."

"I do. Ran into a spot of trouble with Grandpa last year when he got a sword to the gut in the Grand Strand." Even her mother had to acknowledge the easier option. She could subsist on small amounts of blood, enhanced by Toria's innate magic, for a few weeks if necessary, though it wouldn't be enjoyable for either of them as a long-term solution.

"Asaron never told me."

"He didn't want you to know. Kane still has nightmares from Limani's invasion."

"And you?"

Toria knew that if she gave any indication of discomfort, Victory would call off this mad scheme. "Why would I ever regret saving his life?" She forced her body language relaxed, proving this topic held no fear for her. "You can't raise a kid around vampires and expect said kid to be squeamish about vampirism."

"Fair enough. But you'll forgive your mother if she needs time to adjust to the idea."

"You've cared for me my entire life. The least I can do is help carry the weight now that I'm grown."

Victory stood, and embraced Toria. "Thank you."

"You're welcome, Mama."

With the decision made, Toria followed Victory to the guest bedroom. Lines of tension stiffened her mother's shoulders. They settled cross-legged on the bed, facing each other. Even in the low light of a single lamp, it was hard to miss the more minute signs of hunger now that she paid attention. The stiffness in Victory's limbs as she moved, as if her body lacked hydraulic fluid for her joints. Bloodless lips disappeared into the surrounding pale skin.

It was a measure of Victory's age, experience, or power—perhaps all three—that she'd kept this hidden. She clenched her jaw at her mother's freezing fingers. If she showed fear, Victory wouldn't let her help, and they'd be worse off than before.

"Last chance to back out." Victory's voice crested at a whisper.

Her words broke through any lingering hesitation Toria might have. "You know phrasing this as a challenge increases my stubbornness, right?" She pulled her non-dominant hand out of Victory's cool grip and presented the inside of her wrist. "Eat, already."

Victory froze, a delicate statue before Toria that might shatter if not for the steel core within. She touched the pulse-point at Toria's wrist. If Toria's heartbeat echoed through her ears, it must thunder in her mother's.

She cradled Toria's wrist to her mouth, and Toria braced for the initial bite of pain. Asaron had been almost too-far gone when she'd sacrificed herself for him, but Kane's presence and oversight had saved both of them in the end. Instead, Victory pressed a chaste kiss to her skin.

When Victory raised her eyes, Toria fell into the cool blue pools of her irises. For the first time in her life, the force of vampiric attention didn't shunt her away. Victory whispered a single word that Toria didn't hear over the rushing blood in her ears. Unable to blink, unable to move, she surrendered to the embrace of her mother's mind.

Toria woke in her own bed, late the next morning according to the shadows cast on the opposite wall. Her limbs felt loose and heavy, and various joints popped as she stretched under the covers in the cool room. Unfamiliar pressure bound her left wrist, which sported a slim bandage when she raised it to her face. She slipped a finger under the cloth to find two tiny pinpricks, already scabbed over. Victory must have carried her here once she finished feeding.

As if on cue, her stomach rumbled. Hugh better have some bacon stashed away.

The man himself read the paper at the kitchen table when she stumbled downstairs after dressing. He wished her a good morning, but otherwise left Toria to her own devices as she prepared an enormous breakfast.

Once she settled her overflowing plate across from Hugh, with both a steaming mug of coffee for herself and a refill for Hugh, she tucked into the food. Hugh allowed her to make it halfway through her breakfast before breaking in with an apparent non-sequitur.

"So, does Liam still keep that atrocious chest of drawers in his bedroom?"

Toria laughed around her scrambled eggs. "Where the hell did he get that thing? The painted wood clashes with everything else in his apartment." When Hugh smirked, Toria clapped a hand over her mouth.

"No, no." Hugh turned the next page in his paper. "Keep eating. I hope to get hours of entertainment out of this revelation."

Toria snapped off a bite of bacon in his general direction. "You're not funny."

"I'm hilarious." Hugh's deadpan caused her to crack up. "Things are…going well in that department?"

"You don't disapprove?"

"My mother is rolling over in her grave at me letting an unmarried woman in my charge spend the night with a man. But I have the feeling such an occasion is not noteworthy in your life."

"That's true," Toria said. "But I apologize if I made you concerned when I didn't come home."

"There's no one I trust more to take care of herself, so I'm not sure concerned is the best word."

"Well, I appreciate that this conversation could have been way more awkward." Toria shredded the other piece of bacon on her plate, appetite beaten into submission. "Though there is another conversation I've been delaying, and now is as good a time as any."

As if sensing the gravity in her words, Hugh pushed away his newspaper to give Toria his full attention. "What can I help you with, my dear?"

How to phrase this in such a way that Hugh would do what was safest over what he felt best? "It's more something I can help you with. You know that Victory and I have been working on a way to get home?"

"As much as I'll miss having you in my life," Hugh said, "I know this isn't your home."

"I guess this is my turn to return the favor for everything you've done for me. I hope you can understand why I can't give you all the details, but it's a good idea if you leave Nacostina for the winter."

Though his brow furrowed, Hugh gave no other indication of surprise. "I'm guessing this recommendation is based on knowledge you have of future events?"

"Something like that." Toria crossed mental fingers that Hugh wouldn't pry in a way she couldn't answer.

"Natural disaster? Or manmade shenanigans? It must be something citywide, because I know I'm not famous enough to warrant a biography." Hugh must have seen her growing panic. "You know what? Never mind. Your word is good enough for me."

"Thank you." She could float away, this conversation lifting a final weight from her shoulders. "I just… couldn't forgive myself if something avoidable happened to you."

"I know the feeling." Hugh surveyed his kitchen and gnawed at his lower lip. "How much time do I have, exactly? Is this a 'throw everything in the car and we leave tonight' scenario? Or do I have time to close up the house?"

Toria provided the answer with no regret. "A little over a week. Pack what you value, just in case, but there's time to clean the perishables out of the kitchen." Though nothing left would be saved, she had no desire to place such burden of knowledge on her friend. Speaking of friends: "You can tell your poker buddies, too. But I'm trusting your discretion."

"Right. Wouldn't want to cause a panic." Hugh swigged the last of his coffee as he rose from the table. He paused on his way to the sink. "If you and Victory haven't managed to get home before the week is up, you'll come with me?"

Another answer she knew with certainty. "I wouldn't have it any other way."

"Good."

She spent the rest of the day helping Hugh plan his evacuation, discussing what quick and final projects they could finish up, how much he could pack in his old-but-serviceable car, and what his destination should be. She talked him out of holing up in a mountain cabin out west, throwing Victory under the bus by reminding him they needed to be in a populous area to provide for her sustenance, and he settled on a small beach town up the northern coast. Toria wasn't familiar with every detail of the Last War, but she hoped it would be out of the way enough that he'd be safe in the coming years.

Once the working day neared its end, she changed out of her grubby clothes and hopped the trolley toward the museum. She found Liam's parked car and settled against it, huddled in her coat. At least she wore trousers tonight.

Toria didn't have long to wait, and soon spotted Liam's arm raised in greeting. She wrapped herself in his warm embrace, returning his kiss with abandon.

They broke apart when a passing woman coughed in displeasure, giggling into each other's space, foreheads tilted together. Liam leaned away first, touching his gloved fingers to Toria's chin. "You look pale. Are you feeling alright?"

Despite an afternoon snack, Toria knew she still suffered the aftereffects of blood loss. Right now, she craved a steak the size of her head. "Nothing a good meal won't fix. Dinner?"

"It would be my pleasure." Liam kissed her once more before unlocking his car and helping her into the passenger seat.

The silence during the drive was companionable, not awkward, and soon Liam parked near one of their favorite restaurants. As he escorted her into the dining room and accepted her coat, a flutter of shock passed through her. When had she ever felt so comfortable with another person other than Kane? Years ago, perhaps, when Syri was still in her life.

She shook herself out of her reverie when Liam placed their drink orders. "Sorry. I'm back."

"Wherever you were, it was a million miles away." Liam arranged his napkin on his lap. "What had you so distracted?"

"Memories. Good ones." She rushed to reassure him when his gaze sharpened in concern. "Realizing that these are going to be good memories, too."

"I'm glad." Liam passed over the second menu, and their discussion turned to more mundane topics as they decided on dinner and placed orders.

After Toria decimated most of her medium-rare steak, she felt confident enough to broach an uncomfortable subject for the second time that day. Might as well give it the same go as with Hugh. "In about a week or so, Hugh is going to leave town. You should do the same."

Liam's fork skidded on his plate. "I see. Is this related to the notes you wrote for me?"

"Very much."

They ate in silence while Liam contemplated the information. Unlike Hugh, a retiree who had no real ties to the city other than his handful of friends, Liam had a career to keep him here. With his dedication to the museum, this was a lot to ask.

Liam cleared his plate and pushed it away as Toria continued to work on her steak. "Rubin approached me again today, about you."

Toria froze, fork lifted halfway to her mouth. She set her silverware down without taking the bite and folded her hands on her lap. "And?"

"Apparently, he's been doing some digging. No record exists of a resident with your name in Limani within the past two centuries." With hands steady as his voice, Liam refilled their wine glasses from the bottle on the table.

That was both more and less of a shock than Toria expected. "Well, you know the reason already. Besides, the records kept after Limani's independence were crap. How did you play it off?"

"I'm not sure I did, honestly. Rubin is now questioning your arrival here, based on your confirmed magical abilities. The term 'con artist' was suggested."

Toria ignored her wineglass, tempting as the alcohol was. "You know that's not true. You saw me with your magic. How could I fake that?"

"Rubin believes I have been 'emotionally compromised,' and that my judgement is suspect."

"Are you?" They stared at each other over the table, and the restaurant receded in Toria's awareness.

"Head over heels." Liam sipped his wine, and the tension between them eased. "You should come talk to him."

She jerked in her seat. "No."

"It might get you and Jarimis access to the archives again. Help you get home, as much as I dread it." Liam frowned, bracing his elbows on the table. "Rubin is not the easiest man to get along with, but this is your way back in."

A wave of dizziness passed over Toria, and for a moment she was in the Catacombs below Parisii, fighting for her life in a torrent of water and knives. "It's complicated. I'd rather not discuss it here." She'd rather not discuss it at all.

"Alright. Finish your wine while I settle the check." Liam flagged down their waiter, and Toria sipped the red liquid, bold on her tongue after the sweetness of her steak.

Once in the car, he raised an eyebrow at her. "Where to, your ladyship?"

She tucked her hands into her coat sleeves, warming them with her own body heat. "Is your place an option, finally?"

Liam laughed, shifting the vehicle into gear and pulling into evening traffic. "I believe it is customary to offer coffee after a date."

They bantered about tea and coffee and euphemism on the drive to Liam's apartment. Within moments of entering the front door, Liam pinned Toria against the wall to claim her mouth with his.

Between kisses, Toria pulled away long enough for one question. "Even if I don't talk to Rubin, can you help me and Jarimis get into the archives tomorrow night?" She hoped she hadn't ruined the mood.

Instead, Liam slipped his fingers through Toria's hair and tilted her head to the side. His lips met her neck, and a gentle bite sent shivers through her body. "I said I'd do anything to help, love."

When he returned his attention to her skin, Toria pulled at the shirt tucked into his suit pants. Relief washed through her, mingled with intense arousal, and conversation halted when their lips crashed together once again.

They consumed no after-dinner drinks—coffee, tea, or otherwise—as they became distracted with the removal of clothing and skin-on-skin contact. Finally, Toria tugged Liam toward the bedroom.

The topic of Rubin never resumed, and later, Toria kissed a slumbering Liam on the forehead and slipped out of his apartment.

Victory rendezvoused with Jarimis at a café near Hugh's house. He settled into a seat opposite and scanned Victory with frank appraisal. "You're looking well."

Victory pushed the pot of tea across the table. "I somehow managed to raise an amazing daughter."

"This does not shock me in the slightest." Jarimis poured himself a cup, following it with a shot of cream. "Has said daughter had any luck using her connections for access to the museum?"

"She was gone when I woke, so I was unable to confirm." Victory nudged the bowl of sugar toward Jarimis, who scoffed at it. "Worst-case scenario, we break into the museum and steal the artifact."

Jarimis twitched as a pained expression crossed his face. "Such a suggestion borders on blasphemy."

"I don't remember you—" Victory snapped her jaw shut with a click of teeth, but the damage was done. She'd gotten too comfortable.

He sipped his tea. "As I suspected."

"I'm not sure I know what you're alluding to."

"Your discomfort around me. The fact that Toria has made it clear she has never met me, when I would hope to be a presence in your adopted daughter's life." Jarimis set down his teacup. "I'm dead in your future."

They stared at each other, a frozen tableau, until a passing patron jostled Jarimis and he averted his eyes. Victory clutched the table edge with clawed fingers. "You know I can't tell you either way." The words rasped in her throat, through the pain she faced in losing him again.

"And you know I'm not an idiot."

His aggrieved look forced a jolt of laughter through her, and even Jarimis' lips twitched into a half-smile. "No. Never that." Victory spread her hands in helplessness. "I can't tell you what happens because I don't even know." One day he'd been in Limani, and the next, gone. Leaving behind Victory, Mikelos, and his daywalker Allesandra. Despite years of searching, Allesandra had grown old and died without ever knowing his fate.

"Fair enough." Jarimis gave a sharp dip of his chin, marking the conversation closed. "So, the first goal is to return you and Toria to your time, no matter what obstacles we must overcome to access the artifact. What is our backup objective?"

"We leave Nacostina within the week." She raised her hand again when Jarimis opened his mouth to object. "Another example of something for which I can provide no context."

Jarimis prepared a second cup of tea with clipped movements, which Victory knew covered his need to choose his next words with care. Once finished, he did not drink. "I'm not sure I like this dichotomy between us, when I am so used to your trust."

His words punched Victory in the gut. "It's not a matter of trust."

"Yes. You must preserve the timeline to avoid contaminating your own future." Jarimis twisted his teacup in its saucer. "However, there is no way to determine whether the Jarimis of your past did not, in fact, receive information about his future from you. Perhaps that is the way he survives what is to come." He lowered his voice before continuing. "I was in contact with your predecessor before she left the city. I am well aware that war is on the horizon."

"You're putting me in an uncomfortable position, Zvi." Victory leaned forward and placed her hand over his on his teacup. "You know I would never do anything to put you in danger."

"Mother, my short-lived mercenary career was one long string of you putting me in danger." Jarimis' words broke the tension between them.

A familiar heartbeat pattern slipped into the background noise. Victory turned in her seat as Toria wound her way through the café and approached them. She snagged a chair from an empty table and sank into it, stealing Victory's teacup. Though her clothing was presentable, Toria's scent mingled with elven pheromones.

It was on the tip of her tongue to tease her daughter about her evening, but she resisted in Jarimis' presence. In another life, they might have been family enough for her to get away with it.

Once Toria set down the teacup, the tea and cozy café had returned the redness of warmth to her cheeks. "Liam will let us into the museum tomorrow night."

Jarimis clapped his hands together. "Excellent news."

"And I told him he had to leave Nacostina soon. He wasn't thrilled, but I'd already laid the framework. One more person to deal with tomorrow." Toria braced her elbow on the table, propping her head up. "How the hell am I going to convince a woman with a newborn to leave her home?"

Victory and Jarimis exchanged helpless expressions. Jarimis spoke first, patting Toria on the shoulder. "I'm sure your friendship with her will overcome such obstacles."

"Cross your fingers anyway." Toria straightened in her seat, stretching her arms over her head until something in her back popped. "So. Research. Museum tomorrow."

"Quite." Jarimis dug a packet of papers from the bag slung over his chair and spread them across the table. "We should organize our plan of attack tonight, to maximize our time in the archives tomorrow."

Victory waved for the waitress. Her children would need more tea.

When the café kicked Toria and the two vampires out at closing, they moved next door to the pub. Though her mother soon abandoned them in favor of beer with Hugh and his friends, Toria and Jarimis remained intent on their work.

After their abrupt dismissal from the museum, Jarimis spent his time at the city library. While he didn't have access to research about the museum's holdings, he had given himself a crash course on the current published research regarding meteors and meteorites.

Toria, limiting herself to nursing a single beer, dug through the recesses of her mind to fill in some gaps. When the pub shut its doors at the end of the night, they had a working list of metals and minerals, Toria adding what she knew of each of their arcane properties and how they reacted to magical energy. This would help them narrow their search as soon as they had access to the records and analyses on the artifact that had caused this mess.

Every moment, she wished for Kane by her side. Despite her degrees and experience, earth magic was in his blood and soul in a way she could never touch.

The next morning dawned bright and clear, and Toria woke long enough to tug her curtains shut. A few hours later, she forced herself out from under her warm quilts and into the shower. Hugh was out, and Victory slumbered on in her room. Jarimis had returned to wherever he stayed in the city the night before, with a promise that he would meet them at the museum soon after sunset.

Fortified by tea, Toria set out on her final mission. As the future bore down, she saw her cabbie, the drivers of all the other cars, and the people they passed on the streets as walking ghosts. She couldn't save all of them. She *shouldn't* save all of them. But she could save those she cared most about.

Instead of her usual generous tip, Toria left the cabbie with a far more reasonable one. Hugh would need the money. Soon, the driver wouldn't.

She toyed with the ends of her scarf as she climbed the stairs to Lyra's apartment. Once outside the door, she paused. Magesight didn't work through walls. She laid decent odds on Lyra home with her new baby but had no idea whether Kojo stayed with her.

She bet the man had no interest in sleep disturbed by a newborn.

After a gentle knock, Toria flinched at the wail that followed. Not an auspicious beginning to any conversation. Her heart sank further when the door opened to reveal a haggard Lyra. Her friend wore a clean dressing gown, hair tucked into a patterned scarf, but the circles under her eyes drew Toria's attention even before the tiny bundle in her arms.

Before Toria could apologize for intruding, Lyra's entire face brightened. "Oh, you are a sight for sore eyes." She grabbed Toria's elbow and pulled her inside. She shut the door and thrust the baby at her. "I'll be right back."

Toria had no choice but to accept the infant before Lyra shot away. She tucked him, swaddled in a green blanket the color of spring leaves, closer to her chest and sank into the first seat she came across, a plush armchair in the parlor. As if stunned by the change in location, the baby quieted and stared at Toria. He didn't seem much bigger than when she'd first seen him in the hospital. Unable to help herself, she pulled up magesight. His power was strong, but muted, and tendrils of his aura stretched toward Toria.

She slammed combat-level shields around herself before they made any sort of connection. "It's not our time yet, little one." The temptation to poke his tiny snub nose with a finger almost overwhelmed her, but she could not risk direct physical contact, even if her own energy longed for it.

"What did you say?" Lyra reentered the front room, tying her dressing gown closed. Without waiting for an answer, she held out her arms and collected her son. "Sorry about that. You have perfect timing. I was desperate for the toilet, but he screams whenever I try to set him down."

"Glad I could help." Toria fidgeted as Lyra settled into the over-stuffed cushions of a brand-new sofa, arranging pillows until she cradled the baby just so in her arms. "He's adorable. Did you settle on a name?"

"Kojo Junior. But he'll go by KJ." Though a wry expression accompanied her answer, Lyra's face softened with love as she looked at the baby.

What a shock. Toria resisted the urge to roll her eyes. "That's sweet. Mostly I came to check in on you. See whether you needed anything."

"That's so kind of you, but Kojo has organized everything. I have meals delivered, and a girl comes in the afternoons to keep up with the housework."

She left unsaid whether Kojo himself had anything to do with his new son. Considering both the norms of the era and what Toria knew of the man, she doubted it. His son would be a status symbol and heir, not a beloved child to be doted upon. She braced herself, but asked her question anyway. "Have you considered living somewhere else for the winter? Since KJ was born early, how developed is his immune system?"

Lyra pursed her lips, staring past Toria's shoulder. "I don't think leaving is a good idea. Kojo has so much work to do here, and he already doesn't see his son enough."

Since this confirmed Toria's theory that Kojo maintained his own household elsewhere, she mentally threw up her hands.

Toria declined Lyra's offer of coffee, and they made awkward small talk for another few minutes. Lyra had subsumed herself into the identity of "mother," and other than a glimpse or two, Toria's friend the independent, sarcastic barkeep had disappeared. But they managed as if nothing was wrong until Toria committed the cardinal sin.

"Would you like to hold him again?" Lyra lifted the dozing infant an inch in offer. "Everyone else who has stopped by has snatched him from me the instant they could."

"Um, do you need me to? I'm more than happy to help with any chores while you rest instead." Toria didn't have a maternal bone in her body, so it wasn't as if she'd craved another chance to snuggle KJ.

"No, it's okay. Just thought I'd offer." Lyra tucked the blanket around him again, while Toria studied the landscape painting above the fireplace. "I'm a bit tired. I should nap while he does."

They rose as one, and Lyra showed Toria to the door. Toria would have liked to hug her friend one more time, but Lyra held KJ before her like a shield. After the briefest of goodbyes, Toria stood alone in the hallway.

She leaned against the stair rail as grief poured through her. This wasn't how this ended, because this little boy grew up, lived a full life, and had a child of his own. As would that child, and so on, until Kane grew up and bonded with Toria.

Toria knew little about Kane's history, but she remembered one particular story because it was so much like her own. Nalamas, so named because the elves fostered him as a child. Toria's original fate, too, before Asaron stepped in.

Perhaps she shouldn't leave little KJ's life to chance after all.

As soon as possible after sunset, Victory left with Toria to meet her progeny outside a staff entrance to the Museum of New Continental History.

Victory held herself apart as Toria and Jarimis chatted about the subjects they would each tackle. Her role here was moral support and general errand girl, so why did anxiety prickle her skin?

Toria rubbed at her arms in the cold, a scarf wrapped around her neck and cap pulled low over her ears even as Victory and Jarimis waited with their coats unbuttoned. "Liam should be here to let us in soon."

Ah, that explained it. This was the first time Victory found herself in a position to judge her daughter's romantic interest. Both of her vampire progeny had bonded with their daywalkers before Victory met them (though this Jarimis had yet to meet his Allesandra), leaving her little say in the matter, and Kane had also made it clear his water mage was there to stay when Archer set up shop as the new head of Limani's mage school. On the other hand, Toria had never had more than a casual relationship.

But she suppressed a laugh when the staff door opened to reveal a tall elven man wearing a tailored suit, his blond hair tied in a neat queue. He greeted Toria with a kiss and offered a handshake to Jarimis before turning to Victory.

Even though he kept his focus over Victory's left shoulder, she read his trepidation as he offered his hand to Victory as well. "A pleasure to meet you, ma'am. I'm Liamacorin, but you may call me Liam."

Victory's own nervousness evaporated as she accepted his handshake. "Same to you. Please call me Victory." She already knew this man, in his future and her own past. He lived in Limani decades ago, even helping to establish Victory as the Master of the City. Toria had never dropped Liam's full name, so Victory hadn't wanted to presume it was the same elf.

Not that she'd ever doubted it, but her daughter had good taste in men.

"Yes, yes, this is nice. I'm cold." Toria tugged Liam inside by the elbow, holding open the door for Victory and Jarimis to follow. "Are we clear to work?"

"Everything should be fine. Rubin has a dinner with some tentative sponsors for a new exhibit, and security knows I'm working late in the archives." Liam led them through the museum's hallways, down service stairs into a basement level, past laboratories and storage rooms darkened for the night.

They flipped on the lights in the archives room, and Jarimis and Toria set to work right away. As Jarimis darted around the room, pulling books and folders from shelves and directing Liam to do the same, Toria retrieved the notes from Jarimis' bag and organized piles. They worked together like a well-oiled machine, and Victory spared a moment to enjoy the sight. She would treasure this memory, regardless of whether she and Toria made it home or they spent the rest of their lives in the past.

Once both of them had their heads buried in books, Liam touched Victory's elbow. "We should leave them to it. Walk with me while I grab Toria the dinner I left in my office? She'll forget to eat, otherwise."

He already knew her daughter so well. "Sure." She rose to follow him out of the archives room and up flights of stairs to more formal office spaces. The silence between them strained heavy with expectation.

Victory didn't want to jerk him around, so she put him out of his misery. "Thank you for watching over Toria after she got here. I'm not sure what she'd have done without your support."

"I believe her backup plan was to force her way into the Mercenary Guild by whatever means necessary." The dry humor in Liam's immediate response proved without a doubt that he paid attention to Toria. Even if blind to the essential facts of her presence, he'd figured out the important details below the surface. They stopped by an office labeled with his name on a placard, with the title Deputy Curator, and he unlocked the door.

Victory trailed him inside, noting the organized space and catching the scent of paper and spiced tea. "Well, she's already done that once in her life, so I have no doubt she'd have managed it a second time." She accepted the small sack of food Liam handed her from the credenza along the wall. He collected two glass bottles of juice and led her into the hall.

They made their way toward the archives. "I'd better bite the bullet," Liam said. "When Toria met me for lunch today, she seemed upset and distracted. Is there something else going on I don't know about?"

His question startled Victory. "Not that I'm aware."

"That's what I'm afraid of." Liam halted in the middle of the corridor, and Victory drew to a stop and faced him. Jarimis wouldn't overhear their conversation this far from the archives. "Your daughter likes her secrets, and I know she's lived a delicate balancing act these past few months. But I hope you know I'm here to help both of you. I can't do so if I don't know what's going on."

"You assume I know what's going on as well." Victory rubbed her neck. "My daughter is a grown woman, and I haven't been able to tell her what to do for years."

"You're quite correct. I'm sorry."

As they neared the archives room, Victory heard the shuffling of book pages but not her daughter's heartbeat. She shoved past Liam and pushed open the thick wooden door.

It seemed like a paper factory had exploded over half the room. Jarimis stood over one of the tables, comparing a sheaf of notes with multiple books. A wide grin split his face when Victory entered. "Despite the lack of specific research about the artifact, I think we've got something here."

"Where's Toria?" Victory asked, as Liam stumbled on her heels.

Jarimis had already returned to his books. "She left to find you. I can't believe we might have come across a solution so soon. Toria answered some of my questions about semi-igneous rocks—" Now he broke off mid-sentence. "What's wrong?"

Victory scanned the room. "Did you not notice she had her coat?"

Jarimis glanced over his shoulder to where he'd draped his. "Ah. I see."

Liam dumped the drinks on a table. "I'll find her." He jogged out of the room, dress shoes squeaking on the worn wooden floor.

Victory sank into the nearest seat and dragged fingers through her loose hair. "Okay, Jarimis. Tell me what you've found." She already knew Liam's search for Toria would be futile. The girl was familiar enough with the museum that she'd know the most direct route to Liam's office. If they hadn't come across her, it was because she aimed for a different destination.

Jarimis waved her closer, so she heaved herself out of the stiff wooden chair and joined his side. His speech about the magical properties of semi-igneous rocks, how it reacted to magical energy, and something about earthquakes washed over her head.

Liam reappeared, interrupting Jarimis' incomprehensible explanation. The dark expression on his face might have rivaled Victory's own. "Front desk security said she bolted past them, and Comstock said he didn't bother to give chase since she was on the way out, not in. She knew which emergency door stays unlocked."

"You sure you don't know what's going on?"

Liam flinched.

"I'm sorry." Victory tempered the sharpness of her voice. "But you saw more of her today than I did."

Liam rubbed a hand over his face. "She visited her new friend's baby before lunch, and…Lyra and the baby. She couldn't convince her to leave town. There are issues with the child's father."

Of course. Her other friend in Nacostina, the bartender whom Toria had spoken of with such affection. "I don't suppose you know where this woman lives?"

"Perhaps the general neighborhood of the city, but nothing specific."

Victory accepted a book from Jarimis. "Then searching would be a waste of all of our time. She'll come back when she comes back. Let's get to work."

Toria huddled in a cab outside Lyra's apartment building as she waited for the meal deliveryman to leave, the mechanical ticking of the taximeter loud in the silence of the powered-down vehicle. Her mother was going to kill her. Hell, Liam might kill her for this fool stunt. But once the idea had occurred to her that afternoon, she'd thought of nothing else.

After striking gold in a geologist's field notes and pointing Jarimis in the right direction, she'd hightailed it out of the museum. The invisible countdown to the end of Nacostina weighed on her like a cloak of stone.

A military truck rumbled down the street, the third since the cab idled here. This was no longer about saving the people she cared about here and now. By saving this child, she also saved Kane's future.

When a man stepped out of the front entrance to the apartment and swung into his delivery van, Toria leaned toward the driver. "Okay, I'll be right back. Please wait for me."

The cabbie flipped to the next page in his newspaper, reading by the light of a streetlamp. "It's your money on the meter, lady."

Toria exited the car and darted across the street. As she climbed the steps to Lyra's apartment, she gathered ambient energy from the air and strengthened her magical shields to full combat strength. She'd miss the excess magic that permeated this world when back in her own time.

Toria paused outside Lyra's door. Anchored energy in the tips of her fingers until they tingled. And whispered a prayer for forgiveness to whatever gods or spirits might be listening.

She knocked.

No baby cries rang through the apartment, which eased part of her fear. He was much too young to remember this, but if KJ slept through his own kidnapping, all the better. Steps echoed through the front room, and their owner yanked the door open.

Lyra wore a loose housedress, but the scarf still bound her hair. She'd dressed for the deliveryman, not to go out. "Did you forget—Toria! What are you doing here?"

"I'm so sorry, Lyra." Toria took Lyra's hands, and the other woman grasped them by reflex.

"I don't—"

Toria forced power into the other woman where their skin touched, knocking her unconscious. She collapsed as if cut off at the knees, and Toria lunged forward to catch her around the waist.

Even post-pregnancy, the woman was too light. Toria secured her grip and pulled her into the apartment, kicking the door shut behind her. She deposited Lyra on the couch, organizing her limbs so that none hung off the edge. She would wake soon, in comfort, with no painful aftereffects.

Physical ones, at least.

Toria kissed Lyra's cheek. "I'm so sorry. But if I can't save you, I have to save your son." She'd spent all afternoon contemplating and discarding scenarios where she took both Lyra and the baby. Each ended with Lyra insisting she remain with Kojo, or go back to save him, or Kojo learning the truth about Toria and attempting to use the knowledge for his own gain. She had no other choice.

She followed the hallway off the front parlor to Lyra's bedroom. A bassinette sat at the foot of the bed, resplendent with white lace. Another sign of Kojo's excess compared with the genteel shabbiness that marked the rest of the room, with old furniture and faded curtains. Baby KJ lay inside, slumbering through the night that would change his life forever.

Toria hoped he stayed asleep for a while longer. She had no clue how to handle a screaming infant.

She found a bag hanging behind the bedroom door and filled it with the cloth diapers atop the dresser and what little infant clothing she could find. A spare quilt lay on a chest in the corner of the room, so she snagged it and unfolded it on the bed. Time for the final step. She slid her fingers under the baby, depositing him on the quilt in one gentle swoop.

He didn't stir. She looped the bag over one shoulder and tucked the thick quilt around KJ to shield him from the cold weather outside. The baby snuggled against her chest with a gentle whine when she cradled him to her, but otherwise slept on.

She avoided Lyra's body as she exited the apartment and pulled the door shut behind her. Her brain whirled until her vision almost grayed out, and she had to pause on a landing. She couldn't afford to trip and drop the baby. This was crazy. She was crazy. What if the elves didn't believe Toria and wouldn't accept the baby? How was she supposed to care for KJ and get him out of the city before it was too late?

Hell, how would she even keep him fed? She wasn't sure whether baby formula existed yet.

No one stopped Toria as she exited the building and slipped into the waiting taxi. She slammed her shields up to full levels, allowing them to encompass the baby in her arms. The magic embraced him with an almost audible purr, as if her innate power had missed linking with Kane as much as she did. Either way, this kid wasn't dying in a car accident in a world before child safety seats.

"Where to, lady?" The driver shoved his paper onto the passenger seat atop the remainder of his lunch.

"Tia's Clothier, please." Toria had no idea where Liam might be, whether still at the museum with Victory and Jarimis or if they searched the city for her.

But odds were good that Granny Tia was at work or had retired to her apartment behind the shop.

Also, the woman was the kindest elf Toria knew. Not the type to turn away a child in need.

The driver squinted at her in the darkness. "Never heard of it."

"It's near the Oak and Hazel Tearoom."

"That in the elven district?"

"Yes, it is." KJ squirmed in her lap, and she lowered her voice. "Drive, please."

The man put the car in gear and pulled out in the street. KJ had settled to sleep in her arms, so Toria didn't call the driver on his long route around the river. The man might recall the strange fare he'd made decent cash on, but the less trouble she caused, the less chance he'd think anything of it later.

Toria had her money ready when the man pulled to the nondescript front of Granny Tia's shop. The driver didn't offer change, and she didn't ask. She heaved herself out of the car and slammed the door shut with her hip. KJ whined at the noise, and she froze for a beat before shaking her head and walking to the shop's front door. She freed one hand, hefting KJ higher in her other arm, and tried the door.

Locked.

She blew air between pursed lips. A quick peek showed KJ awake, staring at Toria as if deciding whether to howl his head off or not. Toria pounded on the shop door, louder.

It swung open, and her hand passed through open air. Granny Tia stood at the foot of the stairs, wearing a plush dressing gown with her long hair loose about her shoulders. She gaped at Toria for a moment, drawing to her full height.

"Why in earth's name do you have a baby, young lady?"

"It's a long story. Can we please come in?" Toria hoped her pleas wouldn't fall on deaf ears. She had no idea where else to turn.

Granny Tia stepped aside to let Toria enter. Her gaze burned as she followed Toria up the stairs, and her silence hung heavy in the air.

Though he didn't cry, KJ's squirms grew stronger as Toria entered the second-floor shop. She dropped the bag from her shoulder and collapsed into a seat. For such a small child bundled in blankets, the kid could writhe. She freed him from the thick quilt now that they were in a warmer space, and that's when the smell hit her. "Oh, shit."

"Quite astute." Granny Tia shut the door behind them and placed her hands on her hips. "Are you going to do something about that?"

Toria's hands clutched KJ's swaddling as helplessness rushed through her. "I don't think I can."

Granny Tia scoffed. "Nonsense. Changing a diaper is easy."

"No, you don't understand. I can't risk touching him. Our magic is calling to each other, and I can't risk bonding with him." Toria held KJ out to Granny Tia. "Please help us."

The elven woman's eyes flashed a brighter gold in the room's lamplight as she used the elven version of magesight, and realization dawned. "I've never seen anything like this."

"I'll explain everything. But can you please help him?"

Granny Tia gathered the infant into her arms and accepted the bag of supplies from Toria. "Does the child at least have a name?"

Toria swallowed. "Nalamas. His name should be Nalamas."

"That's an elven foster name." Granny Tia settled KJ against her as her eyebrows raised toward her hairline. The baby still didn't cry, instead babbling to Granny Tia in wordless noise.

"I know."

"I shall expect an explanation, young lady." With that pronouncement, Granny Tia swept into her personal rooms at the rear of the shop.

Toria curled in the corner of the sofa and tried to empty her mind. It didn't work. Her hands shook, but she had no idea whether due to panic or because she hadn't eaten in over eight hours. Saving KJ—Nalamas—was no mistake, of that she was sure, but where did things go from here? On top of this, guilt wracked her for abandoning Jarimis to the work at the museum. She thought she'd pointed him in the right direction once she'd seen the records of the artifact's geological composition, but what if she'd been wrong?

The uncertainty of it all tore at her.

Minutes or hours could have passed as Toria let the emotions sweep through her, but the lack of privacy prevented her from letting loose the threatened sobs. When a door opened, she expected it to be Granny Tia emerging from her rooms with the baby.

Instead, a familiar weight settled next to her on the couch and pulled her to him. Toria pressed her cheek against Liam's chest and wrapped herself in his comfort. "How did you find me?"

"Granny Tia called and I broke a few driving regulations to make it here before you disappeared again." Liam dropped a kiss to the top of her head. "Did you really show up here with your friend's child?"

"That she did." Granny Tia returned to the room. A blanket of smooth elven weave cocooned the baby, fast asleep in the older woman's arms. She offered him to Toria, but Toria declined. The closeness she'd already shared with him was too dangerous. She couldn't risk it.

Granny Tia kept hold of the infant and sat in the armchair. Toria scrubbed at her face, trying to regain her composure. By the time she could speak without bursting into tears, the two elves appeared to have finished an entire unspoken conversation.

Liam must have drawn the short straw. He turned in his seat and gathered Toria's hands in his own. "This puts me in a very difficult position."

Toria yanked away her hands. "Seriously? Your role in this is what concerns you?" From what she knew of elven culture, the lives of children were the most precious resource in the world. Had things changed so drastically between her time and now?

Liam ran his hand over his face. "You misunderstand, love. Choosing a child to be fostered with the elves is a delicate decision, not to be made lightly. Many factors must be considered. We do not steal children from living parents, and this one still has both."

"My full name is Torialanthas." Liam jerked in shock, but Toria pressed on. "I know how it works because I was one. Except I almost slipped through the cracks, and vampires saved me instead."

"Impossible." Granny Tia's voice rang like cut glass, and Toria might have laughed at the affronted expression on her face at any other time. "We don't choose wrong, and we don't lose the children we do choose."

"Things are...more complicated where I'm from." Toria ached for Liam's hand, but she couldn't afford to draw from this source of comfort with so much at stake. "Liam, those notes I gave you? Please trust me when I say this is just as important."

"I can't kidnap a child!" His eyes darted to the side toward the baby, and he lowered his voice. "You realize that's what this is, yes? Kidnapping?"

"Or life-saving."

"Yes, but I thought we were focused on saving your life right now. Instead, you left Jarimis to the work and disappeared."

Toria jumped from her seat to pace the limited room between the door and bookshelf. "Did Granny Tia tell you what his name is?"

"Yes, Nalamas. You can't pick a name and tell us he's to be a foster. Like I said, that's not—"

Toria whirled on him. "My partner's name is Kane Nalamas. This kid's dad has my partner's nose. Now try to tell me saving this baby isn't the most important thing right now."

Granny Tia gasped. "You're not from…."

"We don't have time for this." Toria threw up her hands. "You and Granny Tia need to leave with this child. Tonight, if possible. He's going to need to eat soon anyway."

Liam rose and approached Toria. He placed a hand on her shoulder and used his other to tilt her face to meet his. "If we leave, I can't help you anymore. If you and Jarimis didn't solve the problem at the museum, I can't get you back in. You and Victory could be stuck here forever."

So be it. Because some changes to the past were worth risking, but not this one. Not the life of her partner. She squared her shoulders. "I know."

Shadow hooded Liam's face, but Toria imagined the brightness there was reflected by the tears in her own eyes. "Is that a choice you can make for Victory?"

And that was the final piece, wasn't it? If Toria never made it home, she lived out her life and died here. Saving KJ wasn't about the future, because Kane would fade away and die without her. This was about saving the past, giving Kane a chance to exist in the first place.

But Victory would be stuck here as a shadow of herself. Her mom had been so supportive when Toria knew she had to be desperate to make it home to Dad. And she'd been too damned selfish to even ask. Guilt curdled her stomach. "No. But I have to do it anyway."

Liam embraced her, and she wrapped her arms around his waist and held on tight. Now, she let the tears flow free to soak into his wool coat, because this might be it. He lessened his hold on her enough to kiss her, for the final time. In the dim corner of her awareness, Granny Tia gathered Nalamas and left the room.

Toria soaked as much of this moment into her skin and mind as possible, imprinting this into her memory. His warmth, his touch, his smell. His taste, as their mouths met in a desperate kiss. She might never get this back, but the cost was worth it. Kane's life was worth her happiness, every time.

When they came up for air, Liam rested his forehead against Toria's. "Be careful."

Toria cupped her hands around his neck. "Remember my letters."

"I will." Liam released her to pat his coat above his heart. "They're the most important thing in the world, after you."

"And after the baby." Toria pulled away, slipping her hands into Liam's and grasping tight. "I wouldn't have done this if I didn't think it important. Just like I wouldn't have lied to you in the first place."

"And the crazy thing is that I trust you." Liam kissed her once more, but Granny Tia poked her head in the room before they got lost in each other again.

"I've made some calls." One-handed, carrying the infant in her other arm as if the most natural position in the world, Granny Tia gathered two notebooks from the desk in the corner. "Time to go, Liam, before the child gets hungry."

Toria turned to her. "Thank you for this. Liam will explain everything."

The elven women inclined her head. "I trust he will. It's best you leave now, before our ride gets here."

"Yes, ma'am." Toria wanted nothing more than to embrace the woman who'd shown her so much kindness since she'd arrived in Nacostina, but it appeared she'd overdrawn her supply of compassion. She hoped Nalamas would not suffer for her decisions, but trusted Liam to be his guardian in her stead.

Liam squeezed her hands. "I'll walk you downstairs."

"No. It's easier if you stay here." Otherwise he would walk her downstairs. Then wait with her for a cab, or walk her to the nearest trolley station. Then he'd be tempted to go home with her, and she needed him to stay with Nalamas.

Didn't make it easy, though, knowing he wanted to stay with her as long as possible.

"All right." Liam kissed her hard on the lips once, twice, before she pulled away. "Goodbye, Toria Connor."

Toria paused with her hand on the doorknob, forcing the words through her tears. "No. It's only goodnight."

And she walked away.

Either the temperature dropped while Toria had been at Granny Tia's, or her sadness made the world seem colder. Going to the museum was futile without Liam there to sneak her in, so she directed the taxi driver to the bed and breakfast.

Lights blazed within the house, and Hugh called out from the kitchen as she slung her coat on the hook in the foyer.

When she entered the kitchen, making a beeline for the tea kettle, books and folders towered between Victory and Hugh on the table. "Where's Jarimis?"

Hugh responded first, flipping back and forth between pages within a book. "Did you know rubies and sapphires are the same mineral?"

"I did know. Mom?"

"Jarimis is off to beg a resource from a private collection and will return here as soon as possible." Victory shut the book in front of her. "I believe a more relevant question is where were you?"

Toria suppressed the automatic guilt inspired by the tone in her mother's voice. "I had something to take care of." She resisted the urge to cross her arms. Defensiveness would invite more questions. "Once I figured out altitude affected the meteor's properties, I knew I could point Jarimis in the right direction."

Victory's eyes darted toward the front door, hearing something beyond the reaches of human ears. "He's back, at least. You two still have work to do."

When Toria moved away from the counter, Hugh raised a hand and stood up. "I'll let him in. I don't understand any of this technical stuff, anyway."

As he exited the kitchen, Toria avoided her mother's gaze by hovering her hand outside the edge of the kettle and speeding along the boil. Such a superfluous use of magic appalled her in her own time, so she might as well abuse it while she could.

She asked Victory if she wanted tea too, a possible peace offering, but Victory's focus remained toward the front door.

Why hadn't Hugh come into the kitchen with Jarimis? Before Toria asked what her mother heard, Victory launched herself off the bench and out of the kitchen.

Toria spared a second to turn off the stove and pull the kettle from the burner as shouting started.

Kojo's voice echoed through the house as he howled over Hugh's calming tones. "I don't care, old man. *Where the hell is my son?*"

Oh, fuck. Toria ran for the hallway as Victory shoved herself between Kojo and Hugh. Her mother dropped to a defensive stance between the two men, snarling at Kojo as he filled the doorway. "Back off."

"You back off, lady!" Kojo found Toria, where she lurked at the end of the hall. "You! I know you have him here!"

Hugh's attention swung between them, and Toria stepped forward. A touch to her mother's shoulder told Victory she was right behind her. "Hugh, go upstairs, please," Toria said. By his receding footsteps, Toria knew he stopped at the first landing, with its perfect view of the foyer below. Good enough for now.

Toria tilted her chin in defiance at Kojo, but his greater height placed her at the disadvantage and a trickle of fear traced her spine. Was this how people viewed Kane? "Your son is not here. Please leave."

Kojo stepped out of the doorway, and Toria hoped it meant he would leave. Instead, Lyra came forward in his place. Toria's heart sank at the tear tracks staining Lyra's cheeks.

"I remember." Lyra snatched Toria's wrist with clawed fingers, and Toria's out-flung arm prevented Victory from forcing her friend back. "I woke up on the couch, and KJ was gone. There's a great blank space in my memory, but I saw you!"

That particular magic tended to impart what amounted to post-traumatic amnesia on its victims, but Lyra's own recessive magic had protected her from it. Toria opened her mouth to respond, but no words came. Panic slipped ice through her veins.

Victory pushed forward again, and her intrusion in Lyra's personal space forced the other woman to drop Toria's wrist and move away. "Let's all calm down. I promise you both that there is no baby here. I'm sure there's a rational explanation for this."

"But I remember you." Lyra's pleading cut through Toria like a knife.

Victory placed a hand on Lyra's shoulder. "I know Toria visited you earlier in the day. Perhaps your memories got mixed up?"

"I need to find my son." Lyra wiped away fresh tears. "I'm sorry, but who are you?"

"I'm a friend of Toria's." Victory's voice had achieved a soothing quality, one Toria equated with calming skittish horses and young daughters who woke from nightmares.

Kojo tugged Lyra away. "You're in on it."

Lyra flinched in pain as Kojo gripped her shoulder, which reassured Toria that she'd made the right choice. Perhaps even if she hadn't sped things up, in another life the elves saved the child from an abusive father anyway. That's why they'd slated Toria for fostering, before Asaron came along. "What, do you want to search the house, asshole?" Toria spread her arms wide. "Come on in."

"I have a better idea." Though one hand still held tight to Lyra's shoulder, Kojo dug his other in the pocket of his large overcoat. With one smooth motion, he drew a small pistol and pointed it at Toria. "Tell me where the fuck my kid is."

Toria slammed her strongest shields up, grunting in pain as the power ripped from her core. Brilliant violet prisms unfolded around her, framing her body in spirals of protective energy. The shields wouldn't do much against a shot fired at such close range, but if worst came to worst, the bullet might deflect.

Next to her, Victory whipped out a knife. Toria had no idea where she'd had it hidden.

Lyra gasped, but Kojo's aim didn't waver, though he did shift from Toria to Victory, the more obvious threat. "I will shoot her if I don't get an answer."

Victory's answer was as steady as her grip on the knife. "I have no doubt. But there is no child in this house."

How long could such a standoff last? Toria curled her fingers at her side, siphoning energy from the air around her. A regular bullet would do little damage to Victory, who'd move fast enough that it might not hit her anyway. But Lyra was too far away for Toria to encase the woman in her own shields, and with Kojo still holding on to her, any power she blasted into Kojo would bleed into her friend and hurt her, too.

A shotgun cocked behind her, echoing through the foyer. Toria had forgotten about Hugh in all the drama. "You've overstayed your welcome in my house, sir."

Kojo's attention wavered, and he let go of Lyra's shoulder. Toria jabbed out, channeling power through her physical muscles. Electricity arced, striking Kojo's chest. The man staggered onto the porch as sparks of power showered from his body. The foyer plunged into darkness when the magical electricity blew out the house's power, leaving the streetlamp outside as the sole light source.

Lyra cried out, lunging for him. Toria couldn't grab for her with both hands still charged with energy. A gunshot rang out and a body brushed by, both of which sent her shields into overdrive. Violent purple light flashed, visible even to human eyes, leaving Toria temporarily blinded. She froze in place and ground the excess power into the wooden floor beneath her feet.

Footsteps pounded behind her, and as Toria's vision cleared, the house lights flickered on. Everything seemed dim and over-saturated where it didn't dance with spots.

Kojo sprawled on the porch. Victory crouched next to him, cradling Lyra. She already had one hand pressed to Lyra's chest, but seeping blood stained the front of her dress.

"Oh, gods." Toria fell to her knees next to Lyra. Blood bubbled between her friend's lips, and when she coughed, the air rasped. She'd seen this before. Lyra's lung had collapsed. Even if they had time to get her to a hospital, she didn't know whether the medical expertise of the day could save her. Her friend was already dead. She just didn't know it yet.

Hugh stepped around them and kicked the pistol away from Kojo. He knelt to one knee and pressed fingers to Kojo's throat. Shook his head.

But Toria hadn't used enough energy to kill him. She hadn't used more than what knocked Lyra out earlier.

"Toria."

Lyra's voice was weak. Toria gripped her friend's hands. "I'm here."

"Find my baby." Lyra's eyes clouded.

"I promise your baby is safe." Toria brushed blood from Lyra's chin. She wanted to say goodbye, but couldn't find the words. She could only offer platitudes, and pray and trust that she'd not misplaced her faith in Liam. "Your baby is safe, and he'll grow up and live a happy, full life. I promise, Lyra."

She was beyond hearing. "Find him, Toria. Bring him home to me." She repeated the words until her voice faded away, and Lyra's head fell as she went limp in Victory's arms.

The silence of the frozen tableau overwhelmed Toria. She hadn't said goodbye. Like she hadn't been able to say goodbye to Syri.

Like she hadn't said goodbye to Kane.

Heedless of her bloodstained hands, Toria pressed them to her mouth and fell back on her heels. None of this was meant to happen. She might not have been able to save Lyra, but she'd been meant to die a painless death in a fiery ball of fire, not bleed out beneath Victory's hand. "Neither of them were supposed to die. I don't know what happened."

Victory's calm tones broke through Toria's roiling pain. "His muscles contracted when you pumped him full of electricity. Your friend got in the way."

Toria avoided Kojo's eyes. She seared Lyra's face into her brain, penance for mistakes upon mistakes. "But what about him?"

"You couldn't have known. He probably didn't either." Victory eased out from under Lyra, settling her on the porch. "I heard his arrhythmia. The man was a heart attack waiting to happen. Toria, where is their child?"

"Safe, I swear it. I sent him away with Liam. They should be far from the city by now."

Hugh interrupted Victory's response. "Ladies, we need to take this inside." He used the doorjamb to heave himself to his feet and pointed toward the curb, where a car had slowed to a stop.

Toria leapt up. If not for the bodies arranged around her, she could explain the gunshot as a car backfire. She squinted into the darkness beyond the porchlight as a tall figure emerged from the car.

Jarimis froze at the bottom of the porch steps, nose flaring. "What the hell did I miss?"

Sirens wailed.

The harsh noise shocked Toria into motion, forcing her mind from its fugue state. But this wasn't the blare of a police siren. It seemed to come from nowhere and everywhere, blanketing the neighborhood with sound.

Victory and Jarimis flinched in unison as each high-pitched wail rose in crescendo. As Jarimis pressed his hands to his ears, Victory's cry rose above the noise. "What the hell is that?"

Hugh's face paled in the bleak porchlight. "Tornado sirens. But this isn't the right season, the right weather."

Toria knew her storms, and tornadoes didn't happen when brilliant stars punctured the sky. The weather sirens could be warning the people of Nacostina of something worse to come, if the city didn't have air raid sirens, but this was all wrong. She grabbed Victory's shoulder to capture her attention beyond the noise. "But it doesn't happen tonight!"

"Not tonight." Victory gathered Lyra's body in her arms and rose to her feet in one smooth motion. "Jarimis, tell me that car is disposable."

He dropped his hands. "You weren't telling me everything. Are we looking at a repeat of the Battle of Matrice?" Victory's face contained too much expression for Toria to interpret, but Jarimis read it loud and clear, and his own face hardened. "I see. Yes, the owner of that vehicle will never have a chance to miss it."

Memory surfaced, half-forgotten history classes. The Battle of Matrice had involved days of air raids before a concentrated blitz of firebombing reduced much of the city to rubble. She hadn't known Nacostina was attacked before its final destruction. It made sense that Victory might have knowledge outside of the history books.

Houses lit as the sirens woke the residents. This wasn't the way Toria wanted to treat the body of a friend, but Victory and Jarimis had to leave now to avoid the complication of witnesses.

Jarimis slung Kojo's body over his shoulder as if it weighed no more than a bulky pillow. He held his free hand out to Hugh. "The gun, please."

Hugh passed over the small pistol, wiping his hand across his sweater after. "Is it safe to go out there?" He pitched his voice over the sirens.

Victory cradled Lyra to her chest. "Safe enough, but you two should go to the cellar. We'll be back as soon as possible."

He accepted her instructions, wrapping his arm around Toria's shoulders. He allowed them to wait until Victory and Jarimis stashed the bodies inside the car and drove out of sight.

Once inside, Hugh collected the shotgun leaning inside the front door and snagged the two blankets folded over the living room sofa. Toria raced upstairs to collect her rapier and Victory's bastard sword from their bedrooms. She gathered the research material on the kitchen table. Everything else, she and Victory could do without.

With a final glance around the kitchen, she followed Hugh into the cellar he used as cold storage, into the darkness.

The sirens rang on.

Toria jolted awake as a door slammed above, echoing through the floor and into the cellar. She threw the blanket off her shoulders and snagged her sword, positioning herself at the bottom of the steep stairs. Hugh freed himself from the blanket around his legs, snagging his shotgun as he pushed up from the antique rocking chair.

Victory's voice rang through the house. "We're back! It's safe to come up."

Hugh's shoulders slumped in the same relief Toria felt. "Be right up!" she called.

Toria collected the neat stack of papers and second sword. When she climbed to the kitchen, the overhead light blinded her after the dimness of the emergency lantern Hugh kept in the cellar. Jarimis slumped at the kitchen table, with no sign of Victory.

"She went up to change." Jarimis left the reference to her bloody clothing unspoken. "If tea could be arranged, I would be forever grateful."

"That I can do." Hugh emerged behind Toria and placed his shotgun on the counter as if he carried the weapon as a matter of course. He put the kettle on.

Toria leaned the swords against the wall and settled across the table from Jarimis. She dropped the stack of papers between them with a thump. "I think I've found something."

Jarimis straightened in his seat with a pop. "Brilliant. Tell me."

"Wait!" A thump echoed, as if Victory had skipped the final few steps of the staircase, and she entered the kitchen moments later. She slipped onto the bench next to Jarimis and folded her hands in front of her. "I imagine I won't understand a word of it, but tell us both."

Toria tried not to stare at Victory's hands, knowing she imagined the bloodstains. "Can I ask—?"

"No." Despite the interruption, her mother's voice was kind. "It's neither here nor there."

Toria pushed a page of handwritten notes toward Jarimis. "Here are my final thoughts about the artifact based on what you found earlier this evening."

The museum's analysis of the meteor's composition of magnesium and silica, combined with someone's handwritten notes about the magical echoes emitted by the meteor, had reminded Toria of technology under development in the scholarly halls of Oxenafor in Britannia. She'd attended a few lectures last year—decades in the future—at the invitation of a group of chemistry students with whom she'd struck an occasional correspondence.

With Victory peering over his shoulder, Jarimis studied the notes. He trailed his finger across the words as he read, occasionally returning to previous sentences for clarification. "This is not what I expected."

"Researchers first found the meteor in the mountains near Skye, but the time travel incidents didn't start until they brought it to Londinium, and they continued in Nacostina." Toria traced her finger under the relevant passages as she spoke. "So, radiative recombination in the lower altitudes."

Both vampires stared at her. Jarimis blinked first. "What does that even mean?"

"That's funny, because—" Toria slammed her mouth shut.

Jarimis tilted his head to the side. "That's funny why?"

"Nope. Not going there." Because Toria based the other half of her conclusions off a half-written paper she'd discovered in her mother's library. A treatise on nuclear properties and their effect on certain natural structures. A document written by Jarimis, based on this exact situation. But she wilted under the vampires' combined stare. "I hate time travel."

Jarimis cackled with laughter, scratching his cheek. "Having a chicken or the egg moment, are we?"

"Something like that." Toria's mind whirled at the implications. If she explained her thoughts to Jarimis further, did he write his abandoned article based on her idea, or did she have the idea because Jarimis wrote it either way? Knowledge didn't spring into the world, fully formed, without guidance from sentient brains. Or perhaps it did, and this was an example. She laughed, despite the lack of humor in the situation. "If only I'd known that all I had to do was touch a stupid rock again to go home. But Liam and Rubin were so convinced that I'd just jump to the future, so I was terrified I'd go further back into the past." She shoved down a burst of familiar fear.

Victory leaned forward, bracing her elbows on the table. "So where do we go from here?"

Toria and Jarimis exchanged the briefest of glances, acknowledging shared thoughts without words. She turned to her mother. "Now we break into a museum."

Dawn crept on the horizon, but Victory made sure the plans and tea flowed. Toria had woken Hugh from where he dozed in the parlor, drawing him into the conversation to mine his decades of knowledge regarding the museum. He acknowledged the news of their plotting with aplomb, which both raised Victory's estimation of the man and explained so much of his easy friendship with her daughter.

Their timing could have been better. According to Toria, Liam had been helping to coordinate a major gala to be held that evening. A discussion followed about slipping in with the crowds or waiting until after the event was over, but the benefits of the distraction of a major event outweighed many of the points against it.

As Hugh and Jarimis continued their animated discussion regarding the current state of the museum's evening security patrols, Victory touched Toria's elbow and gestured her down the hallway. Though Toria furrowed her brow, she followed without argument and settled herself cross-legged onto the sofa in the parlor next to her mother. Dark circles under her eyes highlighted her daughter's pallor, the result of stress and lack of sleep. She understood why Toria had thrown herself into this new project, because Victory was no stranger to avoiding emotion during difficult times. She hoped her daughter held on until they made it home to their own time or escaped the city, whichever future came to pass.

But right now, Toria stretched her arms above her head. "What's up?" Hesitancy colored her question, as if she dreaded whatever topic Victory might put before her.

"We need to talk about Jarimis."

This didn't appear to be the answer Toria expected, and she dropped her hands into her lap and gave her mother her full attention. "What about him?"

"He can't come with us tomorrow night. It's better if Hugh doesn't, either." Victory needed to make that clear now, before they hammered out details that incorporated the men.

"Between Hugh's knowledge of the museum and the experience I know Jarimis has based on your bedtime stories, I don't know why you'd suggest that."

Victory slouched, resting her head against the sofa. "It's less about them and more about us."

"You know he can hear us, right?" Toria pointed in the kitchen's general direction. "I'm not sure why you dragged me away for this conversation."

Jarimis' shout rang down the hallway. "I can absolutely hear you, Mother!"

Victory rolled her eyes as she stood and returned to the kitchen, Toria traipsing behind her. Though Hugh appeared confused next to him, Jarimis drummed his fingers on the table. She pointed to her progeny. "As far as I'm concerned, you and Hugh need to get as far away from the city as you can after sundown."

Toria dropped into her seat at the table. She sipped her tea and scowled. Considering she'd last made a round over an hour ago, it must be cold. She popped up again to rummage in the cupboards. "If that's the case, I'm using the last of the eggs to make ridiculous omelets, Hugh."

Hugh returned to his drawing of the museum's first floor in a large sketchbook. "No mushrooms in mine, please."

Jarimis picked up a pen from the table, jaw clenched.

Victory didn't sit, maintaining the dominance of height. "I'd rather you be safe."

"I hope you don't miss the irony in wishing for my safety now, when you once protested my career change." Jarimis twirled the pen between and around his fingers.

Victory knew he performed the trick on purpose, to remind her he could do the same with a knife. "This has nothing to do with your safety at the museum and everything to do with your safety in the years to come." She plucked the pen away. "There's no guarantee you'll be able to leave the city tonight, and you know what's coming in less than seventy-two hours. You and Hugh need all the time we have."

Hugh leaned over to steal the pen. With its different ink color, he returned to his drawing. "Perhaps a compromise is in order."

"I'm open to whatever suggestion you might have, sir." Jarimis' narrowed eyes dared Victory to argue.

From over the stovetop, Toria snorted with laughter.

Hugh made a final notation on his drawing and spun the sketchbook toward Victory and Jarimis. "While I also agree that I'd like to head up the coast as soon as possible, Jarimis and I will still be useful to you ladies in entering the museum. Each entrance strategy will have different requirements, and on a personal note, I'd like to see you safe, as well." Hugh accepted a glass of juice from Toria. "We'll get away."

The kitchen plunged into silence, broken by the sounds of Toria chopping vegetables at the counter. Jarimis tilted his head from side to side, weighing all options in his head, but Victory stopped him before he got too lost in the variables. "I don't want to be tempted to bring you home with me. I'm afraid that from my perspective, saving your life will outweigh the importance of maintaining the timeline."

"Why couldn't you say so, Mother?" Jarimis threaded his fingers through hers.

She was helpless to explain how much seeing him here, sitting opposite him, brought back so many memories. He was a ghost from her past, and though he'd disappeared into time, she knew herself well enough to want to cling to him in the here and now. His black eyes, warm with love and affection, bore into hers, and she broke away first before he had to.

Hugh cleared his throat, breaking the moment and drawing them to the matter at hand. "If you'll direct your attention to the map, there are multiple routes inside. All of these will depend on the state of security and how busy the museum is once we get there."

Toria brought two heaping plates to the table. She set one next to Hugh, and settled next to Victory with her own breakfast. Planning and discussion claimed the next hour or so, with a short break for Hugh and Toria to close the door to the sunroom and pin an extra blanket over the kitchen window as the sun rose.

Jarimis took copious notes between arguing with Hugh about the museum's hallways and debating the relative successes of past missions he'd gone on with Victory during his short-lived mercenary career. They all suggested and dismissed various plans both simple and outrageous, from forcing an evacuation of the museum with fake gas to faking Hugh's kidnapping for access.

When the morning paper hit the front stoop, Hugh retrieved it. *FALSE ALARMS WAKE CITY: QIN PLANES LOSE WAY IN POOR WEATHER*

Below the headline, the article detailed a story about two Qin military pilots intruding on Nacostina airspace on their way to a scheduled visit to Calverton in the north. Officials encouraged residents to maintain their regular schedules; there was no cause for alarm.

"What the hell?" Toria voiced their shared shock.

Jarimis scoffed low in his throat. "British intelligence isn't what it used to be."

"That's not it at all. This isn't the full story." Victory combed fingers through her hair, but it didn't distract her from the roiling in her gut. "I lost track of the days."

"Oh, shit." Toria's elbow knocked her plate, rattling the ceramic against wood, as she lifted both hands to her mouth.

Victory tightened her ponytail, searching for the words. "Wan City was destroyed last night. Firebombed by British forces. The diplomatic packet wasn't wrong, just carefully worded. British intelligence knows more than they're telling the public, but doesn't want to cause a panic." The Qin planes had run a scouting mission, a test run for the real attack.

"Makes sense." Hugh poured cream in his new cup of tea. "I know I'm ready to panic. Can you tell us what's happening?"

What happened was the opening shots of the Last War. But Victory shook her head, wordlessly, and Toria echoed the action.

Hugh pursed his lips. "Let's get to work so I can get the hell out of here."

They hammered out the details of a plan, and a backup plan, within the hour. Victory sent Hugh and Toria, both fading from sleepiness, to their beds. She led Jarimis to her own protected room. They'd shared much closer quarters to hide from the sun.

Once tucked away, Jarimis handed a scrap of paper to Victory. It listed a ranked order of towns, scattered in both the British and Roman colonies of the New Continent.

The second-to-top suggestion was a familiar name, and Victory pointed to it. "That one."

She'd just ensured Jarimis would meet Allesandra at a small bar in a town that would soon border the area known as the Wasteland. The woman who would go on to become his daywalker. The woman who initiated both their eventual move to Limani and Victory's purchase of a nightclub there.

The nightclub where Victory met Mikelos.

Night fell, and Victory woke to Toria banging on her bedroom door. She and Jarimis dressed and met Toria and Hugh in the foyer, where Hugh opened the front door and gestured them outside. Victory appreciated the man's willingness to walk away from the home in which he'd expected to spend his retirement. She trusted Jarimis to see him through the coming war in comfort.

But once down the sidewalk, Toria froze with her hand outstretched for the car's door handle, causing Victory to run straight into her daughter. She snagged Toria's coat as she tread on her heels. "You okay, love?"

Without answer, Toria dropped her hand to her side. Hugh and Jarimis passed her and settled into the front seats, leaving the women on the sidewalk.

Victory wrapped her arm around Toria's shoulders as the car's engine rumbled to life. "We're so close to getting home."

Shocked laughter bubbled from Toria's mouth. "Oh, it's not that. I can't wait to get home. I'm just thinking about last night."

When she and Jarimis moved the body of Toria's friend. She rubbed her daughter's arm and spoke in soothing tones. "It was a different car. And I promise we treated both bodies with respect, and left them in a place that will do the same." Without discussion, Jarimis had driven to a funeral home a few miles away. The odds of the bodies being prepared and buried before time ran out for the city were slim, but it wasn't as though they'd dumped them in the river.

A steadying breath lifted Toria's shoulders. "Okay. Thank you." She pulled the door open and slid across the backseat. Once Victory joined her and shut the door, she called forward to the front. "Let's do this, gentlemen."

Hugh shifted gears and pulled away from the curb. Toria twisted in her seat to watch the bed and breakfast fade from view. She groped for Victory's hand in the darkness, and Victory curled their fingers together.

These could be the last moments of stillness Victory had with her daughter. "I want you to know something."

"Yes?"

"From here on out, I'm not letting anyone get in our way." Victory lowered her voice. Jarimis would overhear with ease, but this wasn't a conversation for Hugh's ears. "I know you're worried about our effect on the timeline, but we're approaching zero hour. For the people around us, it makes no difference whether they die today or two nights from now."

Her daughter stared out the window, at the passing cars and people on the streets. Victory heard the low crush of enamel as Toria ground her teeth in frustration. "I know. You're right."

"Think of it this way. You hired me for this mission. It didn't turn out to be the mission we thought we'd be on. But now you've got the best bodyguard money can buy."

"Lucky me. You were pretty cheap." Toria blew air from both cheeks. "You're right. We have a new mission. Let's stick to it."

"We're here, ladies." Hugh lifted a hand from the steering wheel and pointed ahead as they moved along in creeping traffic.

The front of the Museum of New Continental History shone with spotlights. A banner hung over the front entrance, proclaiming the official opening of a new exhibition on fossils from the west. Below, a crowd milled across the front steps, shifting in patterns of conversation. Gentlemen wore tuxedoes, while ladies sparkled in ballgowns, fur wraps their concession to the cold.

Hugh drifted past the front of the museum in the flow of cars until pulling out of traffic into a spot across the street. He shut off the engine, and silence reigned as the four of them craned their necks at the sight.

"Oh, hell. Spotted already." Toria pressed a finger to the window, pointing out a dark figure who trotted across the street toward the car.

The man didn't pass them by, and the nearby streetlight revealed his security uniform. He knocked on the driver's window.

Hugh rolled it down. "Hello?"

"Mr. Hugh Ainsworth?" His breath fogged the air as he peered past him into the darkness, at the others in the vehicle.

"Yes, that's me. Can I help you?"

"Mr. Rubin wishes to speak with you. Come with me, please."

Toria's whole body tensed as Hugh twitched in surprise at the man's words. Hugh glanced over his shoulder at them, but his companions wore equal expressions of confusion. Hugh turned to Toria.

Toria and Victory had originally planned to use the cover of guests to make their way into the building. This could either make getting inside easier, or backfire in their faces. Either way, they couldn't sit here. Toria nodded once.

Hugh turned to the window. "Sure. Happy to see him."

The unfamiliar security guard backed away as Hugh stepped out into the street. Displeasure emanated from his posture when the three others did the same, but he shut his mouth on a half-started argument when Hugh locked the door and crossed his arms. "Ah, this way, please."

They waited for a break between the passing cars, all slowed to gawk at the museum's spectacle, and followed the guard across the street.

Rubin, cutting quite the figure in his tuxedo, broke away from a conversation as they made their approach. After he thanked the guard and directed the man back to his crowd-control post, he narrowed his eyes as he surveyed them. Toria's skin crawled, but she gathered strength from Victory's stalwart presence and Jarimis' unflappable calm.

Rubin ignored the other uninvited guests for now. "Mr. Ainsworth. I spotted your car. I fear you're not dressed for tonight's gala, however."

"A pleasure to see you, Mr. Rubin. The mail must have lost my invitation."

Rubin ignored the jibe. "Nevertheless, your appearance is fortuitous. I don't suppose you know the whereabouts of my deputy? Liam did not show up for work this morning, despite his role in preparation for this exhibit's opening."

Jarimis, without concern for the conversation at hand, circled behind Rubin. The elf flicked his attention to Jarimis once before dismissing the vampire and raising an expectant eyebrow at Hugh.

"I haven't seen Liam in a few days, sir."

"Is that so. What about you, girl?"

Toria froze under the weight of Rubin's gaze. Victory's fingers brushed hers, and she swallowed once before finding her voice. "I'm sure Liam would only miss work due to emergency."

"And I suppose you have no idea—"

Hugh broke into a coughing fit, staggering against Rubin's shoulder. Rubin recoiled in disgust, and Jarimis caught Hugh by the elbow. Rubin plucked a spotless handkerchief from his pocket and wiped his hands as he took an obvious step away from the group, as if afraid they might infect him with more germs. "What a nasty cough, Ainsworth. You should get that looked at. Thank you for your time, but I must return to my guests."

True to his word, Rubin dismissed them with the turn of his back. By some miracle cure, Hugh straightened, shifting his weight from Jarimis. He gestured them away with a quick wave, and the group faded into the crowd.

Once through the throng of partygoers, they moved alongside the museum gardens. Toria touched Hugh's elbow. "Are you okay?"

Hugh let out a belly laugh and pointed to Jarimis. "I'm fine. Thought he could use the distraction."

With a flourish, Jarimis produced a small keyring from his pocket and presented it to Victory. "In your honor, Mother."

Victory accepted the keyring and kissed Jarimis' cheek. "I see you haven't let academia rust your skills."

"Nice job, guys," Toria said. "Maybe we can salvage some of this plan after all."

"And this is where we must take our leave of you." Jarimis bowed low to Toria. "A pleasure to make your acquaintance, little sister."

When he rose, Toria threw her arms around his neck. After a beat, Jarimis returned the hug, holding her close to his slim frame. In a whisper, she made one last request of the man she never thought she'd know. "Please, take care of Hugh."

"I will." Jarimis spoke low in her ear. "And if I can, I will ensure Liam and the child are safe as well."

Toria thanked him again, and they broke apart. She left Victory and Jarimis to a moment of privacy, knowing this particular farewell would be painful to her mother. She turned to Hugh. She couldn't blame the sudden moisture in her eyes on the chill in the air.

"Don't cry, kid." Hugh wiped her cheek with the pad of his thumb. "I suppose this is where I should say something sappy, like you're the granddaughter I never had?"

"I'd have to say something about you being the grandfather I never had, but I have a grandfather, and he could kick your ass." Toria's chest ached. "Thank you for taking care of me, Hugh. I couldn't have managed without you."

"It's been a genuine pleasure." Hugh spread his arms wide. "C'mere."

They hugged tightly, and Toria borrowed strength from his confidence in her. When Victory touched her shoulder, Toria drew away from Hugh. Standing under the streetlamp and stars, they had no words left to be said. The men turned one way, to Hugh's car. Victory followed Toria in the opposite direction.

"Rubin knows we're here, but we have other options." Toria burrowed her hands in her coat pockets, out of the cold. "The east wing service entrance is closest to the geology exhibit."

"Sounds like a plan." Victory dug Rubin's keys from her own coat pocket and offered them to Toria. When Toria didn't sacrifice her warmth to grab them, Victory rolled her eyes and shoved them past Toria's hand into her pocket. "It's not that cold out here."

"I believe you're not one to talk on such matters." Toria curled her fingers around the cool metal. "Why aren't you trying to take control?"

Victory flinched. "Why would I bother? You're the one with more knowledge of where we need to be right now. If we're going with the flow, I'm going with your flow."

"You didn't hesitate to take over the flow on the way to Nacostina with Kane and Mikelos."

"I have no idea what you're talking about." For all her years of experience, Victory did not play innocent well.

Toria snorted in laughter. "From your perspective, that was barely a week ago."

Before Victory could defend herself, they rounded the final street corner to the freight entrance. Toria had expected quiet silence in this area of the complex, not the bright lights and bustle that greeted them. "Oh, hell."

Two large catering trucks clogged the entrance, and dozens of people swarmed between them and the museum, carrying boxes of supplies and wrapped platters under a supervisor's shouted directions. Victory grabbed Toria's elbow and pulled her into the shadows of the shrubbery. "This is a hell of a party. Too bad we're not dressed to sneak in with them."

"We'll have to go the long way around." Toria jerked her head toward the back of the museum, and Victory followed her through a break in the bushes. Deserted gardens surrounded the museum, shrouded in darkness that seemed even blacker after the caterers' lights. "Still following my lead?"

"More than happy to." Victory tucked her arm in Toria's, and they meandered the garden paths.

If anyone stumbled across them, they'd be out for an evening stroll, and weren't aware this area was off-limits, so sorry, Officer. Though anxiety drove

Toria to pick up speed, she matched her pace to Victory's sedate perambulation. Resuming their previous conversation added to their guise, where sneaking in silence might attract attention. "Guess I don't feel much like a leader after these past few months." Toria's breath curled white in the cold air. "You know how weak I've been. Hell, you saw yourself what a mess I was when you first got here."

"That's not it at all, love." Victory clutched her arm tighter. "You could have given into the weakness. Curled in a little ball and refused to leave Hugh's house. Or taken the easy way out and left town with Liam. Instead, you're here with me."

"Mom, I'm holding it together through caffeine and sheer force of will."

"And that's how you know you're a proper mercenary. It's not an adventure unless you're cold, hungry, and have to go to the bathroom."

"None of that even applies to you."

"I am a bit peckish."

Toria batted Victory with her free hand, and their walk descended into comfortable silence. The north wing entrance, outside the café, was shut tight and deserted, but Toria didn't want to risk running into security who might patrol the public areas of the museum during the gala. Even Victory picked up the pace, and they halved their time on the walk to the west wing.

This side of the building was empty, as Toria expected. Victory kept watch with her stronger senses, while Toria tested Rubin's keys until the smaller door next to the freight garage swung open.

Once inside, Victory led them through the darkness. They entered the service hallway behind the ground floor's main exhibit, and paused to check their bearings.

"I hear loud voices in the distance." Victory cocked her head to one side, illuminated by a desk lamp left on in a lab. "But it's muffled."

"The party must be in the auditorium under the rotunda." Toria weighed the risk of going anywhere near the crowd, considering and discarding potential routes.

She led Victory to the service stairs, and they climbed through the darkness on soft feet, minimizing the echoes of their footsteps on the metal stairs. Once on the third floor, they crept past the biology wing's offices and laboratories, Toria murmuring directions behind her mother.

Noise crested, voices and the clatter of drinkware, as they approached the rotunda. The women positioned themselves on either side of the hallway to peer out. The open space two stories below echoed with conversation, underlined by the gentle tones of a string quartet. The balcony on this level, however, remained uninhabited. Toria gestured for Victory to follow, keeping close to the far wall as she circled the rotunda.

They could have descended one level using a public staircase, but Toria had no desire to press their luck. Instead, better to creep through the top level of the geology wing, passing offices and storage rooms filled with rocks, rocks, and more rocks. Halfway through their slow progression, Victory grabbed Toria's coat and hauled her into an open doorway. She allowed her mother to shove her behind the office door and didn't make a peep when Victory drew a knife from the depths of her coat and positioned herself in the shadow of a bookshelf.

In the darkness, Victory's body became another shadow. A piece of the furniture, a trick of the light. With no movement, no need to breathe, she might be a statue.

Through the crack in the door hinge, a flashlight beam bobbed down the hallway. Two sets of footsteps, out of sync. After what seemed like ages, two security guards passed their hiding spot. Neither of them paid any attention to the office that held Toria and Victory tucked away.

Toria stayed still even after she no longer heard them, until Victory gestured her out. She stepped away from the door.

They slipped through the hall and down one level of the service stairs. The main doorway to the exhibit hall remained bolted against them, but Rubin's keys gave them access at the next minor service entrance Toria tried.

Moonlight streamed through the tall windows along one side of the hall, brightening the space and easing the strain on Toria's eyes from peering through darkness. This was familiar territory, and she marched past the display cases toward her goal, Victory close on her heels.

She planted herself in front of her destination, scanning the case. Iron meteorites, polished to reveal their banded patterns. Stony meteorites, blobby chondrites and textured achondrites. But where the bane of her current existence should have sat, the case held a small placard: "This artifact removed for cleaning."

"Fuck," Victory said, an echo of Toria's frustration.

"Hold on a second." Breaking into a jog, Toria darted toward the exhibit hall's front entrance. The museum displayed the stars of the collection, examples of more valuable precious metals and minerals, up here for easier access for tourists to hit the highlights. A quick check confirmed her suspicion.

The faceted aquamarine as long as her forearm. The pink topaz the size of her head. And the enormous hunk of raw platinum. All gone, all displaying the same note about cleaning. The angle was wrong for Toria to see around the main security fence, but she guessed the 45-karat diamond displayed within the museum wall right outside the main exhibit had been the first to go.

"Someone knows that something is going down," Toria said. "All the most expensive items are gone."

"And the most powerful, apparently." Victory's pursed lips were bloodless. "We're too late."

"We're not too late."

"With all due respect, love, how in the world are we going to find one rock in this whole museum? Assuming it's even still here?"

"If it's still here, I can find it." Toria offered her palm to Victory. "Give me your knife."

Victory passed over the small blade from the depths of her coat without argument, though curiosity warred with doubt on her face. But explanation needed too much time. After so long studying the artifact, along with her knowledge gleaned from the notes she and Jarimis found in the archives, Toria knew everything possible about the stone. Since it also had to be a unique magical object, a chance existed that she'd be able to track its signature.

Toria moved off the wide carpet that stretched down the center of the hall. In the space between two display cases, she dragged the tip of the knife over the marble floor. No way to treat a blade, except under such dire circumstances. The quick-and-dirty way in which she traced out the space would horrify Kane, but she imagined Archer's benevolent wave of approval, and that was all the encouragement she needed. Once she had a rough magic circle sketched around her, she dropped cross-legged in the center.

Victory positioned herself in the middle of the gallery.

Secure with the knowledge of her mother's protection, Toria unfolded her shields with a mental twist, spinning them to the boundary set by the ritual circle, enveloping her in a sphere of crystalline power. The circle allowed her to delegate the structure of her shields, releasing extra concentration from her mind. Confident in her dual methods of impenetrable security, Toria prepared to drop into trance.

And found the trance wouldn't come.

She shifted, but the hard floor wasn't the distraction. Anxiety plucked at her nerves, which threatened to turn into a feedback loop of too nervous to fall into trance and too guilty about being too nervous and on and on and on.

Toria emptied her lungs and drew in cool, clean air. When was the last time she had felt calm and relaxed?

Easy.

She summoned the memory and settled into its warm embrace. Curled on her side in Liam's bed, the single night they spent together. Liam's warm body, elven blood hotter than human, pressed to her back and his arms wrapped around her. His lips, chapped from the change to cold weather, kissing the curve of her shoulder.

Instead of falling in the trance, she stepped into it, pulled in by the comfort Liam spurred within her. For a moment, it was even as if he sat next to her.

She opened internal eyes, and Liam was there. He stared out at the night sky, above the passing tree line, from the passenger seat of a truck cab. The bundle in his arms stirred, revealing Nalamas' snub nose and full cheeks.

Relief rushed through her, and her body re-centered within the confines of the museum. Wherever they were, Liam and Nalamas were out of Nacostina. They would be safe.

And she had work to do. Deep inside the magic that permeated the here and now, she had to find the needle in the haystack.

In trance, this level of magesight verged on overwhelming. The magic overlaid the physical world, but existed within it, as well. Even the plain glass and wood display cases to either side burned with inner fire. Pressing outward, she escaped the confines of the exhibit hall, the physical space she inhabited. Her mind expanded to fit every nook and cranny of the museum. She drew back once the gardens, though dormant for the coming winter, threatened to drown her senses in pure earth magic. It teased with its familiarity and Toria's yearning for connection with Kane.

She had to pull this off if she ever hoped to be with him again.

The earthen element was part of it, but not her primary goal. She dove through the layers upon layers of surrounding magic, dismissing the granite and marble and concrete of the museum itself. She shoved away the living auras of the people who crowded the auditorium below her. Skated away from ghostly remnants that clung to the thousands of samples kept in the biology wing.

After ricocheting away from the sensory minefield of the human historical artifacts kept in the anthropology section, she burrowed into the storage rooms below the geology wing. Pinpricks of earthen energy represented every element and compound in existence. Since she hoped—doubted—the museum contained no other time travel artifacts, she wandered through each unique energy signature.

Magesight didn't limit itself to one sense, though often Toria found vision to be of particular use to her. Now, deep within this astral plane, the magical signatures of each artifact assaulted her whole being. This one pricked her with cold. This one smelled like polished brass warmed in the sun.

The one that tasted like a cheeseburger tempted her curiosity, but she couldn't afford the distraction. Even as time moved faster within this plane, the clock ticked on.

She almost missed the spinning ball of electric power, not because it was small, but because it was so familiar it faded in the background of her awareness. As she circled the artifact's magical representation, aspects of its signature revealed themselves one by one. There was the igneous rock that echoed with her own element of storm. Here was the weight of age that meshed it so well into the unending flow of magic.

And here was the energy that set it apart. So unrecognizable as to be undetectable. Shadowy tendrils linked the meteor to yet another plane Toria could not access. She memorized every detail possible, as this might be her one chance to examine what had to be temporal energy. The shadows felt like nothing, drifting away into oblivion even as those nearest screamed against her skin.

This was it. Toria marked her relative location, closed her inner eye, and vaulted back into her body.

When she opened her physical eyes and stretched feeling into her arms, Victory no longer stood before her. Toria pushed to her knees and leaned around the display cases.

Her mother knelt, checking a security guard's pulse. Two additional guards lay around her.

From the outside, it looked like nothing happened as Toria crossed her legs and closed her eyes. After all this time, centuries of age and experience, the idea of an entire separate world outside of Victory's perception still fascinated her. More so, that her daughter and foster son saw and manipulated the untouchable.

Put a sword in her hand, or a council table in front of her, to defeat an enemy she could see any day.

As if summoned by a mental cue, footsteps passed through the rotunda. Victory maintained her position as Toria's guard, balanced on the balls of her feet.

But the steps didn't bypass the exhibit hall. Three security guards entered, joking about drawing the short straw to patrol rather than supervising the guests downstairs and sneaking hors d'oeuvres. Perhaps due to her stillness, or because they didn't expect anyone to be here, the men didn't spot her until they'd moved farther into the hall.

The lead guard shone the wide beam of his flashlight over her. "Excuse us, ma'am. The party is downstairs. I'm afraid this area is off-limits to guests."

They didn't see Toria, tucked away behind a display case. Victory met them midway. Her coat flowed open at her movement, and she placed her hand on the hilt of her sword.

As a group, the men drew away while Victory stalked toward them.

One gave a sharp inhale. "She's back."

"Who—?" The lead guard broke off when Victory continued moving toward them. "Ma'am, stop right there!"

"It's the woman who broke in last week! Jasper said she conked him with a great bloody sword!"

She stopped two paces from the men, still in silence. One drew his own flashlight and whipped the light around the exhibit hall. "Hey, is someone back there?"

This wouldn't do. Victory lunged forward, punching him in the face.

He collapsed under the strength of her blow, flashlight rolling from limp fingers. For a split second, neither of the other two men moved. While one hesitated, flashlight beam quavering, the second lunged for her.

Victory's adrenaline kicked into high gear, and he moved as if through molasses. She braced herself, hand away from her sword. His shoulder slammed into her chest.

She spun with his momentum, catching him under the arms and tossing him to the side like a sack of flour. Most of him landed on the center carpet, but his head hit the marble floor with the pop of wet melon. She whirled toward the other man, now frozen in shock. "I don't want to hurt you."

They'd all be dead soon anyway. Victory ignored the needling voice. When the man raised the flashlight as if to bludgeon her with it, Victory ducked and caught his wrist in one hand. Holding his arm high, she forced herself into his personal space and locked their eyes. "Sleep."

His eyes rolled back in his head, and his knees crumpled. She released his arm as he sagged to the floor, unconscious.

She swept the hall for sign of more guards, tuning her hearing for running footsteps. Nothing.

She eased over to the man she'd thrown and leaned to check his pulse. Fluttering and sluggish, but there. Blood pooled where his forehead rested on the marble tile, creeping in one direction and soaking into the edge of the burgundy carpet in the other. Nothing to do for him, or the others. She and Toria would be long gone by the time they woke.

Victory straightened, sensing movement. Toria stared at her and the body, wide eyes glinting with moonlight. She lifted her hand. "We're safe."

Toria pushed herself to her feet, catching herself on the edge of a display case. "I see that."

197

"Any luck?"

Her daughter stretched her whole body, fingertips aimed at the ceiling. "I know where we need to go."

They hauled the three guards out of sight between another set of large display cases. On casual glance, the bloodstains shouldn't be visible from any entrance.

As Victory followed Toria's purposeful stride to the service stairs, one of the heartbeats behind her stuttered and fell silent.

Her stomach hardened, but she forced the guilt away before it could build. She had a mission, a daughter to protect, a daywalker to return home to.

They both jerked in shock once Toria pulled open the door. Rubin stood on the landing, pleasant smile plastered on his face. "Good evening, ladies. I trust you've found your tour of my museum educational? I sensed your little trip through my wards, and thought I should come answer any questions you might have."

Victory sprang at the elf but collided with an invisible wall that flared Toria's familiar violet in the dim light of the stairwell. "What the hell?" She pounded her fist, and the violet shield crackled under her touch.

When Victory spun on her, Toria shrank away.

"He's just going to keep getting in our way!" With a snarl, Victory turned back toward Rubin.

Toria grabbed her arm before Victory pounded the shield again. "We need him. I know where we need to go, but it's one of the storage rooms. We don't have time to search the whole room if he's hidden it away."

A muscle twitched in Victory's cheek, but she loosened under Toria's hand, snatching her arm away without a word.

Rubin inclined his head in Toria's direction. "I appreciate your aid, but I assure you that your protection is unnecessary."

Red dimmed her view. This time, she summoned the memory of Rubin's brains exploding out of the back of his head intentionally. "Get us to the artifact. You know which one."

"I fear my curiosity has gotten the best of me." Rubin spun on his heel and proceded a few steps down the staircase. He paused, glancing up at them. "Coming?"

Toria relaxed the shield she'd created between Victory and Rubin. But she kept herself between them as they descended the service stairs. Victory might see Rubin as an obstacle to their path home, but he was the one person in Nacostina they couldn't kill tonight.

Rubin kept his pace to a casual stroll, when Toria wanted nothing more than to shove him faster. "I do find myself surprised about one thing, Ms. Connor. I'd have expected you in the company of Jarimis if you were to be with a vampire."

"What's that supposed to mean?" The question escaped before Toria could stop it. She balled hands, digging fingernails into her palm. *Do not engage the elf.*

"Such uncivilized creatures, aren't they? Jarimis puts on a good show, but most of their kind are a mere step above savage beasts. Of course, you're still carrying a silly sword yourself, so perhaps your judgement is suspect."

"Doesn't seem to stop you." Toria blamed her jangling nerves when the retort slipped out. She bit her tongue, tasting blood.

Rubin craned his head over his shoulder, not missing a step as he continued downstairs. "What was that?"

"Nothing. Keep walking."

"What a curious statement. Perhaps I see a bit of what so intrigued Liam about you."

Toria shuddered at the idea of anything about her intriguing Rubin. Her fingers itched to draw her rapier and thrust it in his back, through his ribcage, through his black heart. Even the subtle brush of her magical shielding against his in the enclosed stairwell caused her stomach to churn with nausea.

They made it to the ground floor. Toria's back screamed with tension, and her hand darted for her sword when Rubin paused outside the service door and held his palm out.

None of them moved, until Rubin rubbed his fingers together. "I'd appreciate the return of my keys, unless you are content to spend the rest of the night in this stairwell."

Toria offered the keyring, careful not to let her skin touch his.

Rubin selected the correct key and pushed it into the lock. He paused as his eyes bore into Toria's. "You do realize the futility of your actions, yes?"

"She said to keep moving." The growl in Victory's voice made the skin on the back of Toria's neck crawl.

"Even if I bring you to the artifact, what do you intend to do with it? You can't get home. You'll jump forward in time, to a world even more alien." He ignored Victory. Toria met his gaze head-on, daring him to blink first. He did, focusing on the door once again as the keys jangled in his grasp. "I suppose it's your mistake to make."

Toria could have made any number of quips, but settled on silence. They couldn't reveal their actual goal, or Rubin would figure out she'd time-traveled from a different direction the first time.

They followed Rubin in tense silence through a series of storage rooms, flipping on light switches as they passed. Toria stared at the spot between his shoulder blades. Questions tumbled in her mind. Despite her best efforts, Rubin had now had plenty of interaction with her.

Years ago (a hundred years hence), did he recognize (would he recognize) her when she entered the historical site for the former Parisii Academy of Mages with Kane and Archer in search of Syri? If so, he'd had his own reasons for hiding it. If not—the thought unleashed another whirlwind of queries regarding the nature of temporal logic.

Pushing it all out of her mind, she came face to face with a skull, and froze. "Toria?"

Her mother's voice came as if from a great distance, but all Toria saw were bones. A row of skulls on a shelf, a stretch of femurs below it, a pile of finger joints collecting dust nearby. She squeezed her eyes shut, but that was worse, as images of the Catacombs, deep beneath Parisii, replaced her view.

Thunder roared in her ears, the museum shaking and caving in, until the sound of her name burst through the noise. The thunder was her heartbeat, and the earthquake was Victory jostling her shoulder.

Rubin leaned on a filing cabinet, arms crossed and eyes alight with mild curiosity. "Interesting."

This wasn't the Catacombs. Toria was five feet below ground level, not a hundred. Rubin was a dead man walking, he just didn't know it yet. "I'm fine, I'm fine." She pulled out of Victory's grasp. "Let's keep going."

Her wrist burned, and she rubbed the names tattooed there as they passed through the long storage room and out the other side.

They turned two more corners in the labyrinthine maze beneath the museum, until Victory ducked around her and grabbed Rubin's shoulder. "Wait." But she made no other move, so Toria didn't shield him. She wasn't certain she could bring herself to.

Victory cursed as two more security guards rounded the corner at the end of the hall. She wound back with her free hand, but Toria lunged forward, sliding between the two pairs.

"Mom, wait." She turned toward Comstock and Brinkley. "Hey, guys."

The men stared between her and Rubin. Comstock spoke first. "Boss, what's going on?"

"Please restrain these two women, gentlemen." Rubin gave the order the same way one might request an extra helping at dinner, polite and perfunctory.

200

This was his museum. Though she had sensed them nearing the artifact, Rubin had led Toria and Victory along this circuitous route to time this encounter. Too bad Toria held the trump card.

The guards shared expressions of confusion, and Comstock rubbed at his bald spot. "Mr. Rubin, you want us to arrest Toria and her friend?"

Brinkley laughed, his high-pitched voice echoing. "I mean, I know she's not dressed for the party, but that seems a bit harsh."

"By the way, have you seen Liam today? He didn't come to work this morning, and the day shift was concerned," Comstock asked Toria, oblivious to the outrage darkening Rubin's face.

"This is ridiculous." Rubin slipped under Victory's grasp, twisting in her grip until he had her arm bent the opposite direction, leveraging her own joints and strength against her.

"Mom, don't kill him!" Toria hoped Victory caught her warning even as she held out her hands toward the guards. "It's not what it looks like, guys." She flinched as a fist struck skin, unsure of who attacked whom.

She might consider them acquaintances, but Rubin paid their checks. When Comstock attempted to push by Toria to come to his aid, she grabbed his wrist and shoved magic from her hand into his. Electricity crackled in the enclosed hallway, and Comstock collapsed to the ground with the smell of singed flesh.

She whirled toward Brinkley, who backed up, hands lifted. "What did you—?"

Toria lunged forward, slapping her bare palm to Brinkley's. Power arced between them. He stumbled against the wall and slid down, unconsciousness claiming him.

She spun, recharging the power in her fingers with a high-pitched whine she felt in her skull. Victory controlled Rubin, the tables turned as he sagged to one knee to relieve pressure in his wrists. "You didn't kill him."

"You told me not to. I do listen, you know." Amusement curled the corners of Victory's mouth.

Rubin's snide comment surprised her even more. "Apparently, your friends didn't warrant the same respect."

"They're not dead." Toria studied the men at her feet. Not dead yet, at least. Brinkley got engaged at the end of summer. A few weeks ago, Comstock had accosted her with the joyful news of the impending birth of his second grandchild.

How could she be so selfish? Why did Hugh get to live, but not these men?

She already knew the answer. Because Hugh had no descendants, and she trusted him to live out the rest of his life in obscurity. Who knew if Comstock's next grandkid might cure cancer decades before Toria was even born?

Kane's birth mother died of cancer.

"Let's go," Toria said.

Victory followed her, maintaining her hold on Rubin as he staggered along behind. "Should we expect any other nasty surprises?"

He remained silent until they neared another storage room. "This is it."

Toria reached for the door handle.

Wait. Pausing with her hand an inch from the metal, she brought up her magesight. The brass flared with a decrepit orange swirl, heralding a nasty trap for anyone who came into contact with it. "Take it down, Rubin."

Victory shoved him forward, but Rubin smoothed his tuxedo coat. "And what incentive would I have for such a thing?"

"Try this one." Victory drew her knife and jabbed its tip to his jugular.

"Is that supposed to be a threat? You've already made it clear my life is to be preserved for some arcane reason." He paused. "Not that I don't appreciate it."

They ignored his sarcasm. "It's okay, I've got it." Toria dropped to one knee and hovered her hands above the doorknob's surface. With her magesight still active, she sent tendrils of energy into the set spell and teased it apart, digging out its roots with brute force and cascading miniature shields within shields to prevent any excess power from escaping and tripping whatever trap Rubin had laid.

She backed away, standing, as the last of the orange faded. Her heart raced as if she'd sprinted a mile, and sweat dampened the hair at her temples. Dismissing her magesight, she gripped the doorknob.

Nothing happened.

Opening the door without incident, she waved Victory and Rubin inside. Victory kept the blade at his neck, prodding him to move with nothing more than a poke. Toria braced herself for more bones when she followed them inside.

To her immense relief, making her knees wobble for a split second, nothing more than metal filing cabinets and wooden cases lined the square walls of the room. The space should have felt musty, abandoned, but instead the cabinets gleamed with polish and the air inside smelled fresh. An innocuous end to a grand quest.

"Okay, show us where it is." Dropping the knife, Victory shoved Rubin into the clear center of the room.

Tugging his jacket straight once again, Rubin faced them. "I'm still not sure what you hope to accomplish. The artifact will not send you to the past. Going further into the future seems a great risk." He spread his arms, gesturing to the room, or perhaps the entire museum. "What might greet you when you arrive?"

Victory drew a hissing breath between her teeth, a human action Toria almost never saw in her stalwart mother. "You know what's coming."

Rubin tilted his head and considered Victory. "Interesting. So, it seems, do you."

Toria ignored him. "That's the point. The meteor survives the initial explosion, probably due to a combination of distance and the magical and physical protections of the museum. It's the aftereffects of that specific type of explosion that change the inherent magical properties."

Pained realization dawned on Victory's face. "The fallout."

"You've killed many more times the number of warped creatures from the Wasteland than I have," Toria said. "It's the same principle. Just on a magical item rather than a regular animal."

"This is interesting, but I fail to see the relevance." Rubin stepped toward a filing cabinet. Both women tensed, but he did nothing more than slide open a drawer and withdraw a wrapped package.

It was the right size to be the meteor, under many layers of protective paper. "You want access to the stone?" He turned to them and lifted one hand. "Come get it."

Brilliant shields sprang to life, encompassing Rubin in indistinguishable, twisting layers.

Not even bothering to summon her magesight in the face of such potent magic, Toria sprang forward and shoved both hands into the shields before they coalesced. Pain whipped up her arms, lighting nerves on fire, but the physical contact gave her the access she needed. She dropped to one knee as a pained scream that might be hers danced at the end of her hearing, and brute-force shoved her own magic into Rubin's power.

She couldn't go for Rubin. The elf maintained shields upon shields, layers of intricate protections built over the hundreds of years of his life. That way spelled certain death.

But she had a chance with the meteor. Toria's mind slipped along twisting pathways of grass, evergreen, and sunlight, chasing the center of Rubin's elven magic. Rubin's *life* magic, which might be similar in color to Kane's familiar shields, but life and earth were two distinct beasts. And storm vibrated on a frequency all its own.

The meteor itself bled murky greens and purples, the color of a day-old bruise. Though Rubin was old, this power felt ancient in comparison. Toria dropped into this sphere of influence, inside yet separate from Rubin's shields, and tapped its shoulder.

Mistake. Big mistake. Pain blossomed, mental, psychological, existing on a separate plane from the body she'd left behind in this desperate bid for control. The artifact might have storm as part of its magical signature, but it was an ocean-spanning hurricane compared to Toria's brief summer rainstorm.

She braced herself against the power that buffeted her from all sides. She constructed shield after shield, but each shattered or disintegrated in moments. Rubin's own power swirled tighter around her, but she had to keep him from the meteor at all costs.

The world outside vanished as Toria threw everything she had at control. But it wasn't enough. The meteor fought them both, the rock shuddering within its core and generating more volts of power that stabbed her soul. Despite the power of this past world that staggered her with its excess, limits still existed to her control, and she stretched them past breaking.

She couldn't control the artifact. She could fight off Rubin, but not overpower him. Stalemate. No going forward. No going back. The physical world faded away, leaving her within this maelstrom with no escape.

Swirling light emanated from the meteor, overpowering Rubin's unnatural greens and her own comforting violet. Science and magic merged as the ground beneath her shifted, grinding together and ionizing the oxygen in the room. She choked on the raw power, the taste of obsidian coating her tongue.

The light intensified, shifting wavelengths from one side of the spectrum to the other, rising in a feverish pitch from cyan to blue to violet and on into the infrared, blinding her vision and encompassing her mind with magic too strong for her to comprehend.

It was too much, too overwhelming, and as she thought she would die in a blaze of archaic magic, the world darkened.

Her shoulder hit the ground, the pain barely registering after the constant exposure of raw nerve endings. Toria lifted her cheek from the scuffed wooden floor and squinted through the pallid dullness of the real world.

Rubin sprawled next to her, limbs crooked and hair askew, but chest rising and falling. Victory stood above him, her sword reversed in her grip. She stared at the body, as if daring Rubin to have the audacity to regain consciousness.

Toria groaned as she pushed herself to a sitting position. Focusing on anything without the added definition of magic was hard, and the meteor pulsed ominously at the edge of her tattered shields. She felt no desire to regain its attention. "What...happened?" Her voice cracked on the question, as if her throat was raw from screams. Maybe it was.

Victory extended her free hand. She hauled Toria to her feet, catching her when she staggered on uncooperative knees. "You dove for Rubin, then froze. I could tell magic was happening, but I didn't want to interfere." She returned her sword to its scabbard and caught Toria's face between both hands, as if reassuring herself Toria remained unscathed. "Light bounced around the room, and all the air got sucked away. I bashed Rubin on the head before you could suffocate. You both collapsed when the air rushed back in."

With no more of Rubin's power to push against, Toria's own energy had backlashed against her. Her heart skipped a beat as she realized how lucky she'd been not to burn herself out. "Don't *ever* do that again." Kane would have known better, known the danger involved in interfering with active magics. "But I think you saved my life."

"What are partners for?" The warmth in Victory's voice banished the lingering tremors within Toria's body.

"Thanks, Mom." Toria nudged Rubin's body with the toe of one boot, but he didn't twitch. If this worked, she at least knew this was the last time she'd ever see the elf.

Too bad he would live. But she knew it was necessary, if she wanted a chance at returning to the same world she'd left.

"We can't leave this here," Victory said, checking the hallway. "Otherwise he'll take it with him when he wakes."

Toria's exhausted brain needed a second to put the pieces together. Right. Then the stone wouldn't be in the ruins of the city for them to find. Paradox. "Check the specimen drawers for other rocks that look like this one. Mess up *everything*."

Toria ripped a section of lining from the inside of her coat, wrapping her hands with it before approaching the innocuous package on the floor, as if it had not also participated in the battle for its control. With her bare skin protected from contact, she tugged the paper aside, revealing the chunk of stone.

Both of them slammed drawers open, searching for anything similar and disrupting the careful organization. With luck, Rubin would never have time to inspect every rock before he had to evacuate.

"Here!"

Toria moved to Victory's side at her call, and they stared into a crate of dull gray stones. "Perfect."

"Won't he use magic to pick out the right one?"

"Not if I do this right." Toria moved to the artifact and lifted it from the packaging. She brought it to the crate and tipped it, keeping hold of the layers of paper until the rock fell. It sat among the other specimens, indistinguishable—at least physically. She dropped the packing material to the floor and held both hands an inch above it.

She summoned her magesight and opened her shields, falling into the magic that surrounded her and permeated this world. She reveled in the final moment she would have access to so much power.

In the future, an illusion charm that masked magic required hours of ritual preparation. But here, and now, Toria scooped magic from the ether and dumped it into and around the stone with nothing more than a wish and pure will. *Be quiet. Be invisible. Stay here, so I can find my way home.*

It had to be her imagination, but she swore the artifact heard her. It shimmered with a burst of magical energy, then fell still. She strained her magesight, but even she, the illusion-caster, found no sign the artifact was more than a hunk of rock.

Victory shoved the discarded packing material behind a cabinet and moved to Toria's side. "You're sure this will work?"

"The spell worked. I have no idea about the next part." Toria grabbed her mother's hand, lacing their fingers together and holding tight. "But wherever we end up, this time we'll be there together." Bracing herself, Toria touched the tip of one finger to the roughened surface of the meteorite. She half-expected it to fight her again, but this time, it almost seemed welcoming. Without prelude, pressure built behind her stomach and yanked her up and out of the world.

WITHIN

Nothingness surrounded them, in contrast to the primal power Toria knew the artifact contained. Not a vacuum, because she could breathe. Not a storm, because no wind buffeted them. Other than the pressure of Victory's hand in hers, she felt—absence.

No light and no darkness. No sense of movement, even as Toria's gut told her she hurtled through space.

No ability to move, she found as she tried to turn her head.

In panic, she strained for her shields. But she had no power to draw from, no energy in this shadowy field of naught. Just Victory's hand, clutched in her own.

She opened her mouth to scream, then slammed into a pile of rubble.

AMONG

"But wherever we end up, this time we'll be there together."

Victory kept watch. No security guards poured through the door. Rubin's breath roared in her ears, but his body showed no movement.

Without warning, the same mysterious force jerked her away through a gray void. She squeezed Toria's hand, solid within her own. The stillness pressed in, like invisible hands grasping at her clothing and limbs.

The silence screamed in her ears. The voices she'd heard in the shadows the first time coalesced into words. Not Loquella, not Qin, nor any of the other languages she'd learned and forgotten over her lifetime. But she understood nonetheless.

One comes.

We know this one.

One is too early.

She couldn't move, else she'd have clawed at her ears to force out the voices.

One does not know us.

Shock reverberated through the impenetrable void, as if the entire universe experienced outrage at such an oversight.

The oppressive touch shifted. Now, hands caressed her in mingled curiosity and affection. She felt no difference in the pressure on her clothes, on her body, within her skin.

One will.

Victory's entire sense of self spun away, twisting itself inside out, until her organs were outside of her body, or was she seeing in?

Visions came, overlaying her twisted sight. They spooled out of the void and pummeled her with images. Dreams, memories, scenes—familiar and not. A life both lived, and unlived.

We will return one to whence one came. We will wait for one.

A cicada chirped, and Victory doubled over in pain, clapping her hands to her ears. She dialed back her senses, which seemed to have expanded for miles.

Once secure over control of her sight, she straightened and opened her eyes.

The rubble of Nacostina surrounded her, and summer air warmed her exposed hands and face instead of winter frost. Toria sprawled at her feet, but her daughter already moved arms and legs, drawing them toward her core.

"I think a truck ran over me." Toria moaned as she pushed herself upright. "Are we home?"

"I don't know." Victory tilted her head to the night sky and spun in a slow circle. "I think so."

Footsteps disturbed rubble, and a familiar heartbeat spurred Victory to dash across the space where the Museum of New Continental History once stood. She skidded around a heap of masonry and threw herself into Mikelos' arms.

He caught her with a muffled grunt and returned the embrace. "Victory? Where the hell were you two all day?"

"All day?" Toria limped toward them.

Victory and Mikelos broke apart, and she locked her knees against the force of her relief.

Mikelos' eyes shone in the starlight. "Kane had some sort of seizure last night, and both of you vanished—"

With a sort of high-pitched squeak, Toria bolted in the direction of their camp, coat flapping behind her.

"—and he woke up a few minutes ago." Mikelos stared after his daughter through tousled bangs. "Right when I saw a great flash of light, and—what the hell are you wearing?"

With a laugh Victory would deny was a sob, she shucked off her wool coat and draped it over her arm. She linked hands with Mikelos and tugged him in the direction of camp. "We've been gone for a hell of a lot longer than a day, love."

Toria dropped to her knees amidst the flattened grass of the camp they'd set up before her life had gone diagonal. Kane sat atop his bedroll, hands braced on his temples. He exuded a pained whimper when she threw her arms around his shoulders.

"Too much, too much." But he shifted until he could return the embrace, more than matching the relief and love Toria shoved across their mental link to him. "What the hell happened?"

She pressed a lip-smacking kiss to his cheek before settling on her heels. "I was so worried I'd never see you again."

Kane's pupils were large in the dim light of the scattered lanterns. "I have no idea what you're talking about, and my head hurts." Even as he spoke, confusion colored the love in their connection.

"I'll explain everything. But I need you to check me with magesight. Do you see anything wrong with me?"

Kane's lips twitched, his physical tell that he'd activated his magesight, as familiar as the way he tugged his ear when embarrassed. She held her breath during his examination.

She'd assumed returning to her own time would fix whatever had scared Liam so much. Either Kane would tell her she looked fine, or he'd freak out about her life force getting sucked away into the void.

Instead, Kane tilted in Toria's direction, caressing her aura with his palm. "You are dripping with excess power. No wonder you're wound so damned tight. Seriously, I'm missing something."

Toria drooped like a puppet with its strings cut. That had been the final dilemma. Sweat dripped down her neck, and with a snort of disgust, she shucked off her heavy coat.

Her partner was right about one thing, though. The showdown with Rubin should have exhausted her, but she felt energized enough to run to the museum ruins and back.

But she couldn't bear to leave Kane's side again so soon, keeping her attention on him instead of her surroundings. Nacostina's downtown district had bustled with life and energy mere hours ago, and never would again.

But. The meteor.

Toria launched herself to her feet, ready to return for it at once, but Victory and Mikelos entered the camp's pool of light.

Victory dangled an object wrapped in her own useless coat. "It's okay." She set the bundle to the side of the fire and backed away. "I got the damned thing."

"What damned thing?" Kane used Toria to drag himself to his feet, and she hooked an arm around his waist before he fell. "The thing we were sent to find? Did I miss everything?"

Warmth glowed through Toria's body. No matter how content she'd been in Liam's presence, for the first time in months, her soul was complete. In Kane's profile, she saw the shape of Kojo's nose. But under Kane's arm, she felt the warmth of Lyra's friendship. "You know, I'm older than you now."

"You have lost your damned mind." Kane scrubbed at the side of his head. "Does this mean we're going home?"

Toria rested her head against Kane's shoulder. "Yes. Home."

With dawn too close for comfort, they passed a final day in Nacostina before loading the truck with their gear and returning to Limani. Toria and Kane drove toward Limani's Mercenary Guildhall after dropping Victory and Mikelos off at the manor house. This was their contract, after all, and while Kane still seemed unsure of all he had missed during a day spent unconscious, he agreed with Toria that they needed to speak with Guildmaster Max Asher before handing the artifact over to whoever had originated the blind contract. Max met them in his office at the Guildhall.

"Time travel, huh?" Max scratched at his goatee, the silver hair in sharp contrast to his sun-worn skin. "That's a new one. You got proof of this?"

Toria suppressed a sigh. Proof of her adventure had been the last thing on her mind. "Just the coats Victory and I wore back." In fact, Victory's coat still protected the meteor, sitting between them on Max's desk. "But you can understand my concern in fulfilling this contract if I don't know who I'm turning such a powerful object over to. Either they already know its potential, and have plans to abuse it. Or they don't, and I risk subjecting someone to such a fate."

Sometime that day in the world they'd left, the artifact had passed the point of no return. The bomb's effects had permanently altered the artifact's state. Anyone who touched it would be sent to a radioactive firestorm on the heels of Nacostina's destruction. If they touched it again, they wouldn't return from whence they came, like Victory and Toria. They might keep going back in time, farther and farther away from where they'd started.

"Understandable." Max rolled his shoulders, laying his hands flat on the desk. "Now, I don't do this to discredit your experience, so I hope you don't take offense if I ask Kane for his view of the situation."

"Fair enough." Toria shot an accepting nudge to her partner through their mental link.

"I don't know what happened," Kane said, curling his hands around the armrests. "What I do know is Toria still burns with power, too much for the current state of diminished energy, but pretty standard for what we know of back then. That's all the convincing I need."

"Thank you, I appreciate your perspective." Max stared into the distance over their shoulders, lost in thought.

Breaking a blind contract was no small matter for a Guildmaster, and Toria appreciated the sticky position they put him in. As she tried not to let her nerves jangle with anxiety, she reminded herself she was home now. With Kane by her side. She'd go to sleep tonight in her own bed, secure behind the magical shields of Limani's mage school. That is, if she didn't crash on the couch in the front room of Kane and Archer's suite, not wanting to be away from them. She rubbed at her wrist tattoo until Kane snagged her hand.

When Max stood, they followed suit. "Grab breakfast downstairs and hang out for a while. I'll make a call and find out whether the contract originator knew what they tasked you with."

Kane pointed to the lopsided package. "What should we do with that in the meantime?"

"I'll stash it in the safe. I promise I won't send it off without being able to set your minds at ease."

Though Toria wanted nothing more than to see the rock destroyed, she was still technically under contract to deliver it. However, plans already churned in her mind of what to do after they discovered the identity of the artifact's searcher. Toria followed Kane out of Max's office and toward the smell of breakfast. After eating, they moved to the main "living room" near the Guildhall's entrance to continue a raging debate about the best places to eat in Fort Caroline.

In the middle of Kane's impassioned defense of a hole-in-the-wall seafood place, Liam opened the front entrance of the Guildhall and scanned the room. Toria froze, choking on her laughter.

Their eyes met. Toria may or may not have said something about being right back, and the next thing she knew, she stood inches away from Liam.

Barely seventy-two hours for her. Lifetimes for him. Her hand itched for his. She ached to throw herself into his arms, to kiss his lips. "Hey."

Liam's wide grin lit his face, but not the same face she remembered. The expression was lopsided on one side, thanks to a thin white scar slashed across one cheek. "Hey." His hands opened and closed at his sides, as if he also didn't know what to do with them. "Can we talk?"

Ignoring the less-than-subtle stares that followed them, Toria pulled open the door and led Liam outside. She settled at the top of the Guildhall's steps and Liam dropped next to her. For a moment, Toria tilted her face to the morning sun, basking in the refreshing warmth after Nacostina's final winter. "So, this is awkward."

"I'm the one who hired you to find the meteor. Well, you and your partner."

She whipped her head around to face Liam. Despite the scar, she found it easier to focus on his face over the incongruity of Liam in modern jeans and a worn black T-shirt splashed with the logo of a British band. "You kept my letters."

"Of course I kept your letters." Liam made as if to touch the back of Toria's hand, but drew away. "They got me through the Last War. I got Nalamas settled. I meant to find Jarimis, but got caught up with other issues and made my way to Limani after." He paused for a shy laugh, as if unsure how to compress a century's worth of time into a few sentences. "Jarimis even had me teaching at the university he established. And I was fighting by your parents' side when I got this." He touched his cheek.

Something seemed off about Liam's voice, and Toria realized at the end of his speech that he now spoke Loquella contemporary to this time period. "How did you know I'd be here this morning?" Toria asked. "I didn't even know if we'd make it home, much less when."

"Guildmaster Asher called, since I'm the one who set the blind contract. I even put the bug in Max's ear to suggest your mother should go along to Nacostina." Liam smirked at the abject surprise that must have been blatant on Toria's face. "I've stayed away from Limani for the past thirty years or so, because I found the idea of hiding from you too painful. But I moved back two months ago. When nothing happened as the departure date you recorded for me got closer and closer, I contacted the Guildmaster myself."

"Have you been stalking me?"

Liam's lips thinned in embarrassment, and he looked away. "Your entire life, even if I couldn't be there."

Now Toria did give into impulse. His fingers curled around hers, as if no time had passed at all between them. "I told you not to wait for me."

"I didn't." With his free hand, Liam tucked a lock of hair behind her ear. "I took the long way around."

Toria wanted to lean over, cross the inches between them, and kiss him. But even the touch of their hands was strange, and she knew that while she might be able to pick up where they left off, Liam might not. His being here was nothing short of a miracle, and the last thing she wanted was to push him away.

"I guess knowing you're the one who set the contract eases a lot of my concerns about who wanted that damned artifact. What are you going to do with it?"

"Get you to figure out how to destroy it." Liam followed the path of a passing town-car. "I saw too many people die because of a rock."

"Kane says he doesn't see anything wrong with me. But can you check that you don't see whatever you saw back then?"

Liam's gaze shifted somewhere off to her side for a moment. If possible, his smile grew even wider than before when he looked back at her. "You're where you're supposed to be, I guess."

That left one final, unanswered question. "Can...can you tell me about Hugh?" When a ghost of sadness passed behind Liam's expression, Toria braced herself for the worst.

"No, no, it's okay." Liam rushed to calm her obvious fear. "Hugh made it out of the city and tracked me down. Lived to a rich old age, and passed away with his son at his side."

"Son?" Toria had no idea Hugh had any family.

Liam's lip quirked. "His son Nalamas. The war put a hitch in the fostering plans."

Muscles loosened in Toria's back. A final circuit closed, and she let go of life in the past. Returned to the present, and looked to the future.

"Do you want to have dinner tomorrow?" Toria blurted the words before she considered them. "I mean, I need to spend some time at home today, but it'd be great to see you tomorrow. We could get Kane and Archer to help us figure out how to destroy the meteor. And eat, I guess." Brilliant. If she was trying to live up to some idealized memory Liam might have of her, she'd failed miserably.

Instead, Liam raised her hand, kissing her knuckles. "That sounds fantastic." He pulled Toria along with him as he stood, as if not ready to release her hand. "I suppose we should meet with Guildmaster Asher now?"

"Yeah." She wasn't ready to let go of Liam's hand yet, either. "And—would you like to meet Kane?"

Liam cupped her cheek with his warm palm. "I've waited for years to meet him."

BEYOND

Leaving Mikelos with the bags in the manor house foyer, Victory sprinted to the basement apartment. She stopped in front of the couch, where Asaron sprawled with a book, and planted her hands on her hips.

Her sire tilted his head in greeting, not bothering to glance from his book. "Welcome home. How'd it go?"

Victory had a million possible answers to that question, ranging from "Holy shit, time travel is real," to "I saw Jarimis again and I need a hug," and ending with "I beat the crap out of my past self, so I need you to tell me I didn't fuck up the timeline."

Instead: "I'm seeing strange shadows, and I think I spoke to them."

Asaron lurched at her words, fumbling his book. "You what?"

Victory collapsed next to him on the couch. She laid her head against the cushions, so she wouldn't see her sire's disdain at how insane she sounded. "I thought I was imagining things for a long time. That I was going crazy."

She had expected Asaron's silence, but when it extended past a minute, she risked a look over to him.

Pain wrenched his face. "We thought it was just us."

"Just who?" Victory grabbed Asaron's hands. "What are you talking about?"

"Those of us who have seen the shadows. The darkness that shouldn't exist, leeching into our world."

Victory grit her teeth. This was not a problem limited to her own mind. This was something real, something tangible. Something that could be measured. Could be reasoned with.

Could be defeated.

"Tell me everything you know."

Acknowledgements

If I could travel back in time, I'd give extra hugs to everyone who helped me through this massive project. I wrote the first draft of this novel during my first year at a stressful new job, and my husband was away on a long-term work trip for most of that time. Instead, gratitude here will have to do.

David, Julia, and Sarah for their incredible friendship and support during a difficult time in my life.

Chris Stout, Chelsea Stickle, Cara McKinnon, Alexa Grave, Alex Savage, Lana Ayers, Donna Monroe, Kevin Kusisto, Kristopher Campa, and Irene Pynn for reviewing all or parts of this novel. Your wonderful critiques and genuine enthusiasm for this project made for a better story.

Jennifer Barnes and John Edward Lawson, for always encouraging me to stretch the limits of my imagination.

And my husband Erik for his endless support and patience.

ABOUT THE AUTHOR

By day, J. L. Gribble is a professional medical editor. By night, she does freelance fiction editing in all genres, along with reading, playing video games, and occasionally even writing.

Previously, Gribble studied English at St. Mary's College of Maryland. She received her Master's degree in Writing Popular Fiction from Seton Hill University in Greensburg, Pennsylvania, where her debut novel *Steel Victory* was her thesis for the program.

She lives in Ellicott City, Maryland, with her husband and three vocal Siamese cats. Find her online (www.jlgribble.com), on Facebook (www.facebook.com/jlgribblewriter), and on Twitter and Instagram (@hannaedits). She is currently working on more tales set in the world of Limani.

www.ingramcontent.com/pod-product-compliance
Lightning Source LLC
Chambersburg PA
CBHW020630250626
47154CB00008B/2618